2051

BOOK 2

By Dan Peavler

This book is a work of fiction. Any references to historical events, real people, or real places are used fictitiously. Other names, characters, places and events are products of the author's imagination, and any resemblance to actual events, places or persons, living or dead, is entirely coincidental.

Paperback ISBN: 978-1-953686-09-1
eBook ISBN: 978-1-953686-10-7

Library of Congress Control Number: TBD

WWW.LivingSpringsPublishers.com

John Millet Joined the Military service at Minneapolis, Minnesota on September 17, 1940. President Franklin Roosevelt signed a secret executive order on April 1, 1941, approving recruitment of volunteers from active-duty United States Military personnel to help with the defense of the Yunnan Province on the southwestern edge of China from Japanese bomber squadrons. One hundred pilots and two hundred ground crew, with support personnel, became known as the American Volunteer Group. On December 20, 1941, less than two weeks after Pearl Harbor, the AVG shot down four of ten Japanese bombers in the first Allied victory in Asia, for World War II. The P-40 aircraft noses were painted with a wide grin, flashing teeth and the evil eye of a tiger shark. Time magazine heralded the success of the "Flying Tigers", a nickname which stuck.

John Millet volunteered for the AVG and became one of the initial "Flying Tigers". He spent five years in China where he adopted a pet monkey named Riggs. For nineteen months he was a prime target for Japanese fighter planes while he worked in a fighter control station about three miles from the main base in Kweilin. The station consisted of a power generator and radio transmitter hidden in a cave, with the receiver in a separate cave about a hundred feet away. Forward observers sustained a lookout for approaching Japanese bombers and would pass the information to his location. He shared duties with another soldier working twenty-four-hour shifts, before being relieved by the other. When warned of a threat they would telephone the base via three miles of wire run through the jungle. A warning system, using large balls, was utilized to communicate the degree of alert. One large ball raised meant the Japanese planes were approximately 180 miles out; two balls meant 120 miles away. Three balls alert warned to take cover immediately. The fighter pilots scrambled and received further information from the fighter control station.

He received, from the Chinese people, a red silk scarf with his name embroidered on it, presented to him by Madame Chiang Kai-shek. Another of his prized possessions was an additional beautiful silk scarf, he won in a raffle at a banquet honoring the "Flying Tigers" during the war.

On completion of his service, he graduated from St. Thomas College in St, Paul, Minnesota with a degree in English. He taught High School English and Drama for three years before beginning his career in social work. He married his lifelong partner, Margaret Riley in 1947, and they raised ten children together. His fifth child, Helen, became my wife in 1978. Of all the times I had the opportunity to speak with him, very few occasions did we speak of his war experiences. When the subject was raised, he expressed how much he enjoyed the people of China. When asked specifically of his experiences during the war, he always answered, "war is hell". He was a renaissance man who enjoyed painting, reading, music, his church and his family.

This book is dedicated to my father-in-law John Millet.

Main Character List

The Lisco Family

- Colonel Deb Lisco,
- Colonel Ted Lisco, brother
- Nicole Lisco, wife of Ted
- Bill Lisco, son of Nicole and Ted
- Maddy Lisco, Bill's daughter
- Jon Lisco, brother, retired Lieutenant Colonel.
- Gina Lisco, Jon's wife
- Hank Lisco, brother and high school coach
- Jacqueline Lisco, Hank's wife
- Bobby Lisco, Jacqueline and Hank's son

Jacobys from Utah

- Ed and Irene, farmers from Utah.
- Aaron and Ashley, son and daughter-in-law
- Adam and Megan, son and daughter-in-law
- Breanna, daughter
- Seth, Adam and Megan's son

O'Brians

- Jessica, mother
- Emilee, daughter and girlfriend of Bobby.
- Avery and Reagan, daughters
- Christian, former football player of Hank, leader of homegrown rebels, Emilee's father

Others

- Al and Linda Jones, next door neighbors of Hank and Jacqueline, Dentist
- Jason and Kori Jensen, carpenter and friends of Hank
- Dave Jensen, son of Jason and Kori
- Samantha, flight attendant on plane that was forced to land in Utah.
- Travis, pilot on plane that was forced to land in Utah.
- Terrance and Jerry came to farm with Ted after fleeing Utah.
- George Saxton, assistant football coach.
- Tim, ex-football player of Hanks, homegrown rebel.
- Sherry, rebel who originally came to farm with Christian.
- Caroline Sanchez, attack victim
- Julia, physician assistant and her husband Fred Hamilton.
- Harold Hamilton, bricklayer and his wife Becky.
- Irving Huang, retired captain under Jon.

Acknowledgements

A huge thanks to my sister Jaqueline Peavler and brother Hank Peavler for partnering with me to create Living Springs Publishers. Having their expertise and knowledge in publishing "2051" has been a blessing. Also, to my sister Debbie for her help as a sounding board for ideas.

I also wish to acknowledge the encouragement I received from my family while writing "2051". Having those you care about the most in life, being there for advice and honest critique, is priceless.

Prologue

Washington DC
White House war room

More than a million enemy troops from China, Russia, Iran and their allies were playing cat and mouse with the American troops along the United States southern border by crossing over and striking before returning to the protection of the largest cities on the Mexican side. They were biding their time while stockpiling weapons and allowing insurgents planted years earlier to disrupt and cause chaos across America. Russian armed forces crossed over the Bering Strait into Alaska and were being held in check by United States troops. The enemies next phase in the master plan to take over the world came in the form of a message to Washington warning of an impending missile attack.

The lights in the situation room were bright enough to reflect off the large table, where top advisors sat with the President of the United States. The brighter lights were installed so the older members, which included most of them, could read the memorandums and documents.

"So, they warned us," A bead of sweat dampened President Weller's forehead. "Both Beijing and Moscow have sent messages that our country is about to be hit with thousands of missiles. After all the deception and underhandedness, they want us to believe they are now following Marquess of Queensberry rules."

"They claim the missiles are not nuclear. Can we really be sure?" Vice President John Trupp was amazed he would be asking the question about world annihilation to the President, who only months earlier was so proud of his record on promoting world peace.

"They emphasized the missiles are not nuclear," the President swallowed hard. His face was noticeably pale as he thought of the geopolitical and budgetary discussions over the years about the ideas of shielding the country from the treats of intercontinental missiles. He was fully on the side of not spending money on expensive missiles to shoot down cheap missiles. "Bob, do we have an estimate on the damage we can expect from these strikes?"

"We cannot counter advancing Russian and Chinese ICBM threats. When it comes to missiles, we are at a terrible numerical disadvantage. The Ground Based Midcourse system recently was reduced from 44 to 40 interceptors and two-third of the Naval fleets with Aegis are too far away to supply interceptors for short range and intermediate defense. So, we can defend against some of the missiles, but ultimately many will find their way to our soil." Secretary of Defense Maes tried his best to speak professionally and remain non-adversarial. He had passionately and vigorously debated with the President and Congress on many occasions about funding collaborative technologies, hypersonic and direct energy solutions for missile defense. He also knew the President to be an honorable man who, just like all Presidents before him, had to consider many different aspects to détente.

"They gave us a warning. Now we must consider our response," interjected Secretary of State Aida Mahorn.

"I just left the meeting with the Chiefs of Staff," said the Secretary of Defense. "Our first inclination was that we should respond directly to the Russian and Chinese homelands with our own missiles. That would be a political reaction, with many rockets being intercepted and a great waste of our arsenal. We are beyond politics. It is the Chief of Staff recommendations that we hit the Russian forces in Alaska with as many missiles as needed to eradicate the threat. Then to focus on destroying the Chinese ships capable of hitting our land with mid-range missiles. We can strategically hit targets in the Mexican cities along the border with minimal civilian casualties. For the most part we are going to have to use ground forces to fight these battles."

"How many missiles do we have stockpiled?" Vice President Trupp asked.

"That is the problem. If used correctly, we have enough to fulfill our immediate objectives. But before we can escalate an all-out offensive assault on the enemy, we first need to start the process of changing our factories into weapon plants."

"Aida," President Weller was bending over slightly from the effects of his ulcer acting up. "What allies will give us immediate assistance."

"Australia, for sure. They have several hundred air breathing hypersonic missiles ready to go. Canada and Mexico are in the mix and will help to the extent they are capable." The Secretary of State turned to the Director of National Intelligence Barbara Stone, "Who else can we really rely on for immediate support, Barbara?"

"The honest answer. We don't know." She stopped the statement there, rather than going into the past couple of decades where the Chinese and Russians had foiled American alliances by creating economic and diplomatic partners with many of the United States traditional allies.

A singular figure sat in the shadows directly behind

the Director of National Intelligence, completely discounted by the powerful assembly of decision makers. He breathed silently through his nose as he candidly listened.

"How do we respond to Beijing and Moscow?" President Weller measured the reaction of his assembly. "At least they have started a dialogue."

"Sir, with all due respect," The Secretary of Defense leaned forward in his seat at the center of the long table. "The message we received from Beijing is not for negotiating. They only want more data to use for better understanding our mind set. We should be wary of our response, if any."

"It may not be a communication stating they are willing to negotiate, but the message in itself is an implication of discourse," stated the Secretary of State, turning her attention back in the direction of the Director of National Intelligence. "Barbara, what do you make of the correspondence?"

"Actions around the world are not suggesting compromise. Make no mistake here, Russia and China are not our only adversaries." She squinted, bringing her heavy grey eyebrows down over her eyes, "Troop movement is significant in central Asia, India and parts of Africa."

"Eventually we are going to have to deal with the cartels and stop the enemy from advancing through Mexico," stated Vice President Trupp. "We should go on the offense immediately in Mexico."

President Weller gave him an ominous look. Not because he disagreed with the assumption, but because the Vice President's statement implied that he was asleep at the wheel when the enemy first moved into the northern cities in Mexico. He understood that as Commander and Chief he needed to make the ultimate decisions for the response from the American Forces. The attack occurred so quickly and unexpectedly that his retort to the enemy was woefully slow.

Unnoticed by several at the table, the clandestine figure came to his feet and brushed the back of the Director of National Intelligence, who rose from her seat and pulled the chair back, allowing him to move around. He placed both hands on the long table. Even with the bright lights pounding down, his eyes and the cheeks on his face were sunken, giving him an undistinguishable, shadowy appearance.

"Hard to kill," the man yelled extremely loud. He moved his dark eyes from one person at the table to another. "We have allowed our enemies to become pre-positioned throughout every region in the world, and within the boundaries of our own country. They have strategically placed multi-domain forces capable of engaging our military establishment in our own backyard. These inside forces are mobile, hidden and resilient, making them…hard to kill. And you all sit here debating procedure."

"Who is this man?" President Weller's voice boomed across the table.

"He's someone we must listen to," stated Stone, the Director of National Intelligence. "His acumen is why we are now in serious discussion about the evacuation of American citizens from nearly two million square kilometers of our homeland."

The President slowly fell back into his chair with his heart beating rapidly. He continued to intently measure the man. He allowed him to speak.

"Survival...our enemies have studied our strengths for many decades and have calculated models and concepts to exploit our weaknesses. Their geostrategic alliances with our traditional allies have isolated us to fight them alone. It is too late for us to deem our homeland a sanctuary with the same benefits of safety and projection of power we once enjoyed. Our aspiration now is to survive." The lines meandering from the sides of his eyes seemed to deepen when he emphasized the word survive. "Rather than bickering about decree and rapprochement, you must immediately start the vital process of creating weapons and food supplies. You, as leaders must have the mettle to do what is necessary, no matter how odious, to make sure we survive. With time we can figure a way to defeat this scourge."

The man stepped back into the shadow as the Director of National Intelligence brought her chair to the table. There was some chatter and grumbling from the council as President Weller sucked in a deep breath and prepared to speak. He took a double take at the wall behind the Director's chair. There was nobody there.

PART ONE

Great Falls, Montana

Colonel Deb Lisco gasped for air as she fell on the seat of her pants into six inches of snow, a good two hundred meters from a cloud of smoke curling from the warehouse used as headquarters for the 2nd Brigade. Command Sergeant Major Tommy Talfoya stood above her with dark smudges of ash covering his face. He had pulled her to safety moments earlier.

She rose from the slush and coughed. Blood was dripping from her nose as she used the back side of her left hand to remove some of the moistness. Soldiers from the command post continued to exit the building as their comrades rushed to help.

"Tommy," Deb's eyes were red and watering. She struggled to speak as she hacked up soot. "What hit us?"

Tommy was unsure. He waved to a medic to render aid to the Colonel. He then addressed a soldier with a pulsnet radio on her wrist. "Corporal, is your radio functional?"

"Yes sir," she answered.

"We need F Company's mobile command center on site immediately."

Colonel Deb's ears were ringing as she tried to focus on the rescue efforts. Her vision was blurred, and the upper right part of her head was throbbing. She held both hands to her ears to try and stop the drumming noise pounding in her head.

"Colonel," Medic Sergeant Condoleezza Sessions approached. She steadied Deb and stared into her eyes. "I need you to come with me."

"I have to stay and help."

"No ma'am. You need to allow me to help you."

Deb felt nauseous as she coughed into her arm while Condoleezza struggled to hold her weight. Two privates rushed to relieve the medic from the burden of carrying the Colonel. They sat her on one of ten beds in the dimly lit, air supported medical tent.

She lay back on the hard bed and closed her eyes, allowing some relief from the sledgehammer pounding on the temple above her right eye. She took in several shallow breaths as she waited for Condoleezza to return. Lieutenant Bridges was placed in the bed next to her, with blood covering his left hand. Only a couple hours before he was the soldier who manned the monitor supplying pictures from a drone as Captain Malkova entered the large warehouse allegedly used to manufacture custom wheels on the outskirt of town.

Inside the tent it was cold enough to see the breath of the people speaking. Deb sat up, placed her feet flat on the ground and rose from the bed. She took two steps, staggered and passed out, landing with a thud on the floor.

Soft voices from the end of the bed brought her back to consciousness. Although it took a moment for her to focus, she knew it was commander of 2d Battalion, Lt. Col. Woodworth, speaking with Command Sergeant Major Talfoya.

"How long have I been out?" she asked with a soft

voice. It was now warmer in the tent, and she had an OD wool blanket tucked around her neck.

"About thirty minutes," the command sergeant major moved to the edge of the bed. He stared into her dark eyes which were wide open and fixed with a large, reddish bruise just to the right of her eye, going all the way down to her earlobe.

"What in the hell hit us, Tommy?" she looked at a bandage on her wrist and felt the hospital gown hanging loosely over her upper body.

"It was some sort of Dewy. Not sure exactly what type of direct energy weapon."

"Were there any fatalities?" she swung her feet to the floor, lowered her head and gently rubbed her temple. She felt nauseas.

"Three," answered Lt. Col. Woodworth, looking away in distress, before turning back to the colonel. "Five with severe injuries have been airlifted."

"Josh, I'm sure you have everyone on high alert and prepared should there be another attack." She swallowed hard, stood up and steadied herself while checking out her surroundings. Injured soldiers were crammed into all the beds inside the tent.

"Everyone is aware and prepared." Josh looked at Tommy, "General Maes is fully informed on our situation."

"Is command center operational?" Deb pulled the hospital gown straight out from her belly. "Where in the hell are my clothes?"

"Yes ma'am, the mobile units are all functional." The Command Sergeant Major was unsure how to handle the colonel's unwillingness to rest.

"Colonel," Sergeant Session yelled from the far end of the medical tent, "you need to lay back down."

"Tommy, find me my clothes. We don't have time to waste." She could see the medic moving toward her.

"Ma'am, please, you have a severe concussion." Sergeant Session placed her hand on the colonel's shoulder. "Resting for a little now will allow you to get back to full steam much quicker."

Before Colonel Deb could respond, a corporal entered the tent and approached Lt. Col. Woodworth.

"Sir, F Company has engaged insurgents. They are at the outskirts of the city and Captain Hendersen is requesting clarification on how far they should pursue." The corporal stared at Colonel Deb dressed in the hospital gown.

"Are the drones up?" Lt. Col. Woodworth asked.

"Yes sir, we have limited visibility, but the forward platoon's cameras are sending vivid images." The corporal remained at attention.

"Josh, see where they go. I'll bet you money they are heading to the factory outside of town." Deb pulled the gown over her head and tossed it on the bed, leaving her standing only in a bra and pants from her combat uniform. "I need my clothes."

Sergeant Session scoffed, "Give me a moment and I will get you a clean shirt."

"Deb, you should rest." Lt. Col. Woodworth momentarily stared at her, even as hard as he tried not too, his eyes lowered to her taut abdomen and large breasts bulging out of the side of her bra. Her biceps were as big as his.

"Something is about to happen. Respond to Captain Hendersen," said Deb. "I'll be there in a moment."

Lt. Col. Woodworth and Command Sergeant Major Talfoya followed the corporal out of the medical tent as

Sergeant Session handed her a clean shirt before continuing to aid the wounded.

Her head was still aching. She either needed to lay down and give her body a chance to heal or bear the brunt of the pain and get back to work. Tommy rushed back into the tent.

"Colonel," his face had a look of pure fear, "missiles have been launched toward the United States."

She followed Tommy out of the medic tent while still tucking in her shirt. Both ends of the large command center tent were open, but heaters kept it warm and comfortable on the inside.

"What do we know?" Deb directed her question to Lt. Col. Woodworth.

The lieutenant colonel looked at Captain Laura Dodson who was standing in the middle of a group of communication tech specialists. Captain Dodson motioned toward the monitor, "Ma'am, thirty minutes ago, we received a message that a missile attack was eminent. Missiles have been launched from platforms in mainland Russia, mainland China and their naval ships."

"Are we talking nuclear?" Deb placed her fingers to her forehead and tried to focus. She considered the captain to be one of the brightest officers under her command, whose husband worked with the Missile Defense Agency. The information she held would be accurate.

"Ma'am, all indications are they are not nuclear. But we are finding several aspects of the Chinese technology are not what we thought they were. We have to wait and see just what they have launched," answered Captain Dodson. "All branches have responded in kind with our own missiles."

"What's the speed and range of the missiles?"

"Theoretically, the Chinese have hypersonic missiles that can travel up to eight thousand kilometers per hour and travel a distance of twelve thousand kilometers." Everyone in the tent seemed to be frozen in place as they listened to the captain. "We have the ability to identify the incoming missiles, but with the number airborne and the rate they are being fired, there is no way we will destroy all of them.

"Malmstrom is the most likely target in our proximity," stated Tommy. "We should secure our perimeter, but also stay prepared to assist the air base if they are hit."

The roar of aircraft flying overhead was deafening as the airbase scattered planes from the runways. Deb looked to the floor, and took in several deep breaths, before rushing out the open end of the tent. She leaned over and vomited. Tommy came to her side and placed a hand on her back. She continued to bend over and spit on the frozen ground.

"You must be a hell of a lot tougher than me, Tommy," she sniffled and looked up. "How did you come out without a scratch? You were standing right next to me."

"You blocked the explosion. I happened to be on the back side." He took his handkerchief and handed it to her.

Looking up into his deep-set green eyes she detected something she had never seen before in the way he was observing her. Or perhaps, in the past she had not noticed the intensity of his gaze. She stood up straight as the ground shook from planes soaring overhead.

"Whatever happens when the missiles hit, we are going to give it right back to them. Most of those fighter jets have the scram jet powered missiles onboard," she wiped her mouth with the handkerchief.

"Colonel, we have incoming on Malmstrom. They are about to be hit." Captain Dodson moved out of the tent and positioned to the side of Tommy and looked toward the airbase.

They heard the whistling sound of the missile approaching before a thud. The missile was intercepted before it hit the base. The lack of an explosion surprised everyone.

"Is that it?" Tommy directed the question to Captain Dodson."

"Yes sir, I have no idea why but, obviously, that was not an armed missile." There are hundreds of missiles on radar that are designated for central or southern United States. The ones heading north already struck or have been taken out. The power-scaling lasers seem to be performing very well."

Deb moved back inside the communication tent and addressed Lt. Col. Woodworth, "It's time to find out what is at the custom wheel factory east of town."

"I'll arrange air support." Lt. Col. Woodworth felt a rush of adrenaline flash through his body. "I'm going to go with Company I."

"If this place is what I think it is, it is about to be wiped from the face of the earth." Colonel Deb was tired of taking a flailing without a response, it was completely against her nature. "I want all companies ready to go within the hour. Let's find out once and for all what is happening in this city."

Eastern Colorado Farm

Hank Lisco stared to the west, across the vast open field as he sat on the porch of the farmhouse. It was too noisy for his liking inside the house, where several people were crammed into the living room. The stars were eerily bright, causing the water in the creek to sparkle as it meandered through the pasture. Life on the farm appeared to be slowing down, which gave him time to think of the predicament he, his family and friends were facing. Being such an optimistic person, he was still having trouble accepting that war was taking place on American soil. As a football coach, he always planned and strategized to prepare for an opponent.

Ted's quick departure to the army base in Colorado Springs, and unsure if Deb was seriously injured or even killed in the blast, caused even more angst. He could see lights flickering in the corrals as the Jacobys handled the chores of taking care of the animals. Terrance was outside the garage piddling with the tractor. The temperature was rapidly falling. A cold breeze blew into his face. He pulled his coat tight around his neck as Bill, Maddy and Samantha came out the front door.

"Do you mind if we join you coach?" Bill moved to Hank's side. He started addressing his uncle as coach when he played football for the Lions, in order to keep the other players from thinking he was getting preferential treatment. The terming carried over to when they were alone.

"Of course, I don't. It's actually a good time to have

some company."

"I hope we hear something from Dad," said Bill. Maddy was holding on to his arm looking at Hank with her mouth slightly open. Samantha crossed her arms to keep warm.

"Bobby, Emilee, Caroline and Sherry are in the garage waiting by the computer. I'm sure Ted will contact us as soon as he can." Hank placed his hand on the side of Maddy's face.

"Where is Grandpa?" Maddy stared at Hank's chiseled chin.

"He is at the army base," Bill squatted down and picked her up, easily holding her in his right arm. She turned and put her arms around his neck, hugging him tightly. "Grandpa is ok," he whispered in her ear.

"I want to help him," she sniffled.

"Your grandpa will be back to help us when we need him," Samantha said, reaching up to rub her arm.

Bill could feel Maddy's cold nose on the side of his face as she shook her head in agreement. He turned to Samantha. "Do you two want to go back inside?"

"No, not really," she said, taking hold of Maddy's hand as he sat her down. "It's really beautiful out here, huh Maddy?"

"It's like when we camped out on the rocks." Maddy looked at Samantha with her big eyes, "Remember you slept by Grandpa."

Bill laughed and looked at Samantha's reaction. She just smiled.

"I don't believe I have ever seen a clearer night," said Jon, stepping out the front door and moving to the edge of the porch next to Hank. He pointed to the west where the glare of lights radiated into the cold night air. "All the lights from the farms sure shine bright on a night like this."

"That has to be good sign," said Hank to his brother. "Jon, I'm really having a hard time dealing with all the uncertainty."

"Dammit Hank, it's uncertain for everyone. We just have to take it one day at a time," stated Jon.

"Did you just see that?" Bill stepped off the porch and onto the driveway. He pointed to the horizon. "There was a flash of light."

Hank and Jon joined him on the driveway. A small, but noticeable flash appeared again, followed quickly by another. A low humming sound came from the south and several greyish black contrails lined the darkened sky.

"Missiles," Jon spoke with a lump in his throat. "They are attacking us with missiles. The explosions we just saw were warheads we intercepted. They never hit ground."

Adam and Aaron walked from the barn to join them. Irene and Breanna exited the motorhome and before long most of the people on the farm were standing in the driveway looking at the dark contrails decorating the bright night sky.

"Are we looking at the end of the world?" Gina asked anxiously, staring at Jon with her lips quivering.

"The ones that exploded weren't nuclear," Jon said in a clear voice. "But this is an escalation of war that there is no returning from."

"Jon, how did these missiles reach all the way to Colorado?" Jacqueline took hold of Hank's arm as they all looked to the western sky.

"It's because they just sent a hell of a lot of them our way." Jon noticed that everyone was looking at him for answers. He turned to Nicole and then Bill before continuing, "What they are doing, is measuring our abilities."

Bobby, Sherry, Emilee and Caroline crossed the driveway to gather with the others as they watched the attack unfolding in the night sky. Terrance and Jerry followed closely behind them, both carrying AK-47s. A bright flash of light, followed by a loud boom made them stop and look to the west.

"That just came from the Brown's farm." Bill stared across the pasture and listened. The low muffled sound of gunshots could be heard. He turned to his uncle Jon. "That explosion wasn't from a missile, was it?"

"No. It was probably a propane tank," replied Jon.

The distinct sound of gunshots continued.

"Someone is attacking them. We have to help." Hank took a couple steps in the direction of the farm to the west.

"We have to secure and protect this place first," Jon went into full lieutenant colonel mode.

"I'm going to his farm and see if I can help Clint Brown," said Hank emphatically.

"No, you are not. You and Bill need to prepare everyone with weapons and then work to set a perimeter around this farm," Jon stated adamantly.

Hank folded his arms at his chest and continued looking to the west.

"Hank, I'm going to go check on the Browns. But I really want you to focus on our families." Jon placed his hand on his brother's shoulder before turning to the crowd, "I need two volunteers to come with me."

"I'll go," said Terrance quickly.

"I will go," Sherry moved right in front of Jon.

Jon glanced back and forth between the two of them. His team was to be a young girl, who only weeks earlier was a member of the insurgents trying to take over the city, and the other, an older man with one leg.

Jon turned to Bill, "Can you get Sherry and me a couple of rifles?"

"I'd prefer a pistol, or an AK. They are the only weapons I have fired." Sherry pulled out a black stocking cap and stuffed her thick, blond hair inside before pulling it over her ears.

"We should prepare to be out the entire night." Jon noticed some dark clouds on the horizon. "It's clear now, but it looks like clouds are building so we will probably be dealing with cold and snowy conditions."

"Uncle Jon, do you want me to go with you?" Bobby glanced quickly at Sherry before bringing his gaze back to his uncle. Emilee was standing next to Sherry and noticed the look.

"No, you stay here and help your father." Jon motioned to Nicole and Samantha who were standing on each side of Maddy, "Have all the kids sleep in the basement supply room this evening."

The three made their way across the pasture in the direction of the neighbor's farm.

Brown Farm

There was a distinct smell of smoke in the bitterly cold air as Jon, Sherry and Terrance advanced forward on their reconnaissance journey. Light from the three-quarter-moon peeking through the ever-increasing clouds made travel over the rough pasture easier than if the night were pitch black, it also created a greater risk of them being spotted as they moved to the Brown's farm. They were within three kilometers of the neighbor's barn where they approached the narrow, live water creek that signified the western edge of the Lisco property.

"There is no way around it. We are going to have to get wet." Jon's face was bright red as he moved to the edge of the icy water. He took four long steps with the water rising to slightly below knee level before making it to the opposite shore. Sherry hesitated before crossing the stream. She was wearing jeans which immediately froze to the lower half of her legs. Terrance's artificial leg worked commendably as he stepped through the water. They waited in the cold wind, listening to the loud voices coming from the farm.

"When we get to the wire fence on the backside of the barn, Terrance, I want you to go about twenty-five meters to the north and hold your location on this side of the fence. Sherry, you go twenty-five meters to the south and hold that spot. I will advance through the fence and find a position to observe on the north side of the barn. Hopefully, I'll have a vantage point where I can see what is taking place without being detected."

Flashes of light from flames billowing into the air past the barn were noticeable near the farmhouse. When they arrived at the barbed wire fence Jon pointed to the north and then to the south. Terrance and Sherry split off, without uttering a word.

Jon crawled through the strands of sharp wire and ran to the back of the red barn. He looked back to see if he could see Sherry or Terrance. No sign of either of them. He scurried along the edge to the northwest corner of the barn and gazed toward the farmhouse. The house itself was nearly three hundred meters away with a throng of boisterous people gathered in the driveway and front yard, grouped around campfires. Several of the intruders had hunting rifles strapped to their shoulders, with no military weapons visible.

All he could see amidst the fog of smoke, past the horde in the driveway, were several people mulling around the front door of the home. He pulled in a deep breath and leaned against the back side of the barn, hidden from anyone who should look his way. The bottom part of his pant legs was frozen solid. He could not tell if the crowd was travelers who found a place to dwell or if they were marauders who overtook the homestead. The wood they were burning must have come from a shed or outhouse on the farm, something Clint Brown would never allow. He thought, for a moment, debating if he should advance to the farmhouse. With the unruly nature of the raiders, he decided to be prudent in his approach and have Terrance back him up.

He returned to the barbed wire fence line and motioned for Sherry and Terrance. A slight wind was blowing, and large snowflakes tumbled from the sky. It was much darker now with heavy clouds blocking the moonlight.

"I'm about to freeze my ass off out here Jon," said Terrance. His white frosted eyebrows were pronounced on his black face. "What is happening up there?"

"I can't tell if they are friendly or not."

"I've never been so cold in my life." Sherry held her frozen gloves in front of her bright red face, "My gloves are frozen solid, and so are my pants."

"Pull your gloves off, you can use mine." Jon removed his waterproof fleece gloves and handed them to her. "There ain't nothing I can do about your pants."

"Something tells me these people aren't friendly," stated Terrance.

Jon stuck his prominent jaw straight out. With his teeth clenched his jaw was more prominent than ever before. His thoughts were with Clint and Peg. They were both in their seventies and the type of people who went out of their way to help others. They were decade long friends of the Liscos.

"I need to find out the situation here before we go back. Terrance, you and I can slip through the corral on the south and enter the barn through the utility door. Sherry, you wait here on this side of the fence. If you see us coming with people on our tail, fire five shots in the direction of our pursuers, then turn and run back to the farm as quickly as you can." Jon's breath created a heavy fog out of his mouth, "You will still have bullets in your weapon but make damn sure you don't shoot us."

"How long do I wait?" Sherry felt much better with the warm gloves. The frozen lower half of her pants was causing a tingling sensation with her legs.

"Until you hear gunfire, or we return." Jon motioned to Terrance. They crawled through the barbed wire fence.

The corral was in full sight of the intruders at the driveway, but the wood fence, along with the increasing snow, shielded them enough to reach the door on the side of the barn without being detected. The inside was cold and dark with a musky smell of wet manure. The large overhanging doors at the west end were wide open, giving an unobstructed view to the farmhouse. They inched toward the light of the pendulous doors, staying close to the horse stalls. The ability to see the Brown's home from the front of the barn was better than the vantage point Jon had on the side, but still not sufficient to observe anything but the mass of people in the driveway and front yard.

"All I see is smoke and a hell of a lot of people," said Terrance. "They sure in hell don't look very friendly to me."

"There are so many of them, I wonder if they would even notice me if I walked up to the house."

Terrance gave him a dubious look and shook his head. "I wouldn't take that chance."

"I don't see any other way. I can't leave without knowing they are safe."

"If I go with you, I'll be the only one with an AK." Terrance was kneeling on his right knee with the rifle pointing toward the barn floor.

The snowfall intensified to where the house could no longer be seen from the barn.

"You can give me cover from here. I'll move along the corral to the south and make my way to the house. This snow will give me some cover in order to get close enough to blend in with the crowd."

"Let's get it over with." Terrance lifted the AK-47 and pointed it out the overhanging door. He remained far enough back to be concealed in the shadow of darkness.

Jon shouldered his rifle and stepped into the heavy snow. He took three steps to the south and yelled, "Oh God."

Terrance leaned out the door and looked at Jon hunched over three frozen bodies. Two were face down but Clint Brown was face up, with snow covering much of his face.

"Is it the Browns? Terrance stepped from the barn.

"Yeah, and their hired hand," Jon's voice cracked.

"There's someone at the barn," a low voice shouted from the driveway, followed by indiscernible chatter.

"We have to get out of here," said Terrance, moving back into the darkness of the barn.

Jon hesitated. When he saw several of the invaders rushing in his direction, he receded inside the barn, raised his rifle and fired three shots into the snow in front of the approaching group. He allowed Terrance time to exit out the utility door, before withdrawing back and firing three more shots out the large opening of the overhanging doors.

Terrance climbed through the wooden fence at the back of the corral and leveled his rifle on the wood railing. The loud popping of gunshots filled the air. The thud of bullets hitting the fence forced him to fall to the wet ground. As Jon climbed under the lower rung of the wood fence, he fired several rounds toward the utility door, hitting at least one of the pursuers, before retreating to the barbed wire fence.

Sherry jumped when she heard the gunfire. She could see the shadowy forms of Jon and Terrance running directly at her. She pulled the glove off her right hand and pointed the pistol in the direction of a cluster of people at the north edge of the barn. She fired five shots in quick succession, holstered her pistol, then turned and ran. She sprinted right through the water of the creek before turning around to check to see who was following. The visibility had deteriorated to the point she could no longer see more than twenty meters. Out of the heavy snow the forms of Terrance and Jon appeared. The three of them jogged together through ankle deep snow across the wet pasture.

Great Falls, Montana

"See if we can get in touch with General Maes." Colonel Deb dreaded having to brief the general. She knew exactly what needed to happen.

"We have a drone ready for support," stated Command Sergeant Major Talfoya, "it is launched and readily available."

Deb gave him a dubious look. She was unconvinced that weaponized drones were reliable. With the unknown capabilities of the Chinese in hacking and reprogramming the intent of our Nonhuman Aerial Vehicle (NAV), she felt better with having an actual pilot in control of firing a missile, rather than a robot. She was appreciative that the F-35 was brought back into the fold after being shelved for several years.

"Ma'am, we have General Maes."

Deb stepped in front of the monitor, "Sir we have a situation occurring here."

"I heard," the general was blunt, "are you capable of continuing command?"

"Yes sir." Deb could not stand this man. To protect herself, she wanted to make sure she informed him of everything taking place within her command. "We were hit by a group sheltered at a warehouse on the outskirts of town. We have I, G and F Companies positioned and ready to deal with the source of the attack. Also, I would like to request 1st and 3rd Battalions withdraw back to Great Falls."

"With missiles being launched in our direction, you

want to congregate troops in one place. 1st and 3rd Battalions are to remain in place." General Maes waited for affirmation. With no reply, he asked, "Anything else?"

"Yes sir, are we going to go on the offensive here at any time, or are we going to sit and let the enemy take pot shots at us?" Deb's head was throbbing.

"All that is in the works." The general accepted her question much better than she thought he would. "Right now, you sustain and secure your location."

"Yes sir."

The monitor went blank. Deb looked at Tommy and shook her head.

"You should take a look at this, Colonel," stated a technician.

She looked over the shoulder of the specialist controlling the monitor. A large group of people were in the streets, about seventy-five meters in front of I Company's forward weapons platoon.

"Are they protestors? I don't see any firearms." Deb stepped back and looked at the images transmitting over the area around F and G Companies. "Lt. Col. Woodworth is with I Company, isn't he?" Deb asked.

"Yes ma'am."

"Get him online," Deb turned to the Command Sergeant Major, "this doesn't feel right Tommy."

"Give us some different vantage angles on the crowd," said Tommy. "I want a 360-degree view around I Company.

Deb noticed one of the technicians standing to the side of the room, typing into the monitor of a four-inch screen strapped to his wrist. She moved two steps closer to him. He quickly looked up, startled and placed his arms to his side.

"Who are you contacting?" She looked at his name tag. "Corporal Turner, who are you messaging?"

"Ma'am, I am just programming my Pulsenet."

"Captain Dodson, can you appease me and check Corporal Turner's computer?"

The corporal looked frantically at his approaching superior. He pulled the screen close to his mouth and said, "Delete last three messages."

Colonel Deb grabbed his wrist as Captain Dodson took hold of his other arm. Tommy grabbed him from behind, into a bear hug, and pulled him to the ground. The corporal continued trying to speak into the monitor.

"Gag him," yelled Captain Dodson emphatically. "Don't let him talk."

Deb pulled out the handkerchief Tommy had given her after vomiting. She pinched his jaw open and stuck it in his mouth.

"Give me his monitor," Captain Dodson moved back as a group of soldiers held the corporal on his back.

Deb looked at the group of technicians sitting at their stations scrutinizing the information displayed on the screens. All the information needed for her to make life and death decisions were relayed to her from these specialists. Her stomach sank as she wondered how many of the operators were enemy operatives.

"Colonel," yelled a technician, "I Company's forward platoon is under attack."

Deb stepped to the monitor. Tommy moved next to her. The platoon was being hit with a massive amount of large and small caliber fire. The high-resolution camera took a moment to normalize through the smoke and cold fog. When it did, the vivid image showed many soldiers from the platoon laying in the street. Traces of gunfire filled the air as the heavy armored vehicles from I Company approached the fallen soldiers.

"Ma'am, I have Lt. Col Woodworth on my screen," stated a technician.

"Josh, F Company and G Company are redirecting to your location. Are you secure?"

There was no reply. The views from the cameras projected on the different monitors showed an eerie scene. There was smoke and fog rising into the dark sky, but not a person visible.

"Josh," Deb yelled.

"It's like they disappeared into thin air." Lt. Col. Woodworth had a blank expression on his face. "We need helicopters to evacuate the wounded."

"They are almost there," stated Tommy. "The NAV is overhead if needed."

"Tommy, have all three companies return to base."

"Colonel," Captain Dodson stepped next to Deb, "Corporal Turner was communicating with the enemy we just encountered. He gave them the position, times of departure and number of troops for the deployment."

Deb swallowed hard as she watched the corporal being led from the communication tent. She thought for a moment and asked, "Does he incriminate any other members of the communication team?"

Captain Dodson blinked several times before answering, "Ma'am, the answer might be yes. We need to examine all computers. I do have three soldiers I want to remove from their duties until we know for sure."

"Ok." Deb was feeling sick to her stomach and her head was pounding. She began to wobble as Captain Dodson moved to her side and steadied her.

"I need some assistance here," yelled Captain

Dodson.

Several soldiers came to her side.

"Take her to her tent," ordered Command Sergeant Major Talfoya, pointing to a soldier.

Eastern Colorado Farm

The temperature was well below freezing with snow falling, even so Hank and Jaqueline remained on the porch looking across the pasture toward the Brown farm. Others would come out to join them but would quickly retreat inside the farmhouse. Jon, Terrance and Sherry were taking much longer to check on the Browns than anyone had anticipated.

"Hopefully, Clint brought out some of his good Scotch, and they are all sitting around the fireplace hashing over old times." Hank forced a smile to his wife.

"The weather is getting really bad," Jacqueline straightened her shoulders. "Only a few hours ago it was the clearest night I had ever seen. Now, the snow is coming down so hard we can't see across the driveway."

"Bobby and the others are guarding the perimeter of the farm. It seems almost futile now with the visibility so poor."

Hank thought how different the situation was with his high school football players now guarding the farm with military grade weapons, rather than celebrating the state championship.

Breanna stepped out of the motor home carrying two cups with steam rising from them. Snow accumulated on the top of her hair by the time she stepped under the overhang of the porch.

"Mom made you some hot chocolate."

"How are your mom and dad doing?" Hank asked. It felt good to take his mind off Jon, if only for a second.

"Mom is doing good. Dad is kind of struggling."

"Ed hasn't been out very much lately." Jacqueline smacked her lips, "My God this hot chocolate is delicious."

"Mom has a knack that everything she makes is tasty." Breanna was much less talkative than usual. "Have you heard anything from Jon, Terrance and the girl?"

"Not yet."

"I'm sure they found shelter somewhere. If the wind picks up this storm is going to turn into a blizzard." She turned her back to the breeze, "I'm going to go back and get out of the cold."

"Tell Irene thank you," Jacqueline watched Breanna leave. She wanted to go inside too but felt an obligation to stand in the cold with her husband as he waited for his brother.

The wind picked up speed. Just before Jacqueline gave up, to go inside, she noticed Hank move to the furthest edge of the porch. Out of the white blanket of snow came three figures moving in unison, side by side. He stepped off the porch.

"Good Lord," Hank moved out of their way as they rushed by.

Jacqueline opened the door to allow them entry. Inside, they stood silently, unable to speak, with the snow slowly melting from their bodies.

Jon pulled out a chair at the kitchen table and helped Sherry into it. He looked at her intently, clicked his tongue, and shook his head up and down. Terrance moved slowly to take a seat. All three pulled off their frozen gloves and placed them on the table.

"It's not good," said Jon hoarsely. He lowered his eyes. A crowd of people was now in the kitchen. "We need to make sure nobody followed us."

Bobby, Dave, Emilee and Caroline were at the front entrance to the door, all carrying weapons.

"Bobby," Jon ran his hand through his hair wringing away the wetness, "take your friends down to the fence and make sure nobody is coming across the pasture. If someone is coming across the grassland, they are not friendly."

"What happened?" Gina placed a hand on the side of her husband's face, "Are the Browns, ok?"

"They're dead."

"Bobby," Terrance looked at the youngsters standing with their weapons, "have Jerry go with you."

"There were probably a hundred people at the Brown's farm," Jon sighed, then continued, "many of them had weapons."

"Are you sure Clint and Peg are dead?" Hank asked in as delicate voice as he could muster.

Jon nodded his head at his brother.

"Their bodies were placed outside the doors of the barn," said Terrance. "There was another body next to them."

"It was Hector the hired hand," stated Jon softly.

"We need everyone aware of the danger we are facing." Hank looked in the direction of his assistant coach and football players, "If they do come our way, we need them to know we can protect ourselves."

"I'll go to the RV and inform the Jacobys," stated Coach Saxton, putting on his coat. He had never seen Coach Lisco so serious, or so uneasy.

Bobby moved close to the kitchen table and watched as Sherry removed her stocking cap, allowing her hair to flow free. Her face was flushed red. He glanced at Emilee before walking out the front door.

"You all need to get out of those wet clothes," said Gina. A puddle of water was forming on the kitchen floor under each of their feet.

"I'll go to my room in the garage," said Terrance. He stood up and stiffly took a couple steps.

"Terrance," Jon's voice was much stronger now, "thank you."

Terrance grabbed his rifle, nodded his head and walked out the door.

"Can I grab a change of clothes for you from the camper?" Jacqueline asked Sherry. "You should go downstairs and get a warm shower."

"I can get them myself. But I do think I will take a warm shower."

"Ok." Jacqueline stared at Sherry, observing the dynamic of beauty and animalism that enveloped the young lady. The skin around her eyes was taut, giving them a depth that generated a depiction of potency as she innocently observed the surroundings in the kitchen.

"Mrs. Lisco," Sherry stood up, "I think I will sleep in the basement tonight. I don't feel good about sleeping in the camper alone."

"All the kids are sleeping in the storage area downstairs. I would think there would be no problem with you sleeping in Avery and Reagans bed tonight."

She pulled her cap back over her hair and stepped out the front door without replying to Jacqueline's confirmation of sleeping in the main farmhouse.

"We need to keep a close watch tonight," said Jon.

"Uncle Jon, we'll take care of it," stated Bill.

"Why don't you get some rest. It will be light in about five hours." Hank placed his hand on his brother's shoulder.

Jon was exhausted. He had just finished an eight-kilometer run in dreadful conditions. He wondered whether he had sufficiently described the horror he witnessed at the Brown farm for the others to realize the danger of the situation. His once frozen pants were now wet and sticking to his leg. He felt a twinge in his back as he made his way to the bedroom.

***

The bright morning sun shimmered on the pastel papered wall of the kitchen. The smell of freshly grilled pancakes mixed with the aroma of coffee and bacon filled the rooms of the house. Irene and Jerry took turns between hovering over the stove and cooking the food. The living room was full to the brim with people. Terrance, Bobby, Emilee, Caroline and Dave were outside keeping an eye on the pasture and the road to the farm. Bill and Samantha were in Ted's office at the garage monitoring his computer.

"Everyone, can I say a few words?" Hank anxiously pranced back and forth in front of the fireplace. "I know the events last night were alarming. At the same time, it should be a wakeup call for us. Clint and Peg were good people who never should have lost their lives in this manner."

"It is very important that we understand the danger surrounding us." Jon moved next to Hank, "We have to be prepared to fight if we are confronted with the same people who took over the Brown's farm."

"Do you think they are still there?" Al made a point of looking at each person in the room. "I'm a dentist, not a fighter."

"I presume they haven't left," said Jon. "Believe me these people will not hesitate to harm us."

"With the sun out, I was hoping to build some more on the apartment," said Jason, holding the tattered cast on his arm out in front of him. He was standing to the side of the sofa where his wife Kori was sitting next to Harold and Becky. "I know Harold would like to lay more block on the tower."

"It would be great to get back to building and improving our living conditions on the farm, but we do need to address the security issue first," Hank looked at Jon.

"We would like for everyone to, at the very least, learn how to load and fire a weapon safely," said Jon. "It would be best to instruct only three people at a time."

"So, we can do both," stated Hank, looking at Jason.

"Um, I have something to say," Coach Saxton stood to the side of the room. "Toby and I, along with the Piersons and Smiths have decided we are going back to the city. It seems to be a safer alternative for us at this time."

"Why?" Jacqueline moved next to Hank. "You know how bad it is in the city."

"I have never been so scared in my life as I was last night, not knowing if people were coming out of the night to kill us," said Toby frantically.

"I'm sorry Hank, we spent our whole life talking about being a team and going into battle with one another. The big difference with a football game is that the other team was not shooting at us," Coach Saxton lowered his head.

"And losing did not mean being killed," said Toby.

"I really don't know what to say here George." Hank moved to the side of the room and stared at the members of his football team. "You are making a huge mistake. At least you know we have food here."

"We made our decision," said Toby.

"How are you going to get to the city?" Jon asked.

"We are hoping to use the old pickup Ted arrived in."

"That ain't going to happen," said Aaron Jacoby sharply.

"Oh boy," Hank didn't want his friend's decision to cause conflict with everyone. "Let's make these decisions after we've eaten breakfast."

Nicole came up from the basement followed by Maddy, Scotty and the other children. They all looked wide awake after sleeping in the food storage area in the basement. Maddy went directly to Irene's side.

She stood with her back straight and her hair neatly brushed as she asked, "Can I help you cook Irene?"

"Maddy we are just finishing with the pancakes." She put her hand on the side of the little girl's face. "But you know what we can do a little later?"

"Make some more cinnamon rolls?"

"Nope, don't tell anybody," Irene leaned down and whispered, "I have a special way of making angel food cake with chocolate fudge icing. Maybe we can have you and Grandma Nicole help."

"And Samantha."

"It will be a girls cooking party."

Hank forced a smile as he poured himself a cup of coffee. He remained silent as he walked out the front door. Although it was a brisk morning, the bright sun felt good on his face as he sloshed thru the snow on the driveway in the direction of the corrals.

Bobby leaned on a wooden picket. "Well Dad, have you got things figured out?"

Emilee and Caroline stood on each side of Bobby.

Hank smiled wryly and shook his head. "I think our

situation is even more confusing than it was last night. George, the Piersons and Smiths all want to go back to the city."

"What, Jesus, it's a terrible time for them to do that."

Terrance, carrying a telescope and Dave holding binoculars came closer to listen to the conversation.

"I can't believe Coach Saxton would want to leave us here," stated Dave, towering over Caroline as he moved behind her.

"Can you see anything at the Brown's farm with that telescope?" Hank asked Terrance.

"Not really," he answered candidly.

"What about the drone?" Hank asked. "Doesn't it have the range to go that far?"

"Bill and Samantha are working on it. It launches but they can't get a signal on the computer monitor," said Bobby, shaking his head.

"Why don't you all go in and get something to eat. I'll keep an eye out here." Hank was looking at Emilee and Caroline as he spoke," there are a lot of pancakes ready to eat."

"I'll stay with you Dad," said Bobby.

"I thought I smelled pancakes," said Terrance, moving in the direction of the farmhouse. "You don't have to ask me twice."

"You sure Bobby that you don't want to get out of the cold?" Emilee asked.

"I'll be there shortly. You guys go ahead."

The father and son waited silently for a moment as they watched Jason and Harold begin to shovel snow off the construction sites. The temperature was rising quickly.

"I needed to get out of the house before I said something to George that I would regret," Hank lamented.

"Did you get into an argument?"

"No," Hank took a sip of his cold coffee, then looked into Bobby's eyes. "Having him tell me he was leaving at a time when we all should be working together, really hit me wrong. But neither of us said anything we might regret."

"Dad, he's your best friend."

"Yes, he is," Hank swallowed hard. The confusion and uncertainty of everything was making it difficult for him to make good decisions. Bobby was correct. If George and Toby wanted to leave, then he would help them in any way he could.

Lone Tree, Colorado

Christian was awake well before daylight. He walked through the foyer of the large home they had confiscated in the ritzy neighborhood. He traipsed into the family room and looked out the picture window. A perfect view of the Rocky Mountains with their snow-covered peaks bathed in sunlight was ruined by several pockets of smoke billowing into the sky from buildings burning across the city.

"Couldn't sleep either?" Jessica, with a heavy wool blanket wrapped around her was sitting in a chair with her knees pulled up to her chest. "It was really cold last night."

"Cold doesn't bother me at all."

"This is beautiful, but…"

"I know, it's not ours and never will be." He was shirtless and the belt buckle was open at the front of his pants.

Jessica stared at his crooked nose and protruding forehead as he stood over her. When they were in high school, she made fun of his caveman head. He was never handsome by any imagination but had a strength to him that always attracted girls.

"What are we going to do?" she asked.

He grimaced. A loud knock came from the front door.

"Christian, open up."

A cold rush of air filled the room as he opened the door. Standing on the porch was Shira and two more of his followers. She pointed across the lawn where hundreds of insurgents dressed in black covered the street.

"They want to talk with you," Shira said. She looked past him into the living room at Jessica.

"What do they want?" he pulled his pants tight and latched his belt buckle.

"They want us to take out the police station on Colorado Boulevard." She stepped back and glanced over her shoulder to the street. "The leader of this group is not very compromising. She wants to speak to you face to face to make sure you are fully aware of their expectations."

Although unofficially so, Christian considered Shira to be second in command of the rebels dedicated to following him. He remained shirtless as he stepped into the cold and marched down the sidewalk to the curb at the street. A group of about twenty of the people dressed in black, some with their faces covered with masks, waited for him. They all held weapons.

"How can I help you?" he asked.

"We are beginning the execution of the next phase of disruption and now have the directives for you to follow," said a man at the front of the group before stepping to the side, allowing a small woman to move in front of him.

"What kind of directives?" Christian felt his heartrate quicken when he heard the word directive. He was smart enough to know it was another word for orders.

Insurgents at the back of the crowd leveled their weapons in his direction. It made no sense why they would show such a blatant display of power to those they considered confederates. He glanced at Tim standing at the door holding an AK-47 with Jessica still wearing only a tee-shirt at his side. Shira stood close to him.

"The police have taken command of the station on Colorado Boulevard. Early tomorrow morning you are to take control back." The lady speaking sounded more like a robot than a person. "Prepare to leave for Colorado Springs immediately after you have control. Get dressed and we will give you the details."

Christian felt the cold wind on his bare chest while he watched her step back and disappear in the group. He was surprised how unbending and rigid her demands were being relayed to him.

"Are we going to follow their orders?" Tim asked as he followed him into the vestibule.

"I don't know," Christian hesitated for a moment. "I guess I'll get dressed and see what they expect of us."

Jessica followed him to the bedroom. "We should take off and get as far away from these people as possible. They are not our friends and never will be. We should all leave now."

"That will be pretty hard to do Jessica with hundreds of them outside the door." He stopped to stare at her for a moment.

"Christian, I'm telling you, this will end very bad for us if you allow these people to make all the decisions." She stared at him while he ignored her musing.

He dressed and put on a light jacket before joining Tim in the foyer.

"They never moved an inch," said Tim. "Aren't we supposed to be on the same side?"

"Theoretically we are," said Christian. "Stay inside the house. I'll agree with everything they say. We can hash it all out after they leave."

Christian pulled the collar of his jacket around his neck as he approached the lady at the curb. He towered over her as he stepped into the street.

"You are to leave at six am and take your soldiers

west to Colorado Boulevard where the police have established a substation. You will take control and eliminate their ability to operate."

"Ok," he shook his head in affirmation. He despised the way she used the phrase "you will". "What do we do then?"

"We have transportation for you and five of your top command to transport to a base we have at a ranch just outside of Colorado Springs, south of the small town of Peyton. The rest of your assemblage will transfer to the location over the following two days."

"Why are we going to Colorado Springs?"

He was surprised at how long she hesitated. She was so used to others taking her orders without query that his question caught her off guard. He waited silently for her response as she continued to stare, never diverting her eyes.

"We are going to strike the North American Aerospace Defense Command," she answered.

Christian could not believe the objective was NORAD.

"I understand," Christian replied as calmly as he could.

"Six am tomorrow morning," she turned and disappeared into the crowd.

He watched the large group peel away in perfect unison.

Inside the house Christian took in a deep breath. He looked at Tim and Jessica, "We have a big problem here."

"We have to take the police station," said Tim. "Then we should leave. NORAD is inside the damn mountain near the Army base. If we try to take it, we will all be killed."

"This is a mess. Attacking NORAD makes absolutely no sense," Christian scoffed. He stared at the floor and shook his head.

"We should leave the city, right now," Jessica pleaded.

"Where Jessica, back to the Lisco farm?" Christian spoke with a rage she had never witnessed with him before, not even in high school. "We stole their car. And by the way you are a real, great mom. You left all three of your children. I don't think they will throw a parade for our return."

She glared at him with a mist forming in her eyes.

Christian turned away and stared out the picture window. About fifty of the rebels in black were visible at the end of the street.

"What are we going to do?" Tim asked. "They are watching us."

"We don't have much choice," Christian moved closer to Jessica. As he tried to make eye contact, she blatantly turned to look away. The mist in her eyes had turned to anger.

Great Falls, Montana

"Colonel."

Deb felt a slight tap on her chin.

"Colonel, can you wake up?" Condoleezza was standing over the top of her.

"What time is it?" Deb noticed she was only half covered with a blanket.

"0900, ma'am." The medic placed her hand behind the colonel's head and helped her sit up. "I need you to drink some water."

Deb placed her feet on the floor. She held the cup of water and took a sip.

"You were nearly airlifted out of here last night. You almost found yourself in Minot, North Dakota this morning. If it weren't for the number of casualties, you would have been," she waited for her to finish drinking and lifted her legs back onto the bed. "Command Sergeant Major Talfoya wants me to notify him now that you are awake."

"I have to use the restroom."

"Go ahead, but then right back in bed."

Deb felt nauseous. Her whole body ached as she crawled back into the bed. She was nearly asleep when Tommy entered her tent.

"Colonel, how are you feeling?"

"I'm tired."

"You can rest. I know you don't want to but maybe a little patience at this time is the best thing."

"I have to ask you Tommy," she raised her head slightly, "did I make a mistake last night?"

"No," the Command Sergeant Major moved to the edge of her bed. "The mission was in response to a low collateral damage threat. We responded prudently, with more than adequate firepower required to take care of the problem."

"How did we not see them before they hit us?"

"Everyone blended in. It looked like townspeople protesting, but they attacked without any warning. In reviewing the images from the camera on the Stryker vehicle we are lucky the damage was not worse. The forward platoon had no chance to counter."

"How bad was it?" Deb held her breath.

"Five KIA."

"Oh my God." She put her left hand to her temple. "We haven't done a damn thing and we have already lost eight soldiers."

"We have eyes on every square inch of this city. The threat just disappeared into the woodwork. We have all the intelligence system maintainers working to find a link to the enemy that attacked. All we can do is sit and wait."

"Colonel," a private placed a tray of food and a pitcher of water on the night table next to the bed. "They want you to drink a lot of water."

"Tommy," Deb waited for the private to leave. "We have a bigger problem within our ranks than we thought. Can you get ahold of General Lauer at Fort Carson and see if others have been infiltrated?"

"I think you are correct on this. We need to bypass General Maes and see if General Lauer will give us some help with rooting out the subversives." Tommy took in a deep breath, "I'm also going to place guards at the front entrance to your tent."

"Do you think that is necessary?" she glanced up at

him. The way he was looking at her was probably no different than the way he had stared at her a hundred times before. Maybe it was the knock to the head that made her think he was looking at her more as a woman and not as a commander.

"Condoleezza is not going to allow you to go back to work today. I know resting like this is totally against your character but a day or two of rest and you will be back at full strength." He placed a hand on the side of her bare bicep. He tried to capture her gaze as he looked indiscreetly into her eyes. She cocked her head slightly away. "I'll keep you fully informed on any developments."

Deb didn't feel like eating. She did drink a full cup of water before crawling into the bed and pulling the covers tight around her neck. Her mind wandered to the times she saw the Command Sergeant Major without a shirt. His chest was massive and solid. She visualized him with only a towel wrapped around his waist. She took in a deep breath and whispered, "What am I thinking? The guy is a career soldier just like me. Besides his damn head is way too big for his body." She chuckled before letting out a deep breath and falling asleep.

Lone Tree, Colorado

The street was full of homegrown rebels friendly to Christian. Walking to the police substation on Colorado Boulevard would take at least two hours. With the element of surprise gone, it would be more difficult to overwhelm the forces protecting the city than when they first started the insurrection.

Jessica felt a pang of anger, verging on loathing, as she watched Christian address the crowd. She hadn't said a word to him since his attack on her character. His statement about her being a bad mother stung much worse than she would have ever thought it would.

"I'm going to stay here. I'm not going to fight the police," she declared with a heavier Irish accent than usual while she waited next to Tim only a couple meters behind Christian.

"Christian will never let you stay behind."

"I don't give a shit what he thinks." She turned and walked back inside the mansion. She went to the back bedroom and emptied her duffel bag on the bed. After pulling a sweater over her shirt she entered a large walk-in closet and rummaged through the homeowner's clothes. She found a ski jacket, ski gloves and stocking cap. She placed a hairbrush and toothpaste in the bag and hurried to the kitchen where she filled the bag with fruit, lunchmeat and water.

As she entered the living room she saw outside the large picture window, Christian and Tim charging up the sidewalk. She grabbed the duffle bag and rushed out the back door. The frozen grass made a crunching noise as she rushed across the neighbor's lawn and climbed over a stone wall. She hit the street running, sprinting until she was at the outskirts of the wealthy neighborhood.

She ran until her body begged her to rest as she came to a hiking trail adjacent to a park. Following the concrete trail to an area with several soccer fields, she made the decision to exit the trail and walk across the open area. Although it would be easier to be spotted, she felt a sense of security in having the ability to see anyone approaching. At the far end of the playing fields was a large building with a brick sign in front of the structure with the words, "Douglas County Library".

The front of the library was mostly glass with a high gable entry made from brick. After shaking the locked front door, she walked around to the back and looked thru a small window. A platform to a staircase going into the basement was visible about a meter down from the bottom of the window.

She went to the front of the building and picked up a large rock from the landscaped entry. She smashed in the window. It would be a perfect place for her to take refuge for at least a day.

Eastern Colorado Farm

It was unusual for all the Jacobys to be inside the house at one time. They were usually working relentlessly taking care of the farm animals. Mingling with the rest of the people on the farm was low priority on their list of things to do.

"We should check on the other ranches around the area. We could all benefit with working together," stated Aaron.

"How can we safely do that?" Hank asked, knowing the Jacobys were a prototypical farm family who would take a chance to support a neighbor.

"There had to be at least a hundred people at the Brown's farm last night," stated Jon. "Once we get the drone up and running, we can use it to get a visual of the different farms. Until then it would be a great risk to travel to these places without knowing who occupies them.

"We need to take care of the Brown's livestock." Aaron looked at his father, "Bring his cattle here and deal with the logistics of ownership later."

"It would be best to notify the sheriff in Limon," stated Ed, reaching down to massage his knee. It was the first time he felt strong enough to venture from the bedroom in the RV. "Limon is on Interstate 70, so there has to be some military passing through from time to time."

"My guess is that it is overrun with people by now," replied Jon. "Traveling there would be dangerous too."

"If there are a lot of people, they need food," Ed spoke

very clearly. "The military has to keep the Interstate open, so I'm sure they have some sort of presence in the town. How about if we offer them food for some sort of protection?"

"Like Jon said, traveling anywhere seems to be risky." Hank thought of the discussion he was going to have with George Saxton about them leaving the farm.

Nicole and Jacqueline entered the room. Aaron and Ashley moved to the end of the sofa so they could sit.

"Has anyone heard from Ted?" Ashley asked softly. She held her head cocked slightly to the right, a condition she was trying to correct from the gunshot wound she received outside Monticello.

"Bill has monitored the computer in his office, trying to contact him," stated Nicole.

"He will get in touch with us as soon as he can." Jon stood in front of everyone with his arms crossed.

"I agree with Aaron. We should take care of the Brown's livestock," Hank stood up.

"We can't do it if the people from last night are still there," said Jon adamantly.

"Can you drive to their entrance and look?" Jacqueline asked.

"Well…" Jon placed his hand to his chin.

"I'd rather saddle up the horses and go across the pasture," Adam spoke for the first time. He moved next to Hank. He was dressed in his western button-down shirt and jeans. "If the farm is vacant, we can herd the cattle back here. If the people are still there, we come back."

"We have eight saddles, but can we find eight riders?" Aaron asked.

"Jon, it would be good if you went with them. Do you feel comfortable on a horse?" Hank asked.

"You know Hank, I haven't ridden a horse since I was ten years old. But I suppose I can."

"Breanna can ride," Ed glanced at his daughter.

"I have no problem going," she stated.

"Bill has been riding with Deb on many occasions." Nicole hesitated for a moment, wondering if she should be volunteering her son, "You can ask him if he is willing to go."

"That would be five. I'm sure we can find three more out of this group. They need only be able to ride along the cattle and push them here to our pasture." Aaron stood up and walked behind the sofa. "We should get this done immediately before someone else does."

"Being able to ride a horse hasn't come up since we arrived here." Hank held his hands out, "I guess we'll find out who can."

"There is one more thing," Jon stuck his jaw out, "if Peg and Clint are still laying in front of the barn, we have to bring them back and give them a proper burial."

"We still haven't found those damn radios," stated Hank. "You'll have to signal that it's safe at the Brown farm and I'll drive there."

"You can use the Ford pick-up Ted drove here," said Ed.

"Ok. Let's get everything underway," said Hank.

Nicole watched the group leave the living room. She was going to increase her effort to contact Ted. Fort Carson was a major target for the missiles, but she never doubted her husband was safe and out of harms way.

"Grandma, are you ready to make a cake?" Maddy yelled across the living room from the kitchen. "Irene and Samantha are already here."

Irene was busy laying out the ingredients on the

counter. Both Maddy and Samantha had their blond hair pulled back into matching ponytails.

"So, what are we making here?" Nicole moved next to the table.

"Angel food cake." Maddy looked at her grandma with dark eyes wide in anticipation.

"It's angel food cake with chocolate fudge icing." Irene gave them a tender smile, "It's a little different from a traditional angel food cake. This one is in a flat pan and will only be about three inches high."

"It sounds delicious." Nicole's heart was pounding as she thought about Bill and the others traveling to the Brown farm, but she didn't want to frighten Maddy. She placed the palm of her hand on the side of a large glass bowl full of fixings and stated, "Them are the biggest bowls I have ever seen."

"What do you want us to do?" Samantha asked enthusiastically. It would be the first time for her to spend a meaningful amount of time with Nicole. She had formed a deep connection with Nicole's husband and granddaughter and was in the process of doing the same with her son. It was time she put her best foot forward and make a good impression.

"This is a team effort." Irene shook both fists out in front of her before pointing in the direction of two large bowls. "I have prepared the egg whites in one bowl and sifted the powdered sugar and flour together in the other. But with all the gadgets we have in this kitchen, I cannot find a mixer. So, we have to beat it by hand."

"We can do it," said Nicole enthusiastically.

"Nicole you can hold the bowl while Maddy and Samantha beat the ingredients. I'll slowly put everything in as you whip it together."

Nicole held the bowl of eggs tightly as Irene used a tablespoon to add the light ingredients of salt and extract while Maddy and Samantha easily beat it all together. It became much harder to stir when Irene began adding half cups of flour and sugar into the vessel with the egg mixture.

"It's getting thicker," said Samantha, "my wrists are getting a little tired."

"Mine too," said Maddy, stirring lightly.

"It's almost ready." Irene placed three flat baking pans on the table. "Most people use a ten-inch table pan for angel food cake. This will make more pieces."

"How long will it take to bake?" Samantha asked.

"About thirty-five minutes on a low heat, or until it's golden brown." Irene smiled at Maddy. "But we do have frosting to make. No hurry though. We'll have to let it cool for about an hour after we pull it from the oven."

Nicole was sitting at the table where she could see outside the kitchen window. There was a flurry of activity as all eight horses waited at the railing of the corral. Hank and Jacqueline were sitting in the old Ford F-250 talking to Bill who strapped a rifle to his back and took the reins of a horse.

Her breathing increased as she changed her perspective from the tense scene outside back to the kitchen. It was obvious by the way Irene had moments of staring blankly into space that the tension of the situation of her sons and daughter facing danger was weighing heavily on her. With true country fortitude she was trusting that everything would work out, leaving her to do what she enjoyed most, cooking.

"Irene and Samantha, would you drink a glass of wine while we wait?" Nicole asked.

"Absolutely," said Samantha quickly.

"Maybe a small one," Irene smiled and clasped her hands together.

"And I have some sparkling water for you," Nicole touched Maddy on the nose.

Nicole took one drink of wine and let out a large sigh and said, "What a wonderful idea this has been."

Samantha held the glass close to her bright red lips before taking a sip.

"Ladies, I haven't had a drink in quite some time. But here goes," Irene took a large swallow.

Maddy sat back and watched. The atmosphere was contagious. She enjoyed seeing her grandma so relaxed, something she had not seen since they arrived at the farm. And having Samantha laughing again, like she had many times on their trip with Grandpa Ted, made her happy.

"Bill said you grew up in the Littleton area," Nicole stared into Samantha's green eyes. Although they had been together for a short time, she knew Bill was becoming infatuated with the beautiful flight attendant.

"Yes. I recently bought a home in Highlands Ranch." She held her wine close to her chest. "God only knows what is going on with that place now."

"And your parents are in Littleton?"

"We stopped on our way through, but they weren't at their home," she took a drink of wine. "I have been discussing with Bill how I might be able to check on them. It would be wonderful to bring them here. We just don't know how we are going to do it."

They all sat quietly for a moment and sipped their wine. Maddy broke the silence.

"I heard Bobby talking with Emilee." Maddy narrowed her eyes and looked at Samantha. "I heard him say that he's pretty sure you and Dad are doing it."

Samantha gritted her teeth. She chuckled and brought her right hand to her forehead, reflexively shielding her face from Nicole.

Irene giggled and turned her head slightly away from the others. She took a sip of her wine.

"Doing what dear?" Nicole innocently looked at her granddaughter. Then it dawned on her what she had just heard. "Oh my gosh. Maybe we should start making the icing."

"We all went through a heck of a lot in the last few weeks." Irene looked at little Maddy. "We have all become good friends. Huh?"

"Yeah," Maddy leaned toward Irene and shielded her mouth. She whispered, "We are best friends."

Irene leaned back and smiled. The warm sensation in her chest from drinking the wine made her feel better than she had felt in a long time. It engendered hope she would live long enough to see her own grandchildren again.

"Ok." Samantha took in a deep breath and finished the last of her wine. Lipstick was noticeable on the rim of the glass as she sat it down. She gave a welcoming smile toward Nicole, and said, "I'm ready to see how to make this fudge frosting."

Irene was able to make everyone feel as though they were the ones making the delicious dessert. She placed everything together and had the others simply beat the mixture.

Nicole, Samantha and Maddy took turns stirring the fudge frosting while Irene removed the pans of cake and inverted them on the countertop.

Brown Farm

Bill made every effort to coax his horse to take the lead after they crossed the creek whilst Bobby, Dave and Emilee cantered alongside of him. But Breanna would have none of it. She rode ahead, making it evident how well versed she was in the art of horseback riding. A pistol was visible in a side holster above the waistline of her jeans.

Jon was extremely uncomfortable riding the horse. He wanted to be in the front, but his mount was a follower and no matter how hard he tried to make it pass the other horses, it would refuse. He stayed at the back riding behind Adam.

"There is a gate in the wire fence about two hundred meters south of the corral where we brought our cattle thru," said Aaron. He felt remorse, remembering, only a couple days earlier, negotiating the purchase of a bull with Clint Brown.

"We need to make sure there is nobody in the farmhouse," stated Bill.

When they arrived at the fence line Breanna stopped and allowed her older brother, Aaron, to move in front of her. He pulled open the gate to the barbwire fence and allowed everyone to ride through. He pulled the gate to the side and left it open. The sky was bright blue, and the sun was beating down on the snow, creating rivers of slush along the beaten path leading up to the farmhouse.

Bill reined his horse to a stop and stood tall in his saddle. He used his binoculars to check for any movement around and inside the farmhouse. He saw nothing. Breanna was already at the picket fence surrounding the vacant lawn in front of the home.

Jon looked in the direction of the barn, then slowly began to ride toward the large overhanging doors. The Browns were laying in the same spot as when he saw them the night before. They were almost unrecognizable with remnants of snow slowly dripping off their clothes. The others gathered next to him.

"I'll see if there are some blankets in the barn." Aaron's cheeks hung loosely from his face and his nostrils widened. He climbed off his horse and hooked the reins to a wooden rail on the corral.

"Good God, who could possibly do this?" Breanna clambered from her horse and continued to hold the reins while she leaned down to the three bodies. She said a silent prayer.

Aaron returned from the barn carrying three horse blankets. He took his time draping the bodies of Peg, Clint and Hector. He neatly tucked the blanket on all sides, then removed his hat and ran his fingers through his thin hair. He turned to Jon.

"We have to go to the west pasture to herd the cattle, so we better get started. The less time we spend here the better."

"I'll wait for Hank and Jacqueline to show up with the truck." Jon looked in the direction of the farmhouse. "We should check the house."

"I'll look with you Jon." Breanna watched the others ride off, without making a move to mount her horse.

Jon kept his rifle at the ready as he opened the front door to the farmhouse. Breanna was close enough behind to brush into him every time he stopped. A large hole at the door of the coat closet in the foyer gave an indication as to what the rest of the house might have endured. After taking two steps into the living room, Jon held up his hand for Breanna to stop.

They waited for a moment as he studied the situation with his rifle at full ready. The living room furniture was all tidily in place and the carpet was vacuumed. He stepped into the kitchen. The refrigerator was humming without a dirty dish to be seen. The distinct smell of cleaning products filled the room.

"Somethings wrong here," he whispered, slowly backing into the living room. Breanna held her right hand on his back as she matched his steps in retreat.

"Is someone living here?" Breanna mouthed the words while placing both hands on her pistol and holding it out in front of her.

"I don't know," he whispered, pointing at the back bedrooms.

They walked slowly to the hall leading to the bedrooms. The sound of her breathing loudly caused him to turn around and say, "Don't shoot me."

She nodded and followed him down the hall to the first bedroom with the door open. Stuffed animals were scattered on top of a neatly made bed. Jon stepped inside the bathroom on the opposite side of the hall. Toothbrushes were in a glass on the sink.

"Someone's here," he whispered.

Breanna's usually beady eyes were the size of saucers as he moved past her in the direction of the closed door at the end of the hall. She walked sideways close enough behind Jon to be touching him. She held her gun aimed at the floor as she rotated her eyes in looking down the hall behind them and then forward again.

Jon held the rifle in his right hand while he leaned ahead and pushed the bedroom door open with his left hand. He stuck his head inside the room. It took a second for his eyes to adjust to the dark conditions.

"Jesus," he yelled, jumping back and leaning next to the wall of the hall.

"What is it?" Breanna kept her back flat to the wall.

"Put the gun down," Jon yelled into the room with his back next to the wall. "We aren't going to hurt you."

Inside the bedroom, at the end of the bed, was a woman pointing a gun in the direction of the door.

"Go away," the woman yelled. A small child began to cry.

"The others are going to be back at any time," shouted a different woman.

"You have a child in there. Just aim the gun somewhere but at us." Jon peeked around the corner. The lady was pointing the pistol off to the side. He stepped into the room. Breanna moved next to him with her gun pointed in the air.

"What are you doing in this house?"

"We are waiting for my boyfriend and his friend to return." The lady looked at two older women crouching behind the bed. "They went to a farmhouse, we passed yesterday on our way here, to see if they have any food to spare."

"So, you murdered the owners and took over their home?" Breanna took a step closer to the lady. One of the older women stood up and placed her body in front of a toddler aged boy.

"There was nobody in the house when we arrived yesterday," said the old lady shielding the child.

"Who were all the people here last night?" Jon sensed

they were telling the truth.

"We came with a large group we met at a camp in Limon. They told us about a commune outside the little town of Kiowa, so we hitched a ride with them in the back of a U-Haul truck," stated the young woman. "There was an explosion and lots of shooting last night so we locked ourselves in this room."

"We decided not to leave with the people we came with this morning," the old lady spoke. "They seemed dangerous, and I didn't want to take the chance of something happening with my grandson."

"Ok, come out here." Jon walked into the living room as they followed.

"We cleaned up the best we could this morning," said the young lady. "We figured it was the least we could do, since they took all the food."

"Well, your friends killed the people who own this ranch," Breanna looked at them with animosity.

"If that's true, we knew nothing about it." The young lady looked as if she was going to cry. "Mom told us we shouldn't go with them when we were in Limon.

"They were definitely not our friends," insisted the mother, looking out the picture window to the driveway.

Hank and Jacqueline were in the old F-150 at the front of the house. Jon quickly exited out the front door.

"They are over here," Jon pointed as he walked around the pick-up in the direction of the barn. Breanna followed him outside with the mother and young woman lingering behind her. The other lady and child remained at the door to the farmhouse.

Hank backed the pick-up next to the bodies.

Jacqueline gasped when she saw the Browns and their hired hand.

The mother and daughter following Breanna looked on in horror as the bodies were lifted into the bed of the truck. By the time the three bodies were placed in the back of the truck the young lady was crying. She held her hand over the bodies with her eyes closed, saying a silent prayer. She looked at Breanna and said, "God knows we had no idea this happened."

"I believe you," said Breanna solemnly.

"What are your names?" Jacqueline was standing next to the door of the pickup.

"I'm Trenda," the young woman sniffled, "my mother is Alice."

"Alice, how long were you at the camp in Limon?" Jon asked.

"We got there real early yesterday morning just as the others were preparing to depart for the commune. The camp was unbelievably packed, and everyone was complaining about not having enough food. There was room in the U-Haul, so we decided to leave with them," she shook her head.

Hank looked at the lady. Her face was as ordinary as any he had ever seen. She was the type of person who would disappear into a crowd. "Did you come from Denver yesterday?"

"Aurora," she moved a finger across a red crack at the center of her lower lip. "We were staying at the high school, but the situation was unbearable. They kept telling us there would be a shipment of food coming at any time, but it never came."

"How did you get to Limon?" Hank asked.

"Sam, my boyfriend and his brother Timothy, are good with cars, actually good with electrical," said Trenda. "They were able to get a van they owned running, but it only got us to Limon before it quit."

Hank wondered if George Saxton would be influenced about returning to the city after hearing the lady's stories. Both ladies were thin as rails, obviously in need of a good meal. He looked at Jacqueline before saying, "We have a place for you to stay."

Fort Carson Army Base

Ted held a black marker in his right hand while he slouched over a large paper map of the Denver metro area. The map covered a large table in the situation room, just two doors down from his office. Neither General Lopez nor Colonel Bonney Myer, having come from the east coast, were familiar with the city, so they were relying on Ted to give them the layout of the main streets and location of schools, hospitals and other significant locations of interest, which would be relevant to them helping the local government take back the urban area.

Colonel Myer's 3rd Brigade was made up of inexperienced soldiers on most levels, many with only a few months of training, but the sergeants and first lieutenants at the squad and platoon level were seasoned veterans. Every indication was pointing to the war being one of urban warfare, something the United States forces were well versed at. Training for the 3rd Brigade was about to become real.

"Reconnaissance indicates the area of turmoil is predominantly south of Hampden Avenue." Ted marked from east to west across the entire map. He then moved to the bottom of the map and placed an arrow. "By coming up through the town of Parker, we can allow the local governments to take back control as we move to the west."

"How dense is the population from Parker into the metro," Colonel Myer asked.

"It's wall to wall people Bonney," Ted circled the area from Parker to Lone Tree. "The threat from subversives in the city of Parker is low, but still there. The last report from reconnaissance indicates that much of the populace are still in their homes. With the availability of food being the biggest issue."

"We are in contact with local law enforcement, and they are aware of our arrival," stated General Lopez.

"What are we going to encounter when we move to the west?" Bonney pointed to the west side of Interstate 25.

"We estimate there are up to 8000 rebels in the urban area, with over sixty percent of them on the south side." Ted stood up straight, "This is why we want you to utilize the full brigade."

"Colonel, we will keep you posted on new intel. You can prepare your soldiers to leave at daybreak." General Lopez turned to Ted, "We have about fifteen minutes before we meet with General Lauer."

Ted was having a difficult time adjusting to his new position as assistant division commander. The new army was focused on utilizing specialized units of brigade and battalion sized forces. Artificial intelligence was utilized far too often by the upper echelon of the Military in making decisions. The commanders at the brigade level still had some semblance of decree in creating strategy and control over their commands. He would trade places with Colonel Myer in a heartbeat.

"I don't know what kind of resistance they are going to encounter tomorrow," said Ted, "she sure has a lot of green soldiers to deal with."

"I'm afraid they are going to have to learn under fire." General Lopez shook his head. "I just received orders that the 99th Division is about to join the fight. 1st and 2nd Brigades are to leave for the southern border on

Wednesday. It is my understanding that several Brigades from the 4th Infantry Division will do the same."

"Part of the 4th Infantry is located near San Antonio," Ted stated. "Do you know if Deb's 2nd Brigade are going to join them."

"Right now, she is still outside Great Falls, Montana, but things are going to change very quickly. We are about to find out what is planned." He opened the door and allowed Ted to go out first. Ted sensed there was something on the general's mind as they began walking toward the command center.

"Ted, I want you to stay here in Fort Carson with 3rd Brigade." The general stopped walking and looked earnestly at Ted. "If Bonney is successful with the mission in the Denver metro area, we want to keep her group in reserve and prepared to relocate to other cities to clear out the rebels. I want to be honest with you. We are hoping you will be willing to help with this part of the war."

Ted remained silent as he walked along side General Lopez down the narrow hallway. They were the last to arrive at the briefing. Major General Lauer was at a podium, ready to begin. He and General Lopez took a seat at the back of the room.

"The Chiefs of Staff and the Department of Defense has drafted a specific plan of action to respond to the threats this nation is facing. I will break down into two parts where we stand as a military at this time. First will be the greater world-wide threat and second is the capacity this military base will have in answering that threat." General Lauer spoke clearly and with authority, "We did receive minimal injury from the missile attack to both military and civilian targets on the mainland, but Guam, the Philippines and Japan all received significant damage. Keeping these allies from falling into the enemies hands is vital to the security of the west coast."

Ted glanced at General Lopez who was listening intently to the commanding general. He then looked at the room full of soldiers. In all his years of service he had never seen so many combatants fixed and absorbed while being informed during a briefing.

"We underestimated the support the Chinese military was receiving from the Mexican cartels. The current estimated number of enemy troops at and near the southern border has been updated to be over two million. They have been able to establish launch sites and take-off points for cruise missiles, nonhuman ariel vehicles, rockets and artillery. It is a stalemate of sorts at the border. We have transported and emplaced PAC-10 and PAC-11 interceptors adjacent to the border. These are vital in keeping the balance of power in missile defense." The general hesitated for a moment and looked out across the darkened room. "Our immediate objective is to protect the interceptors. 1st and 2nd Brigades from the 99th Infantry Division are to collect in Phoenix and redirect to positions in support of the missile interceptors. 1st Stryker Brigade Combat from Forth Infantry Division will move to San Antonio. Fourth Infantry Division's 2nd Brigade will move to an assembly area in the vicinity of St George, Utah. All Battalion commanders must stay mobile and be ready to adjust their position to meet with plans and alterations as deemed necessary."

Ted knew Deb would be happy to be attached with the 4th Infantry again. After the missile attack the base placed a seventy-two-hour moratorium on nonessential radio use. He tried several times under the appearance of military necessity, unsuccessfully, to communicate with his sister. His staff had assured him her name was not on the list of casualties.

"The final objective coming from the Department of Defense and Homeland Security with the directive of the President of the United States is the deployment of the Army to help establish order in our cities. As we have done in Colorado Springs, we will have all units in reserve being utilized to help local law enforcement gain control over their domain."

Ted felt a terrible sense of irrelevance as he sat back in the cushy stadium seat listening to the Major General finish. He made a mistake in accepting the job of Assistant Division Commander. When he and Nicole met with Army Chief of Staff McClinton to discuss his re-enlisting, the general made it sound like he was going to play a significant role in helping to protect the country. He should have remembered the words of his father, "Cemeteries are full of indispensable people."

"Ted," General Lopez brought him out of his thoughts. "I am leaving this evening for Texas. I want to arrive ahead of 1st and 2nd Brigades to help set up command."

"Is there anything specific you want me to do?" Ted asked.

"I think Colonel Myer is prepared for the sweep of the Denver metro area, but you can advise and assist her with any logistics in the morning."

Ted simply shook his head. He continued to sit as everyone exited the room. He dreaded going back to his quarters. It made things worse as he thought of Nicole, Bill and Maddy. He wished he were back at the farm with them.

Great Falls, Montana

A sharp pain in Deb's lower left hip caused her to roll off the bed. The good thing was that the throbbing in her head had disappeared. She was dressed in a white cotton nightgown as she stretched before moving to the door of the tent. The two guards stationed at the front acknowledged her while consciously ignoring her scanty attire.

"Can we assist you, ma'am? I can procure you a jacket." A heavy fog appeared out of the private's mouth as he asked the question.

"That's not necessary." She could see several people inside the command tent with the lights from monitors flickering in the cold night air. "I need you to find Lt. Col. Woodworth and have him join me in my tent."

"Yes ma'am." The private rushed off as Deb moved back inside her tent out of the frigid air.

She sat in a chair and silently waited for Lt. Col Woodworth. She had been out of the loop for nearly twenty-four hours and needed to be informed of any new developments. She felt weak, but for the first time since the explosion she sensed she was recuperating.

"Colonel," Lt. Col. Woodworth stuck his head through the door. When he noticed Deb sitting in a chair dressed in her night clothes he hesitated. He looked away as he asked, "Did you call for me?"

"Come in Josh, have a seat," she pointed to a chair, "I want to be updated."

"I take it you haven't spoken with Tommy this

afternoon." He tried to keep his eyes away from her large breasts with the nipples poking out of the thin material of the nightgown.

"Not since this morning," she poured a cup of water and held it up. "Would you like some?"

"No thanks," he hesitated for a moment and then shifted straight to the point. "General Lauer has reattached us to the 4th and we have orders to leave for southern Utah on Thursday. Tommy has contacted 1st and 3rd Battalions and they should be back here sometime tomorrow afternoon."

"Wow," she shook her head, "that happened quickly."

"Another thing, the drones we launched this morning have encountered a significant amount of interference with returning signals. Captain Dodson is trying to figure out how they are blocking our images."

"What about the warehouse?" Deb asked. "We used the drone when I Company investigated the wheel factory and had no problems."

"We only used the drones over the city. With your permission I would like to send them to the warehouse tonight." Josh stood up, "If we leave without some sort of response to the attacks, we may never know what is taking place here."

"You have my permission. But no matter what you find, I don't want any action until we discuss the scope and nature of the mission." She rolled her eyes down toward the floor in thought. "Contact the Air Force Base and have them place a squadron of armed NAVs on standby. If we get verification that this warehouse is an enemy stronghold, I want it completely destroyed."

"Colonel," the private standing guard in front of the tent yelled, "permission for Sergeant Sessions to enter?"

"Granted."

Condoleezza stepped into the tent carrying a covered plate. She was pleased to find Colonel Lisco still dressed in her nightgown. "Ma'am, I brought your dinner."

Lt. Col. Woodworth moved to the side allowing the medic to set the food on a small wooden table being used as a nightstand.

"Sergeant," he acknowledged the medic, then put on his cap and moved to the door. "I will keep you informed Colonel."

Condoleezza watched him leave before moving uncomfortably close to Deb. "Can you look up and open your eyes wide?"

Deb took in a couple deep breaths and looked up.

"Have you been having any headaches?" the medic looked into her eyes.

"None, as much as I slept this afternoon, I'm hoping I can sleep tonight."

"If you can sleep tonight," Condoleezza thought about telling her to limit the workload for a couple of days, but knew that would not happen, "you'll be back too normal in no time."

"Thank-you Condoleezza."

The medic smiled and left the tent.

Deb did plan to rest but knew, come morning, she was going to be back stronger than ever.

Eastern Colorado Farm

"I would be calling for a framing inspection today if I were building this apartment under normal circumstances." Jason sat across the kitchen table from Hank, cradling a cup of coffee. "I'm going to frame the rooms inside and start running the electrical wires."

"You are doing everything by the book anyway," stated Hank.

"Your sister had the foundation and rough plumbing inspected before all this took place. The permit card was signed off for both the apartment and block tower foundations, as well as the rough plumbing." Jason placed the dirty and battered cast on his arm onto the table. "As long as the foundations are sound, especially with the block tower, we should be ok."

"Harold seems to know what he is doing with laying the block," Hank leaned back in his chair.

"I thought I was going to have to help him with placing the wood joists for the first floor, but he already has them on. He plans to place the floors as he builds each level. He then can lay the block over the wall, using one section of scaffolding to lay the high part, then do the same for the next floor. If he had enough block, he could lay the damn thing a hundred meters high." Jason shook his head, "He has been mixing cement and grout, plus carrying his own block. The guy is amazingly efficient."

"Bobby told me he, Emilee and Sherry are going to start helping him," stated Hank. "They are about to learn what work is all about."

"You're right about that. The higher he gets with the tower, the harder it will be to get him material." Jason slammed the coffee cup onto the table, "I need to get out and go to work."

"Jon placed some concrete blankets and the solar heater up by Carol's grave site last night. He left the three bodies there," Hank spoke in a woeful tone. "We need to have some of your helpers go up and dig the graves. They are going to have to use a pick to get past the frost line."

"I'll have Dave get some help and do it." The giant man stood up from his chair. "Jerry and Terrance are going to help me pull electrical wiring today, so it is a good time to take care of that."

Hank sat at the table contemplating having a bowl of oatmeal when he heard the front door open. George and Toby walked into the kitchen. For the first time in his life, he felt uneasiness in the presence of his best friend.

"Hank," Toby's voice was strained as she moved right next to him. "We are going to leave this morning. Even if we must walk, we are going."

"Sit down and have some coffee." Hank could feel the cold radiating from their clothes, "We can figure this out."

"We don't want to figure anything out," yelled Toby. "We want to go home."

"Ok, ok." Hank held up his right hand. He looked at George. "Let's figure how to get you home. It's much too dangerous for you to walk."

"Have you heard from Ted?" George asked. He pulled out a chair and sat down.

"Bill and Samantha have been trying to contact him, but no luck."

"Can we take one of your cars?" Toby asked sharply.

"No. you can't," Hank licked his lips as he stared at

her. "The Jacobys made it clear that you cannot take either of their vehicles and you sure as hell can't take our only mode of transportation."

"Can someone drive us part way?" George asked in a much more confrontational manner than Hank would have expected him to. "Take us to the edge of the city."

Hank took in a deep breath through his nose. He placed his hand on the handle to the coffee cup but never brought it to his mouth.

"I don't think our request is unreasonable," stated Toby still standing behind her husband.

"There are eleven of you. It will take two vehicles."

"Using the pick-up and another vehicle will allow us to take all our stuff," Toby's tone was still foreboding.

"We need to run this by the others, especially the Jacobys." Hank looked directly at George and tried to relieve the tension. "I'm sorry everything has worked out this way."

"Hank it's not anyone's fault. We are city people who would be frightened out here even if there weren't a threat from some gang trying to kill people." George wrinkled his big nose.

"I hope you are not making a big mistake here," said Hank. "We have no idea what is going to happen with this war."

"We will take that chance." Toby looked away from the two men.

Hank took a sip of coffee and looked at Toby, "It may come down to you having to walk if you want to leave."

"It will be easier to get back than it was to get here." She stood up tall and folded her arms across her chest.

Great Falls, Montana

Even with the heater in her tent on high, Deb was chilled to the bone as she put on her fatigues.

"Colonel," Lt. Col. Woodworth yelled from outside, "are you decent?"

"Yeah, come on in," Deb looked at her watch, it showed 6:15.

"Jesus, it's twenty-eight below." He entered the tent wearing a heavy coat with a hood, "I told the guards to go to the mess tent."

"I should have dismissed them last night."

"I don't think we can be too careful," he continued to stand at the door. "Have you eaten?"

"Not yet."

"He wants to meet us in fifteen minutes at the communication tent."

"I can wait to eat. I could use a coffee though." She pulled on her coat, "Did you deploy the drones last night?"

"We did. We couldn't get closer than four hundred meters to the warehouse without them being jammed," said Josh. "Captain Dodson will be at communications with Tommy. She can better define how she thinks they are blocking the images."

Command Sergeant Major Talfoya was watching a fuzzy picture on a monitor as Captain Dodson pointed to the image. Each monitor in the center had a soldier actively scrutinizing the screen.

"Colonel," Tommy leaned back from the monitor. "We were just looking at the video from last night's surveillance by the drones."

"What are you finding?"

"We can see a lot of activity on the north side of the warehouse. But when we get within 380 meters of the center of the building, we lose the picture. It is the same with all the drones," stated Tommy.

"We thought we were keeping up with the Chinese technology with jamming our pictures, but obviously we weren't."

"Have we tried a larger NAV?"

"No ma'am." Captain Dodson looked at Lt. Col. Woodworth, "If they have the PS-4 tracker scout available it will eliminate our guess work about having a drone that will get past their jamming technology.

"I'll request they do so immediately," Tommy replied.

Deb looked across the room. There were unfamiliar faces amongst the crew of soldiers sitting in front of the many screens. If there were dissidents among the soldiers, she was confident they would be spotted.

A private handed her a cup of coffee. She turned to the Command Sergeant Major. He took several steps back, and she followed, to where they were out of earshot of the others. "1st and 3rd Battalions should be here by late afternoon. General Lauer has instructed us to leave early Thursday morning. He'll direct us as to the route we are to take."

"Any idea where we will end up?"

"Southern Utah." He squinted his eyes, "I'm so ready for some warm weather."

"Colonel," Josh yelled across the room. "They launched the NAV for surveillance of the warehouse."

"Is it armed?" Deb moved next to Captain Dodson.

"No ma'am, all armed NAVs are unavailable."

Captain Dodson checked the monitor as the images cleared up on the largest monitor in the room."

The drone made the first pass over the warehouse with pictures being transmitted back without any type of interference. It made two more passes before one of the communication technicians said, "Malmstrom is requesting clarification of how many more passes they should make."

"Inform them we are good with what we have," said Deb. "We can slow it down and look at the footage."

They replayed, in slow motion, the pictures without seeing the slightest movement from anywhere around the warehouse. As they scrutinized the last set of images from the north side of the building, one of the technicians yelled, "Hold it, look at the far window."

Captain Dodson focused her eyes as she tried to identify the protrusion located in the window. She rubbed her chin and shook her head. "I can't see enough of it to tell what it is."

"Look at all the tire marks and footprints in the snow," said a corporal manning one of the monitors. "There has been a lot of recent activity at the site."

"Colonel," Josh motioned to both Tommy and Deb. He stepped to the far opening of the tent as they followed. "With all the troop movement thru this area we have to find out if this structure is a direct threat to our armed forces. It would be a dereliction of our duty to leave without knowing its purpose."

"I completely agree. The mission needs to take place immediately," stated Deb.

"Josh, can you have them ready to go in two hours?" Tommy
asked, looking over his shoulder to make sure nobody at

the monitors could hear him. "I will notify Fort Carson of the operation."

"Captain Dodson," Deb motioned for her to join them, "we are going to shut down this command center. Not another message is to leave this tent. Everything from here on will be communicated through G Company mobile. I want you, and you alone, to observe all messages at this location."

Captain Dodson rushed to the middle of the room. "Everything off, now! Turn off anything that can transmit a signal, including your Pulsenet."

"Ma'am, I'm in the middle of ordering supplies, I'll lose the order if I shut down," said a corporal innocuously.

"Turn it off!" Captain Dodson shouted. Having someone in her command as a traitor made her sick to her stomach. "Everyone is to look at the soldier next to you and verify their devices are completely shut down."

"Tommy, you and I will go with G Company to the farm owned by the rancher who told us about the warehouse," said Deb.

"Walt Blake."

"Yes," she turned to LT. Col. Woodworth. "Are you coming with us?"

"No, I'll go with H Company."

"Is two hours enough time?" Tommy asked Josh.

"I can have fire squads up and ready within thirty minutes."

"We'll release the drones after everyone is in place," stated Deb. "We leave in two hours."

Blake Farm

The low hanging fog allowed for a visibility of six kilometers. The driveway and part of the adjacent field to Walt Blakes farmhouse was covered with army vehicles. The old rancher slowly moved from the front door of his small home, wearing a large, hooded winter coat, and proceeded down the sidewalk in the direction of the massive force of military weaponry. His wife waited at the open door while he made his way toward Colonel Lisco and Command Sergeant Major Talfoya, standing at the side of a light tactical vehicle.

"What in God's name are you people doing out in this cold weather?" Walt asked as he approached.

"We are going to find out exactly who you sold your land too," answered Tommy. He could feel the hairs in his nose freezing.

"You told us when you came to Great Falls to report suspicious activity at the warehouse that you were the one who initially sold the land to the people who built it," stated Deb. "Where is the property line."

"That's their fence line, right across the road." Walt pointed at the dirt road they arrived on, then lifted his arm and pointed over the grassland. "If you look close enough you can see the top of the warehouse. But whenever I get curious about the place, I go to the hill over there and watch them." He pointed to a hill about a kilometer further down the road past his home. "The fog is already starting to burn off so you should have a birds eye view of the place."

"Have you noticed activity lately?" Tommy asked.

"Hell yes, they have lots of people shuffling around down there." Walt placed his right thumb to his nostril, leaned his head back toward his house and blew his nose onto the ground. "Excuse me, but I told you all about that the other day."

"Do you and your wife have some place you can go for the afternoon?" Deb stared at his bright red nose.

"I suppose we can go into town," Walt looked at them suspiciously.

"You need to go immediately," Deb stated.

"Sir," Captain Jensen yelled to Tommy, "F Company is twenty kilometers from the site."

"Captain," Deb pointed to the east, "we will follow you with 1st Platoon and mobile command to the top of that hill."

"Yes ma'am," Captain Jensen stepped back into the mobile command center. The cumbersome vehicle moved down the frozen driveway to the dirt road.

"Thank you, sir." Deb waved to Walt as she hurried to the tactical vehicle. Tommy was already inside and ready to move. The old man never moved an inch as he watched them leave his property.

They drove through an open gate to the pasture on top of the knoll and parked on the frozen grass. The command center vehicle was fifteen meters long and looked like a cross between a tan fire truck and a recreational vehicle. The inside was HVAC climate controlled, making it comfortable to work in shirt sleeves. There were four large monitors situated on the walls.

"Colonel, Lieutenant Murphy will be in charge of images for the monitors." Captain Jensen stood to the side of the lieutenant who sat in a chair in front of the largest monitor.

"Ma'am," said the lieutenant, "we have contact with Captain Henderson with F Company on screen 2. Images from the drones just released from H Company's position are on both 3 and 4 screens. As soon as we get pictures from F Company forward fireteams and squads we will alternatively display on screen 1."

"We can connect visual with H Company at any time," stated Captain Jensen.

"Put Captain Hendersen on speaker." Deb stared at Captain Jensen's hand grasping the back of Lieutenant Murphy's chair. She always considered the captain to be one of the biggest women she ever met, but never really noticed her enormous hands.

The pictures from the drones were crystal clear as they hovered over the rooftop of the colossal building. Just as they started to go to the side of the warehouse the picture turned white.

"They jammed them," Lieutenant Murphy turned to Colonel Lisco.

"Captain Hendersen, what is your position?" Deb rubbed her chin as she looked at the monitor.

"We are on a dirt road approximately two klicks north of the warehouse. We are on the backside of a hill in the grove of trees, so we do not have a visual of the building from our location."

"Do you have direct access to the site?"

"Affirmative, there is a utility road that goes through the trees to the back of the building. It's well used and wide enough for all our equipment." Captain Hendersen looked away from the monitor with indistinct chattering being heard behind him. He directed back to the screen.

"Do you want us to proceed to the parking lot of the warehouse?"

Deb hesitated, she looked out the windshield of the command vehicle down in the valley. The fog had dissipated, and she had a clear view of the structure. The tree covered hill the captain mentioned hid the entire company from her sight. She studied the area while contemplating where best to place the soldiers. The parking lot and entrance to the warehouse was on the opposite side of his position. It might be advantageous to surround the area to limit the ability of the force inside to escape.

"Ma'am?" the captain broke the silence.

"No, stay where you are," she answered decisively. "Are your men in forward positions close enough to give us a visual."

"Fireteam four is located at a gulley about sixty meters northeast of the structure." He hesitated for a moment, "We will relay as soon as they have their camera fixed on the site."

Deb stepped back and stared blankly at the monitors, then stepped out of the vehicle into the ice-cold air. She looked through her binoculars at the warehouse. Tommy followed outside and stood next to her.

"What do you see?" he asked.

"Look at the fields around the warehouse. Those aren't natural hills. Someone dug out thousands of yards of dirt." She lowered the binoculars to her side. "Walt told us there might be hundreds of soldiers living there. I'll bet there is a whole city under that building."

"Ma'am," Captain Jensen's body took up the entire door as she leaned outside. "We have images from F Company's forward squad."

Deb and Tommy hurried back inside the command vehicle. They scrutinized the pictures of the side of the warehouse. There were large casks protruding approximately fifty centimeters out from eight different windows.

"Anyone have any idea what we are looking at," Deb asked.

"No idea," said Lieutenant Murphy. "Could it be part of their ventilation?"

"Put Lt. Col. Woodworth on this monitor," Deb pointed to the first screen. She waited until his face appeared. "Josh, bring up the platoon of MT-3 Bradleys to Captain Hendersen's location."

"Just the tanks?" he asked.

"Yes," she turned to the screen with Captain Hendersen. "Captain, pull all your men back to your present location."

"Ma'am, the image of the roof captured from the drone before it was jammed shows more barrels on the rooftop." Lieutenant Murphy leaned back from screen 3.

"Get the images to Captain Dodson back at base and see if she can get us an answer to what in the hell they are." Deb spoke directly to Lieutenant Murphy and then turned to Tommy. "Check on the availability of immediate air support."

Deb pivoted to the screen with Lt. Col. Woodworth. "Josh. As soon as you arrive, have the tanks locate to where they have visual on the windows."

"We have to assume people inside this place are American citizens," Josh stated, but never asked about rules of engagement.

"Captain Hendersen, are your forward teams back?" Deb did not reply to the lieutenant colonel.

"Yes ma'am," the captain answered.

"Begin broadcasting over the loudspeakers the message that identifies us as the United States Army, and we require all people inside the building to exit immediately. Have Sergeant Chen repeat it in Chinese and then have Specialist Ivanov do the same in Russian. Keep broadcasting until they respond, or you receive further orders."

"Yes ma'am, also, Colonel, we have visual on H Company's tanks, they are arriving at our location," stated Captain Hendersen.

"Ma'am, we have an artillery battery that was on their way to Sunburst, Montana preparing to give us support. The air base can't guarantee immediate support," said Tommy.

"Where in the hell is Sunburst?" Deb looked at him with frustration.

"It's about one hundred and seventy kilometers to the north," stated Tommy. "The battery of long-range cannons are about twenty kilometers away."

"Colonel," Captain Jensen moved next to Deb, "Captain Dodson just responded that Research and Development could not identify the barrels as weapons."

"Damn, that is not the answer to the RFI I was hoping for." Deb looked at Tommy. The sound of the message in the distance could be heard being broadcast by F Company. "It just complicates the hell out of everything. That's all I need on my record is to attack a custom wheel factory in the middle of America because I thought the ventilation system was a new age weapon."

"We are going to have to send a team to investigate," stated Tommy.

"I don't know how they can get much better pictures

than we already have," Deb declared. "Call it intuition or whatever, but I don't like the idea of sending anyone inside this place. They have already surprised us twice."

Before the command sergeant major could reply, a blinding flash of light shot through the windows of the command center. The screens on the monitors all flashed off and then came back on.

"What in the world," Lieutenant Murphy leaned back in his chair holding both arms over his head. "What in the hell was that?"

"Was that an explosion?" Captain Jensen asked anxiously, thinking for a moment a nuclear weapon detonated.

Deb looked through the front window of the command vehicle in the direction of the warehouse and answered, "No, it was an electromagnetic pulse."

"Lt. Col. Woodworth is on screen one," said Lieutenant Murphy.

"I have never experienced anything like that," stated the lieutenant colonel. "With that blinding light we are bound to have some casualties here."

"Do the tanks have the targets in sight?"

"Yes ma'am.

Before she could reply, glaring flashes of light filled the air. She moved next to Tommy at the front window of the vehicle where they could see bright lasers pulsing out of every opening of the building. "We need artillery support," Deb yelled as she took a couple steps back from the window. Fragments of light from the lasers reflected off the walls of the command center. "Have them level the place."

Every five seconds a surge of light would burst from the roof top, compounding the effect of the constant light pulsating from the sides of the building. Flashes from the Bradley tanks could be seen responding to the attack.

Several intense flashes dashed through the air above the command center.

"They are shooting at us." Captain Jensen looked astounded as a beam hit the back top of the vehicle, creating a baseball size hole in the roof. "Should we move from this location?"

Rocket boosted shells exploded loudly as they ripped into the warehouse. The intensity of the explosions shook the vehicle. Within the melee of bursting shells, the blinding lights from the lasers curtailed as parts of the building disseminated into the air. The bombardment lasted for little more than a minute, culminating with smoke and dust soaring from the rubble. The areas visible through the debris of the smoldering building showed that much of the roof had collapsed and the walls imploded.

"Josh, are you still there?" Deb moved in front of the screens.

There was silence before he replied, "Yeah we are still here."

"Captain Hendersen."

"Yes ma'am.

"What is your status?"

"Nothing here was hit directly," the captain's voice was rushed.

"Josh, what about you?"

"The crews are still responding in the Bradleys. We are going to have some damage. We'll wait for the dust to settle and then assess the situation on getting the crew back to this command post."

"Are the tanks still operational?" Deb asked.

"I'll get back to you on that," Josh wavered. "The rest of H Company is moving to this location."

"Colonel, do you want me to direct 2nd and 3rd Platoons to the site?" Captain Jensen asked.

"No, use the drones to give us a view of the inside of the warehouse. Have everybody remain in place."

"Colonel, 3rd Battalion is thirty minutes north of the city," said Tommy. "Do you want them to come here or continue on to headquarters?"

"Have them go to headquarters in Great Falls." Deb grabbed her coat and stepped out of the command vehicle. She stared down at the devastation. "Good God," she said to herself. Tommy came to her side.

"Colonel, are you ok?"

She stared straight ahead and took in a deep breath. The smoke filled her lungs.

"It's freezing out here. Are you sure you don't want to come back inside?" He continued to stand next to her as she remained fixated on the wreckage.

"Is this what war has turned into?" she looked at him with her dark eyes narrowed. "Look at all the damage. It took less than ten minutes."

"Colonel, we need to contain the location."

"Use the drones and nonhuman vehicles. Observe it from a distance but no soldier goes near it until we are positive what we are dealing with." She cleared her throat, "Tommy, contact Fort Carson and see if we can get some assistance with excavating the site. We need combat engineers to work through this mess."

Deb continued to stare at the columns of smoke rising from the valley below. The smell in the air was brackish, like what a person might experience near a volcano in Hawaii. The trees around the premises were all demolished, knocked down like a tornado had rumbled over the site. She was briefed on the massive power of the high energy lasers but never imagined the magnitude of their destruction. One mistake by her, one wrong move and a complete Battalion or even her entire Brigade could have been obliterated in the blink of an eye.

"Ma'am," Tommy yelled from the door of the command vehicle. "A team is on its way from Fort Drum to help with extracting the site. They will be here before nightfall."

"Have all units remain in place until they arrive." Deb looked back toward Walt's farmhouse. The old rancher and his wife were standing in their driveway watching the smoke rise. She turned in the direction of Tommy and said, "Let's go back to headquarters."

Lone Tree, Colorado

Jessica spent a restless and worrisome night sleeping on the carpet inside the library. At first light she poked her head out the broken window. She tossed her duffle bag outside before climbing thru the opening, being extra careful not to cut herself on the jagged glass. Once in the wide-open parking lot she checked in all directions. She felt exposed and vulnerable while considering which way to go. Knowing the Lisco farm was east, she began to run eastwardly.

The cold air saturated her lungs as she sprinted until her legs begged her to stop. The tip of her nose was ice cold, but the sides of her breasts were wet with sweat underneath the winter coat. Although she had a night away from the rebels, she constantly looked back to make sure Christian, or his henchmen were not following. She stopped and bent at the waist and rested.

Her decision to leave Christian was completely unexpected, without any thought of consequence, or a plan. She was familiar with the area on the south side of town to the extent of knowing where she was, but none of the side streets were recognizable.

She began to jog until she came to a major thoroughfare that she recognized as Lincoln Avenue. The remnants of a supermarket and other shops were visible on the opposite side of the street. Her heart pounded in her chest as she sprinted across the wide road and paused at a tavern on the edge of the shopping center. The entire area was eerily quiet.

A bright green sign at the top of a bar, with its front door knocked off the hinges, identified the establishment as Mulligans. She waited at the entrance while her eyes adjusted to the darkness. With the first step inside her nostrils were filled with the smell of stale beer. The place was completely ransacked, picked to the bone with only a blackboard laying to the side with the words, daily special mulligan stew, written in white chalk. She moved further inside and found a partition wall where she had a view looking out a large picture window at Lincoln Avenue. She kneeled on her left knee and pulled out a bottle of water from her pack.

For a brief second, she wondered what happened with Christian when he attacked the police station. Then the images of Emilee, Reagan and Avery appeared in her mind. It felt as though her heart was about to come up through her throat as she visualized them. It was strange that the contemplation about her three daughters centered on Avery and Reagan. Emilee was older and was such a devoted daughter that she would be willing to forgive her mother for abandoning the family. The younger girls were loyal to one another. It would take more effort to gain their forgiveness and understanding. No matter what had transpired in the past she was going to find a way to be with them once again.

She stared out the window lost in thought. Facing the people at the farm, especially Jacqueline Lisco, would be difficult, but something she was willing to endure. The problem was she had no idea where the farm was located. She never paid attention to the roads while riding with the girls in the back of Hank's truck or when she left with Christian in the Lisco's stolen car.

It was still early morning and there wasn't a cloud in

the bright blue sky. Even in the shade of the bar she could feel the temperature rising. In her haste she packed water, food and warm clothing, yet she terribly regretted not taking a weapon. She was completely vulnerable in so many ways, yet she felt some contentment in knowing a solid decision was made to travel to the farm and see her girls.

The loud thumping of helicopter blades brought her out of her deep thought. The noise increased until several of the choppers rushed over her location causing the building to shake. She stepped outside the tavern to witness the massive display of military might filling the air above the city. Two bright flashes of light caused her to lower her head and move back inside the shelter. The sound of muffled explosions could be heard in the distance.

Her knees were trembling as she listened to the helicopters scouring the sky above. Two more bright flashes reflected off the walls of the dark room. She stayed frozen in position as the sounds of explosions followed. In the distance she could hear the roar of engines as a convoy of trucks headed her way.

Fort Carson Army Base

By the time Ted made his way to the base command, control and communication facility, Colonel Myer was already nearing the town of Parker. He felt oddly strange that he was not making any decisions about strategy or maneuverability and was present only to offer advice, guidance or recommendations. He watched images being sent from a camera attached to a forward tactical vehicle. Several screens in the room relayed pictures from the Denver metro area. The conversation between troops could be heard chattering back and forth throughout the large room.

Colonel Myer was in contact with the specialists and technicians at the monitors, relaying the local officials' requests for food and drinking water. Her mission so far appeared to be one of a humanitarian relief effort.

Ted moved to the screens displaying the area to the north and west of the colonel's location. The drones were displaying columns of smoke where explosions had occurred at the newly constructed emergency power stations and temporary police bases. Helicopters were flying in a grid pattern over the area trying to capture pictures of rebels on the ground. There was not one face-to-face encounter between the United States Army and the rebels.

Colonel Myer paused with a platoon of soldiers from B Company at a location west of Interstate 25 on Lincoln Avenue to evaluate the circumstances and process the information of the massive force covering the city. The chatter over the communication channels continued to be constant with many reports of sightings of insurgents who seemed to disappear before their eyes.

Ted moved from monitor to monitor trying to discern the information so he could help Colonel Myer make sense of the hidden enemy. As he was contemplating, a technician summoned him to a screen where Colonel Myer waited.

"Ted, we have a young lady who just approached our convoy." Colonel Myer was sitting in a cramped position in the mobile communication unit. "She has information to give about the rebels but first wants directions to the Lisco farm on the eastern plains. She says her daughters are there."

"Is her name Jessica?" Ted never met her but heard all about how enamored Bill was with the lady before she up and left the farm without her children. He also knew his nephew Bobby was still very much attached to Jessica's daughter Emilee.

"Affirmative, her name is Jessica."

"Tell her that I am Colonel Ted Lisco, Bill's father."

"She is speaking with Captain O'Brian and seems to be cooperative. We will see how much she can help us with pinpointing the location of the rebels she has been working with. Then we will transport her to the base later this evening."

Ted noticed a corporal approaching.

"Sir, General Lopez wants to speak with you," said the corporal.

Ted followed him to a monitor toward the back of the facility where he found some privacy to speak with the general.

"Ted, I want to let you know I will be back on base

Monday morning."

"Are preparations for advancing to the southern border going as planned?"

"I can't communicate anything more until I arrive in person," stated General Lopez.

Ted hesitated for a moment, surprised the general couldn't further the discussion.

"General, I would like to take a platoon and travel to my office at the farm tomorrow after Colonel Myer arrives back to base."

"Remind me Ted, it is about two hours away?"

"It's less than that from here." He was surprised the general would waver in giving permission.

"Ted, go ahead and make plans to travel to your farm. We have been having issues with security on our open communications so I will speak with you after I return to Fort Carson." The general disappeared from the screen.

Ted took in a deep breath and let it out slowly. He wondered what the general had in mind for him. When he first joined the army, he was enamored with the magnitude of the massive, powerful force that gained its strength from everyone working together. The interoperability of all branches made the military stronger. Now he felt it would not matter if he were a part of it, or not. He hated the idea of being ineffectual.

Eastern Colorado Farm

Bobby and Emilee carried eight-inch concrete blocks up the stairway to the second level of the masonry tower. Every third trip they each would lug a five-gallon bucket of mortar to the work area and dump it on a mortar board. Although the temperature was cool, they were working up a sweat.

After placing a five-gallon bucket of water into a mortar mixer, and ten shovels of sand, Sherry hoisted a thirty-two-kilogram bag of cement on to the grate of the powerful machine. After stepping back and allowing the dust to settle she shoveled in ten more scoops of sand. The loud machine would spit out wet globs of cement as it mixed the mortar. She had smudges of cement smeared across her forehead.

Jon and Hank watched the masonry crew as they worked. Harold was visible through the openings being left for windows on each side of the structure as he worked at a frantic pace. He already had the bolts sticking out of the bond beam at the top course of block signifying the second story of the tower was almost to full height.

"I haven't had a time to talk with Sherry since we returned from the Brown's farm," said Jon. "I need to let her know I appreciate the job she did that night.

"Bobby told me she wants to talk with you about the next step she and Caroline need to take with their enlistment." Hank cleared his throat, "Apparently Ted helped them with the paperwork before he left."

"Hell Hank, I'm not sure what the process would be.

I doubt anyone could get into Fort Carson now." Jon noticed Dave approaching.

"Coach," the young man towered over Hank. "We dug the three graves."

"How deep did you get?"

"Close to six feet. Once we got through the frozen part it was easy digging." Dave stared at Sherry while she worked.

"Ask your dad if he will have time this afternoon to make the caskets," said Hank.

"Will do coach." Dave never took his eyes off Sherry as he walked away.

"I am going to check with Bill to see if he has had any luck contacting Ted. I see Maddy and Scotty playing outside the garage, so he and Samantha are probably at the computer." Hank took one step toward the garage when he noticed George and Toby Saxton coming his way.

"Hank," George set a large backpack at his feet. "I need to apologize to you."

Toby remained slightly behind her husband.

"With all we've been through I can't let it end this way," George extended his hand.

"George, this never would have ended our friendship," Hank took George's hand and looked at their belongings. "Looks like you have made a decision?"

"Now that we know where we are going, we figure it will take us a day and a half to reach Franktown south of Parker."

"We are not going to find a warmer day then this," said Toby.

"I wish we had more information on what is happening in the city before you leave. It might be total chaos by now." Hank was genuinely concerned about his friend.

"I'll be honest. I'm a little worried why Ted hasn't contacted us with some sort of update," Jon interjected.

"The young lady we spoke with at the Browns told us her family found it dangerous enough in Aurora to make the journey east." Hank knew his connotation about the people who left the city was meaningless. George and the others were planning to leave and had already disassociated themselves with everyone at the farm. "I know you are dead set on leaving, so let me see if we can't figure a way to get you at least part of the way there."

"No, Hank, I'm not putting you in a situation where you could lose one of the vehicles here at the farm. We are completely prepared for the journey and want to make amends with you before we go."

"We want to part ways as friends," said Toby.

Ted looked at George's big, hook nose and felt a terrible sense of loss. "We will always be friends. You can come back if things don't work out. I'm serious about that George. You can always come back," he reached over and gave Toby a hug. The others in George's group gathered behind them.

"Hopefully, we will see you back in Littleton." George picked up his backpack and led the group away.

Hank and Jon watched them as they walked briskly down the driveway to the county road.

"There goes a quarter of our people," said Jon.

"Jacqueline and I were talking about that last night. That leaves us with thirty-one adults and the six kids," Hank replied. "The good thing is that we have a group of people who are efficient and know how to get things done."

"Case in point," Jon stared at the masonry crew.

"How high are they taking that tower?"

"I guess they are going three stories." Hank turned as he heard horses approaching. Breanna on a beautiful Bay with a white blaze running down his face rode up next to the two men. Avery on a dappled white horse with a dark mane and tail came next, followed by Reagan on a large chestnut horse. Both girls looked small on their giant steeds.

"How far does our property go to the east?" Breanna asked as she pulled back exceedingly hard on the rein to her horse.

"I have no idea Breanna," stated Hank. He looked. His brother shrugged his shoulders.

"I rode out there yesterday. There was no fence," Brenna patted the side of her horse's neck. "I guess me, and the girls will go on an adventure and see if we can find the property line."

"Are you enjoying riding the horses?" Hank looked at Avery and Reagan as they smiled while steadying their mounts.

"Yes," said Avery, holding the reins with her bandaged hand.

"Breanna is a good teacher," stated Reagan. "We are going to gallop the horses today."

Hank thought how odd Breanna had seemed the first time they met. Her constant talking and opinionated views were just her exterior. On the inside she was a caring person who would be there during bad circumstances.

"I agree with you, she is definitely an accomplished horse woman." Jon smiled at Breanna, "I sure couldn't keep up with her on a horse."

"You did pretty good for a city guy," said Breanna

smiling.

"How long are you going to be gone? Jon asked.

"We will be back within the hour."

"I want to have everyone meet right after lunch."

"I'll let Mom and Dad know." Breanna looked at Avery and Reagan than nudged the side of her horse. "We couldn't have asked for better weather for a ride. Come on girls."

***

Hank and Jon decided to have the meeting, with the remaining occupants of the farm, on the driveway in front of the Jacoby's motorhome. Ed was having more and more difficulty walking. Although Irene was as mobile as ever, she found herself spending an exorbitant amount of time playing cards with her husband in the confines of the RV.

Bill, Samantha, Maddy and Scotty carried folding chairs to the location. It was nearly one o'clock when the final group of Harold, Bobby, Emilee and Sherry made their way to the gathering.

"Sorry for taking so long. We had to finish using the mortar," stated Harold, taking a seat next to Becky.

"It is really impressive how fast the tower is being built." Jacqueline looked at Harold and then fixed her eyes on her son and his two friends. Their clothes were covered in cement and all three had blotches of cement on their faces.

"The apartment progress is amazing too." Gina glanced at Kori to make sure she knew how much everyone appreciated Jason's carpentry skills.

"Thanks to Terrance and Jerry we only need a couple more hours to have the rough electrical wiring pulled for the first half of the building," stated Jason proudly.

"Tomorrow, while we still have good weather, we are going to start roofing the final half of the structure."

"I guess everyone knows by now that Coach Saxton and his group left earlier this morning." Hank took a position in front of the crowd.

"Why did he leave?" Al asked apprehensively. "Linda and I were discussing their going. Do they know something we don't?"

"No, they don't. Actually, they have no idea what sort of situation they are returning to in the city." Hank was a bit put off by Al trying to create conflict.

"Could it be that they are correct that things are not so bad in the city?" Al looked at the others. "I know the country is being threatened at the borders, but it might not be as treacherous back home in Littleton."

"Ever since Ted left, Bill and Samantha have been at the radio trying to get information. The news we have received over the radio doesn't give us an accurate description of what is happening in the city. We know it is bad. To what degree we don't know," stated Nicole.

"I guess what I'm saying," Al hesitated for a moment. "Before we put so much into creating a place to live here it would be helpful to know the condition back home."

Hank looked at Jon in search for a reply. Before Jon could respond Ed stood up.

"I know we are not going back to Utah for quite some time," Ed spoke softly, almost too low for everyone to hear. "Why not work to make this place better. It doesn't matter if we leave tomorrow, or we are here a year from now. Colonel Lisco created this place to help others, not for herself. We should all respect that."

"We need to get the hay from the Browns ranch." Aaron wasn't about to deal with the frivolity of whether to make the farm a better place. "If we can take the backhoe to the creek and make a dirt bridge so we can cross with the tractor and trailer, it will save us about ten kilometers a trip."

"Do you need help with that?" Jon asked.

"No, me and Adam can take care of it."

"I agree with what everybody is saying," said Al emphatically, ignoring the Jacoby's thoughts on making the farm more efficient. "We should still find a way to stay informed. To keep abreast of what is happening."

"How do you suggest we do that Al?" Jon asked.

"We could go to Limon and speak with the people who recently arrived from the city. With the apartment progressing so well it might be a good time to find more people." Al glanced at the others.

"I volunteer to go," Bill stepped forward. He looked at Samantha.

"I'll go with him," said Samantha.

"I'll go too," yelled Terrance.

"Me too," Linda surprised everyone, including her husband. Al stared at her with his mouth wide open.

"Is everyone good with going tomorrow morning?" Hank asked.

Everyone answered in the affirmative.

"One last thing," said Jacqueline. "We are going to bury the Browns this afternoon for anyone who wants to attend."

Great Falls, Montana

With the clouds completely dissipated, the sunset glittering over the Montana landscape was stunning. Deb hesitated outside the mess tent to take in the beauty. She hadn't had a bite to eat the entire day, so the aroma of freshly baked bread was invigorating.

After retrieving her food, she joined Lieutenant Colonels Barnet and Wilson at the back of the pavilion.

"Colonel, it's good to see you all in one piece." Lt. Col. Wilson smiled at Deb as she took a seat. "I guess our information about you being on your death bed was a bit exaggerated. You just missed Tommy. He was summoned to the communication tent."

"I'm still kicking," Deb looked back and forth between her two friends.

"What happened out there today?" Teresa looked at the colonel with wide, saggy eyes.

"We shook a hornet's nest." Deb lowered her eyes and continued eating. She could feel her heart racing.

"Colonel," Tommy took two steps into the tent. "General Lauer wants to speak with you."

"Looks like a change of plans." She stood up and tossed her napkin on her food and followed Tommy out of the mess tent toward communications.

General Lauer was standing to the side, with only a part of his back visible on the screen. When his face did come into view Deb was surprised at how tired and haggard he looked.

"Colonel, you are to move with 1st and 3rd Battalions

for southern Utah tomorrow morning via Interstate 15."

"What about 2nd Battalion?"

"They are to stay in Great Falls and assist General Prost with the warehouse situation."

"General Prost?" Deb looked at Tommy. He shrugged his shoulders. "Is she part of the combat engineer team working on the extraction?"

"No, she will be supervising cyber. She arrived in Fort Carson last night with General McClinton and left this afternoon after hearing about the incident at the warehouse." The general's voice was almost monotonous as he gave her the surprising news, "She should be there now."

"Anything else?"

"Specific orders will be relayed on your journey in the morning." She was preparing to ask about Ted when the general disappeared from the screen.

Deb took a couple steps away from the monitor and stared at the Command Sergeant Major. "What is that mousey little bitch doing here?"

"I take it you have a past with her?" Tommy lowered his chin and stared at the colonel.

"She was at a meeting I, along with Ted and Jon, had with General McClinton a couple of years ago. She was a total pain in the ass."

"Colonel Lisco," a tech specialist interrupted. "General Prost wants to speak with you."

Deb forced a smile as she followed the specialist to his monitor.

"Colonel Lisco," the general's face seemed different from two years earlier. It seemed fuller. "I'm hoping I can meet with you, in person, this evening."

"Yes, certainly ma'am." Deb tried not to flounder

with the unexpected request. She turned to Tommy and rolled her eyes, trying to convey her desire for him to make an excuse. "Command Sergeant Major is this a good time, I mean, are we all caught up with preparation for departure tomorrow?"

"Right now, is as good a time as any," Tommy smiled at Deb.

"I'm ten minutes from your location," stated the general.

"Have the sentry direct you to the officer's tent. I'll meet you there," Deb said. As soon as the general went off the screen she chuckled, "This will be interesting, and by the way thanks a lot."

The lighting at the center of the empty officer's tent was bright, with a darkness around the outer edges, closer to the walls. Of the four tables, Deb chose the one farthest away from the door. She sat and waited in utter confusion for the arrival of General Prost, remembering how different their personalities and viewpoints were during their first face to face meeting over two years earlier.

General Prost entered the tent and looked Deb directly in the eyes, and continued to do so, as she quickly walked across the room. She held out her hand and said, "Colonel Lisco, I'm glad you are available this evening."

Deb stood up and took her hand. "Would you like something to drink ma'am?"

"No thank-you," before sitting down the general removed her coat and placed it on an empty chair. After sitting she leaned forward and confidently engaged Deb with her eyes. "I'm sure you wonder why I want to meet this evening."

"Yes ma'am. I guess I do wonder," Deb fidgeted in her seat. She was intimidated by the general continuing to stare directly into her eyes.

"I was scheduled to be in Calgary tonight, but I flew from Virginia to Fort Carson this morning with General McClinton. We had a good talk on the trip that, amongst other things, included recollecting the meeting we had with you and your brothers nearly two years ago."

Deb felt somewhat unsettled in the presence of her diminutive superior. She sat straight in the chair, placed her prominent chin out and listened intently as the general continued.

"When we heard about the warehouse, General McClinton asked me to head the team from cyber command during the excavation."

"Something tells me you are going to find a hell of a lot of information at the bottom that building."

"We believe so too," the general declared. "But that is not the only reason I wanted to take this opportunity to meet with you in person."

Deb cocked her head, "What might that be ma'am?"

"You were right Colonel. You were correct in almost every aspect that you warned us about in the meeting at the Pentagon. We blew it off," General Prost raised her voice. "The situation the country is facing wouldn't be nearly as dire if we had listened to you. I want to let you know how much I regret not investigating more deeply into your concerns."

"General, I misjudged you too. I wasn't entirely correct at that meeting. When you told me that the days of brigade versus brigade warfare were over, I miscalculated the value of your knowledge and experience." She swallowed hard. "Today when I witnessed the high-speed lasers and the power of our own rockets, I realized this war will be much different than any before."

"This is a war that will have decisions made by machines far away from the battlefield. I hope we, as a country, can counter the technological aspects of our enemies. The entire scenario we are facing at this time has come about from models they created from hundreds of thousands of simulations. Artificial intelligence has morphed into not only making the decisions but enforcing them. It's really frightening." The general wrinkled her nose and squinted her eyes, "But Colonel Lisco, the one calculation I think they are missing is that all great leaders have an instinct unavailable to a machine."

"What do you expect to find at the warehouse, ma'am?"

"I expect there to be a cache of information," General Prost inhaled deeply. "Since the place has been there for years, we should find not only information about weapons, but plenty of hard data on the embedded forces throughout the country."

"More information for the machines to create more models," Deb smiled.

"Exactly," she smiled back.

Having someone as knowledgeable as the general discuss strategy and tactics was uplifting to Deb. It was something she relished doing with her father when he was still alive. General Prost was able to give her a better perspective on not only the danger they were to face in the combat zones but also from the ones within the ranks. The compelling discussion covered nearly all topics Deb could think of that might help make her a better leader.

As the conversation ran its course Deb's opinion of the lady was completely changed. She took a moment to think how fortunate she was to converse on equal terms with such a brilliant trail blazer as General Prost. She took in a deep breath and asked, "Can I get you something to drink now, ma'am?"

The general placed her small hands flat on the table. "How about a Scotch? On the rocks."

Deb cocked her head back. She knew exactly where the scotch was located. "Two Scotches it is."

"I didn't see him. But I know your brother is back at Fort Carson," the general remained seated and spoke loudly as Deb fussed around the bar.

"I'm going to try and contact him sometime tomorrow while we are moving." She placed two large glasses of scotch over ice cubes on the table. "Would you like something to eat ma'am?"

"No, I'm good," she took a drink. "Please, call me Ann. We don't need to be so formal while we are having a drink."

"Certainly, feel free to call me Deb." She took a drink of the Scotch whisky. The warm sensation of the liquor flowing down her throat and caused her shoulders to relax. "That is so good."

"The Lisco family has such an interesting history with the Army," Ann stated congenially, obviously feeling the same calming sensation. "Was it your great grandfather who fought in the Battle of the Bulge?"

"Actually, it was my grandfather. He and my father both had children later in life."

Both women were drinking their libations at a quickened pace. As soon as their glasses were empty, Deb went to the bar and returned with the bottle and filled them to the top.

"Ann, umm where did you grow up?" Deb opened and closed her mouth. Her jaw felt a little numb.

"Massachusetts."

"Were your family in the military?"

"My aunt was."

They both drank and told stories neither would remember, not to outdo one another, but to be amiable. Both women were feeling no pain as Deb filled the general's glass and then poured the remainder of the bottle of Scotch into hers.

"Looks like we drank the whole damn bottle," Deb laughed loudly, slamming the bottle to the table.

"I am delighted we had a chance to spend this time together." Ann was speaking loudly as she lifted the glass to her thin lips and swallowed the last of her drink. Her head was moving in a circular motion. "But now that we know each other so well, I have to come completely clean. I made some disparaging remarks about you a couple of days after your meeting with General McClinton. I want to make amends, right now." She put her right hand up by her ear, then slammed it down hard on the table as she stood up.

"What did you say?" Deb was slumping and leaning in her chair.

Ann stared blankly through blood-shot eyes, then stuck her chin way out in front of her and said, "Look at me. Look at me, I'm colonel know-it-all." She relaxed back in her chair and said, "I'm sorry."

Deb started laughing. Pretty soon they were both laughing loudly.

"Ok, ok I have to admit that I have said disparaging words about you too, Ann." Deb tried to focus her eyes.

"What did you shay?" Ann slurred.

Deb tried to open her eyes wide as she moved forward in her chair and pronounced her words slowly and clearly, "Well, I called you a mousey, little bitch."

"When did you do that?"

Deb's head was bobbling slightly as she answered, "This afternoon."

They both burst out laughing.

Tommy rushed into the tent, followed closely by another soldier.

"Colonel, the entire encampment can hear you."

Deb's upper body felt numb as she stared vacantly at the command sergeant major.

"Let me help you to your quarters. The corporal can assist General Prost." The command sergeant major lifted her out of the chair.

"Tommy, that is Ann," she pointed her left index finger in the direction of the ceiling.

"Please ma'am," Tommy whispered. "You really can't afford being charged with another conduct unbecoming an officer."

"General Prost, it was a pleasure meeting with you this evening." Deb wobbled. "Tommy, this is what happens when you stay up all night drinking."

"Come on," he directed her to the door, "it's not even 2100 yet."

"I would appreciate it if you can assist me to my quarters," she spoke softly as she leaned on Tommy's arm. "I don't want another officer unbecoming the conduct charge."

In all the years serving with Colonel Lisco it was the first time Tommy had seen her totally intoxicated. He knew she was aware of the consequences of being drunk and disorderly on base. There was much more to her making the decision to get plastered with General Prost than was on the surface.

Limon, Colorado

Bill steered cautiously over the wet dirt roads in the new car he helped Deb pick out less than a year earlier. Terrance was sitting shotgun with Samantha and Linda riding in the back seat of the spacious automobile. When they reached the frontage road that ran parallel to Interstate 70, he stopped the vehicle. There were several abandoned cars and trucks visible on the highway. They arrived at an exit ramp that would allow them to enter onto the freeway but chose to travel along the frontage road.

Approaching the small town, they crested a large hill where they could see a massive amount of people confined to an area that spanned the road. Orange colored, sand filled, fifty-gallon barrels traversed the pavement in front of a tall fence where people could be seen beyond the enclosure. They stopped the car about four hundred meters from the barricade.

"Any ideas how to approach this?" Bill continued to look in the direction of the compound.

"For one thing I want to make damn sure nobody takes this car," stated Terrance. "I don't want to have to walk all the way back."

"How about if Samantha and I go and check," Linda smiled and nodded at Samantha. "What do you think?"

"Well…," Samantha wavered.

"We go in and ask some questions and come back out," said Linda, opening the door.

"Why not," Samantha chuckled nervously and

stepped out without any more discussion.

"Just a second," Bill hurried out the door and moved close to Samantha. "If something seems wrong, don't take any chances, come back and we can re-evaluate."

"Do either of you want to take a weapon?" Terrance held a pistol out in front of him.

"This is why it will be better for us to go rather than either of you," said Linda confidently. "We are not threatening to anyone."

A cool breeze blew at their back while the two women walked down the black-top. When they were within twenty meters of the sand barrels four figures became visible. They stopped ten meters short of the barricade and spoke with the guards for nearly five minutes before advancing into the community.

Terrance opened the trunk of the car and retrieved his AK 47. He hid it in a coat so as not to take a chance of provoking someone into thinking he was a threat. Both men waited anxiously as the women remained out of sight for over three hours.

"Did we make a mistake here?" Bill asked. "We should have been more specific about having them check back within a certain amount of time."

"You would think they would have figured we would be worried," said Terrance.

"I don't see any place where we could get a better vantage point to look inside the encampment."

"Hell Bill, that wouldn't do us any good. There are thousands of people scattered for God knows how far," Terrance rubbed his chin.

"None of this makes any sense," said Bill. "The people we found inside the Browns farmhouse never did show up at the farm. I would sure like to talk with them about this place.

"The guards here don't look like police or National Guard," stated Terrance.

"I'm going to go and talk with them."

Terrance wavered for a moment as he stared at Bill's facial features. His high cheek bones and pronounced chin were the same as his father. He remembered Ted's intensity when faced with duress. He could see the same strength now in the son. He responded, "Sounds better than just sitting around."

Bill walked quickly. A man and three women greeted him as he approached the roadblock. All four were slight of build and dressed in matching shirts.

One of the women held up her hand indicating for Bill to stop.

"We have some questions you need to answer before going any further."

"I only want to find out about the two women who came through here about three hours ago." Bill tried to be as amicable as possible. He could see a two-meter-high wire fence about fifty meters past the roadblock.

"Have you been sick or around anyone who is sick within the last thirty days?"

"No, I'm healthy and I haven't been around any sick people." Bill decided it would be better to answer the questions than to cause a fuss.

"Do you have any weapons?"

"No," he felt the holster rub the back of his upper hip. "I don't want to enter your communal, or whatever it is. I just want to find out about the safety of the two women who just entered."

"Is that your car on the top of the hill?"

"Yes ma'am." He noticed all four of them had

holstered pistols. "What does that have to do with me wanting to find out about my friends?"

"Both women went to registration," said one of the sentries.

"How long would it take them to register?" Bill noticed a small, red insignia at the upper left of each of the guard's shirts that read FEMA.

"They are backed up, so I would guess most of the afternoon."

"Well," Bill scoffed. He placed his hands up in the air in frustration and looked back in the direction of Terrance. "Could you have someone go and get them for me?"

"You can follow us."

"I don't want to enter," Bill glanced at the gate in the distance behind the sentries. Samantha was tossing her hands and yelling as she pushed the gate open. She walked quickly toward him.

Bill watched her stomp his way until she was five meters away. "Where's Linda?" he yelled.

"They placed her in quarantine," Samantha could not stop prancing as she inhaled deeply. "They literally drug her away."

"We need you to go inside and find our friend, right now." Bill looked deeply into the eyes of the woman guard closest to him.

"If she went to quarantine, she can't come out for seven days."

"Here comes Terrance," Samantha had her back to the guards as she looked down the highway.

Terrance was driving slowly toward them. Three guards from the fenced area moved through the gate and jogged toward the roadblock.

"Sir," said the first guard to arrive, "we are going to

confiscate your automobile. By executive order signed by the President of the United States we have the right to take and use any item necessary for the betterment and advancement of the common good of society. Your car falls into the realm of this order."

"The hell you are," said Bill with exasperation.

"We have the full power of the United States government to seize your vehicle."

"I don't care who you are, you sure as hell can't have this car." Bill reached around and grabbed his pistol. He pointed at the head of the closest guard. Terrance leaped from the driver's seat and moved to the front of the car with his AK 47 at the ready. Samantha quickly climbed into the back seat. Terrance waited for Bill to be in the driver's seat before jumping inside. They sped about two kilometers up the frontage road before stopping to contemplate their options in rescuing Linda.

None of the guards had unholstered their weapons. When they saw the weapons aimed at them, they placed their arms over their heads and retreated behind the sand filled barrels.

Eastern Colorado Farm

Bill slowly maneuvered the car down the driveway to the farm. After much calculation and some debate, they made the decision to return without Linda. Explaining to Al that his wife was in quarantine at the camp was not something any of them were looking forward too.

It was a beautiful day with the temperature well above freezing. It was the warmest day since arriving at the farm. Hank and Jacqueline, sitting on the front porch, were the first to notice the car coming down the driveway. Nicole and Maddy were the first to arrive to greet Bill. Soon the car was surrounded by a crowd.

"Where's Linda?" Jacqueline asked quizzically as the three vacated the car.

"She is still at the compound," Bill looked at Hank. "It's a FEMA run camp and they quarantined her."

Hank looked over his shoulder toward the house. Al was hurrying down the driveway, where he stopped about three meters from the main body of people.

"Where's Linda?" he took in several deep breaths with his mouth partially open.

"Al, she was quarantined at the camp in Limon," said Bill. "They wouldn't release her."

"So, you left her there?" Al's upper lip was twisted. "Why would they quarantine her?"

"Her temperature was over a hundred," Samantha took one step in the direction of Al. "And she had a bad rash on the inside of her right arm."

"She had a rash on her arm from cleaning things

around here with cheap soap." Al puffed his chest out and pointed to the car. "Now get back in and let's go get her."

"I argued with them for an hour trying to get her discharged," said Samantha.

"Maybe you should have argued for two hours, or three."

"I went to find Bill to help, but the guards at the gate threatened to take the car." Samantha looked at Bill, "So, we took off before they could take it."

"You left her behind so you could save the car." Al slapped his hand hard on the hood. "Of all the stupid things I have done in my life, coming to this place has to top them all."

"Let's figure this out," said Hank. "Just calm down for a second Al."

"Fuck you Hank. If that were Jacqueline they left behind, I'm sure you wouldn't be so condescending. Now get in the car. I'm not leaving her there all night."

"If you drive there in the dark, they will see the lights of this car and seize it," stated Terrance firmly.

"I don't give a shit if they take every vehicle here. Did you two try to stop them from taking her?" Al was breathing heavily as he looked back and forth between Bill and Terrance.

"Samantha and Linda went inside the compound while we waited outside," Bill inhaled deeply. "Like Samantha said she tried her best to get them to release her."

"So, you two big brave guys sent my wife into a dangerous situation with this bimbo." Al licked his lips and shook his head up and down.

There was complete silence. Bill's heart was pounding the walls of his chest as he moved his nose a couple of centimeters from Al's nose. Hank moved closer to the two of them.

"You have one chance and one chance only to apologize to her," Bill towered over the dentist. He held his finger right under Al's chin. "I mean right now."

Al didn't say a word, as he stood his ground. Hank placed a hand between the two men.

"It's alright Bill, calm down here."

"It was Linda's idea for the two of them to go alone. Samantha was the brave one in this whole ordeal," said Bill angrily, pointing at Al. "I won't sit back and allow you to call her names."

"Did you say it was a government compound?" Ed asked, limping forward to the center of the crowd. "I'm sure they have strict rules but at least they are responding to this mess. Why don't we sleep on it tonight and go back in the morning?"

"Terrance was right about them taking the car." Bill glanced at Samantha as he moved next to her. "The guards told us that the President signed an executive order stating they can take anything that is necessary for the betterment of society."

"That's all the more reason we should go talk with them before they come here and take all our livestock," said Jon. "I'm willing to go in the morning and speak with whoever is in charge to see about them releasing Linda. Also, to see if we can make a deal with us supplying beef for protection."

"That was exactly my thought too," said Ed.

Al looked menacingly at the entire crowd before stomping in the direction of the house.

Hank thought how his good friend and neighbor's Napoleon Complex was brought out into the open for all to see. He chuckled to himself when he thought about

Linda being held in quarantine at the FEMA compound. The only time in her entire life that she took a chance and now she was missing. He knew her well enough to know she was happy to have a change of pace. As far as Al calling Samantha a bimbo, that would take some mending for the relationship between the dentist and Bill to ever become amicable. Samantha did not seem to be distraught in the least from the remark.

Fort Carson Army Base

Ted reached the departure location on the western edge of the base just as Lieutenant Hanson of Company E, 2d platoon arrived. He had a large smile on his face as he escorted Jessica.

"Sir", he saluted, "Colonel Murphy requested I personally escort Ms. Jessica O'Brian to your location."

Ted saluted the lieutenant, "I'm ready to leave immediately." Jessica remained silent as she stepped in front of Ted.

"Did you arrive last night?" Ted noticed Jessica's hair, pulled back in a ponytail, looked freshly washed. All she was carrying was a small duffle bag.

"Yes, I slept in a guest apartment," she spoke with an Irish accent while staring at Ted for several seconds with her bright blue eyes. "Thank-you, it was more than adequate."

"Is this all your gear?" he sensed she was nervous as he stared at the duffle bag.

"That's it, I didn't take much when I left." Ted's easy disposition gave her cause to relax. She looked at the vehicle Ted was standing nearby. "Are we riding in this truck?"

"This is a XM 4400 Electric Survivable Combat Tactical Vehicle." Ted smiled warmly as he looked closely at Jessica's face. With her hair pulled back she looked young. Nicole told him how enamored Bill was with her, now he could see why. With her high cheek bones and bright red hair, she was a beautiful woman. His wife also told him about her leaving behind her children, so he planned on finding out all about Jessica O'Brian on the trip to the farm.

"Sir, we are ready to go when you are," said Lieutenant Hanson.

"Let's go," Ted opened the door to the tactical vehicle and allowed Jessica to enter the back seat. He followed her inside.

After several minutes of small talk as the platoon made its way into the countryside Ted decided to break the ice about Jessica's children.

"Are you worried about how your children are going to react to you going back to the farm?"

She stared at him for a moment, then lowered her gaze. There was wetness in the corner of her eyes.

"Have you thought about what you are going to tell everyone?" Ted continued without receiving an answer.

"Not really," she whispered. "I just want to be with my girls again."

"Why did you leave?"

"I guess because for all my life I have been strapped down with something or another. I had a chance to leave and be free," she sighed, "I took it."

"I take it, you now regret the decision?" Ted stared at her as she continued to look away. Colonel Murphy told him that she was helpful in giving information about the movement of Christian's rebels, and now he wanted to help her. "Can I give you some advice?"

"Of course."

"Don't be the victim."

"I don't think I am."

"Your daughters deserve to have a mother who can admit a mistake." Ted thought for a moment, "The others at the farm will be more likely to accept you if you don't make excuses."

Jessica stared at him for a moment. It was completely against her nature to submit. But Emilee's relationship with Bobby complicated the need to be accepted by the Lisco family.

"What I'm trying to tell you, is that at this time, there is less tolerance being given for bad decisions. With all the unknowns with the war, everyone is scared and confused."

"I've been that way my entire life." Jessica raised her eyebrow and slanted her head toward the colonel.

"I don't doubt you have gotten the short end of the stick on many occasions." He could see why his son had become so enamored with the woman. She had a toughness that could easily be taken for confidence. "I hope you will take my advice and show vulnerability without complaining. Take responsibility for your actions."

"I'm tired," she took in a deep breath and relinquished it. "When we get to the farm, I will try my best to not blame others for my mistakes."

"I know my family," Ted gave her a reassuring smile. "They are willing to forgive."

"I hope they will," she smiled softly as she lowered her chin.

Ted knew he had reached the point where any more advice would be counterproductive. He wondered how Bill and Samantha's relationship was developing. Before duty required him to leave so quickly the flight attendant and his son seemed to be getting along quite well. But, according to Nicole, before Jessica left the farm, Bill was under the assumption that he and the beautiful Irish lady were a couple. It would all be an interesting scene when

Jessica showed up unannounced.

"Sir," said the private driving the vehicle. "There are cars blocking the road ahead."

Ted leaned forward to look out the windshield. "Wait for the lieutenant to handle the situation."

Lieutenant Hanson had the infantry soldiers exit the vehicles and fan out on both sides of the convoy, as he and two privates approached the roadblock. A Humvee was blocking the view to the area, so Ted stepped outside the safe confines of his tactical vehicle. "Stay here," he said to Jessica before closing the door. He advanced to the area nearly twenty meters from the cars blocking the road where the lieutenant was speaking to a group of five people. Behind the cars of the barricade there were between thirty and forty more people pointing their weapons in his direction. The soldiers of the platoon were spaced on both sides of the road.

"Sir, they say they are members of the farming community," said the lieutenant. "I asked them to move the cars so we can proceed."

The three men and two women speaking with the lieutenant were all dressed in black. Ted looked past them to the others standing behind the cars. They all wore the same black clothing.

"Lieutenant, bring the Nyalas up to this location." Ted looked directly at the people the lieutenant was speaking with. He didn't say a word to them as Lieutenant Hanson spoke into his radio. Two RG-35 Nyalas with manned open-air 0.50 caliber heavy machine guns pulled within two meters on each side of the group.

"Now," Ted looked directly at the rebels in front of him. "Tell us who you really are."

"We are farmers."

"I don't think so.'

"We work for the farmers."

"Who hired you," Ted realized they were within thirty kilometers of Deb's farm, and he might recognize the name of a farmer.

"All of them did," said one of the women.

"Right," Ted scoffed. "I don't know who you are, but I want this roadblock out of our way."

A powerful gust of wind blew into the agitator's face before they turned and walked back to the roadblock. Within a minute the cars pulled to the side of the road. It was disconcerting to Ted as he looked out the window of the tactical vehicle. The rebels brazenly stared at the convoy of soldiers as they quickly passed through their blockade.

FEMA compound Limon, Colorado

Hank drove the Jacoby's antique, Ford F-250 right up to the sand filled barrels blocking the entrance to the FEMA camp. It was predetermined that they would let Jon and Jacqueline out at the outpost and Hank would drive the truck back a kilometer to the west and wait for them to take care of business inside the compound.

The air was crisp, and the morning sun was peeking over the top of the wire fencing on the back side of the barricade. Jacqueline pulled the wide lapel of her pea coat tightly around her neck and followed slightly behind her brother-in-law as he confidently gauged the lone sentry waiting at the roadblock. Jon wore a trench coat which gave him an aura of intrigue.

"Can you tell the head of the incident management assistance team that Lieutenant Colonel Jon Lisco requests a meeting," Jon spoke first. He was cleanly shaven, and his hair was neatly combed.

"FEMA headquarters is located on the northern edge of the compound in the town." The guard was an older lady, "You can get there through the compound."

"Are you with FEMA?" Jon asked authoritatively.

"Since Monday," her approach was good-natured. "Last week I was the town librarian. FEMA hired several people from the area to help with all the travelers stranded here, so I guess you could say I am with them."

"I need to speak with whoever is in charge. Could you please call ahead and inform them we are on our way?"

She spoke into a radio as Jon and Jacqueline waited patiently. She finally lowered the radio.

"Go to the gate and one of the guards there will take you to the operations center." She pointed to the gate at the tall fence about fifty meters to the east.

The people inside the compound were wandering around the grounds like a flock of ducks trying to find a morsel of food in a large lake. Jon and Jacqueline walked briskly through the mass of lost souls for nearly twenty minutes before arriving at a gate on the northern fence line separating the throng of travelers from the citizens of the town of Limon. They continued past the guards at the gate and walked to a dilapidated hotel about a hundred meters south of Interstate 70.

After entering the atrium of the hotel, the guard stopped and pointed in the direction of an old man with chalk white hair.

"That's Deputy Director Garrett. He should be able to help you." The guard quickly turned and exited.

"Sir," Jon said loudly as he approached the deputy. "Can I have a moment of your time?"

"What do you want?" The deputy director asked curtly without looking at Jon. He continued shuffling papers on a desk.

"My name is Lieutenant Colonel Jon Lisco." Jon could tell the guy was a real hard ass. "I would like to speak about a proposition I can offer that will get some beef to this location."

"Retired?" The deputy raised an eyebrow and glanced at Jon. "I take it you are retired. Anyway, we have a team already appropriating cattle from the area ranches."

Jon stared at the man for a moment. He knew immediately he should discontinue speaking about the situation at the farm with the man who was obviously former military. Appropriating meant he was seizing the property of others.

"Where is the ranch you are speaking of?" the deputy stood up tall. He was several centimeters taller than Jon. When Jon failed to respond he said, "Sir."

"Several ranches north of here, by Last Chance." Jon looked at Jacqueline to see how she would respond to his blatant lie.

"We are overwhelmed right now and would appreciate any help we can get." The man sniffled and wiped his nose with the back of his left hand. It was almost as cold inside the lobby as it was outside. "We have never experienced a disaster of this magnitude. The only way to survive here is for local people to step up and help."

"Are you going to be able to keep up with feeding all these people?"

"We probably can here but it will affect the others in the Denver area." The man-made eye contact with Jon. "This is the eastern border of FEMA's region 8. More than seventy-five percent of deliveries to the region by truck from the east come through here, so we have first chance to replenish our supplies. To be honest, transportation is a bigger issue right now. Although the cities east of the Mississippi are disrupted it is not the same degree of chaos we are experiencing in our metropolitan zones."

"Transportation?" Jon looked at him skeptically. He thought about it for a moment. "Of course, there wouldn't be a problem if the people weren't here."

"Exactly, we have had five different electromagnetic pulse incidents in the last week. Most of the people are stranded because their vehicles have been disabled. Some have walked over eighty kilometers to get here. The town of Limon had a population of six thousand three weeks ago, now there are four times that amount."

"Have you been briefed on the EMP weapon that is being used by the insurgents?"

"No, but we know it is small enough to hide quickly after it's employed. You would think it would be easy to catch the people responsible in a town this size, but local law enforcement has no idea who they are. The flash of light is so intense that it is hard to find the exact location it was fired from. The sheriff here calls them magicians because they disappear into thin air immediately after discharging the weapon."

Jon glanced at Jacqueline, "Linda," she mouthed. He nodded that he had not forgotten.

"I would like to come back in a couple of days and assist you with finding these rebels," Jon spoke convincingly. "I have some familiarity with the EMP weapon."

"I'm sure the sheriff would accept any help he can get. Mechanics are ready to work on the cars as soon as we stop the EMPs."

"Also, we have a friend of ours quarantined at your medical facility who we would like to have released to us."

"Are you taking her out of the facility?"

"Yes sir."

"Inform the sentry at the gate that Deputy Director Garrett gave permission to release your friend. If there is any problem, have them radio me," the deputy looked sternly at Jon.

"Thank you, sir," Jon motioned to Jacqueline that it was time to go retrieve Linda.

Upon hearing the deputy director gave verbal

permission for releasing Linda, the guard at the gate to the quarantine area was more than willing to set her free. It took less than ten minutes before Jacqueline and Jon saw her hurrying in their direction. Her hair was disheveled, and there were bags under her eyes, but she smiled when she noticed Jacqueline.

"Hello neighbor," Jacqueline gave her a hug as she exited the gate.

"Oh my God," Linda chuckled, "what an experience."

"Well, you are out now," stated Jacqueline.

"Thank God," Linda seemed in good spirits. "I take it Samantha made it back?"

"Yes, Al didn't take it very well when they showed up without you last night."

"I can only imagine," Linda scoffed.

"You'll hear all about it when we get back to the farm," Jacqueline glanced at Jon.

"Samantha was so good when they took me into quarantine. She screamed and yelled at them, and she actually slugged one of the guards," Linda laughed out loud.

"You'll have to give her a hug and thank her when you get back," said Jon knowingly.

"I will do that," replied Linda.

"Hank is waiting in the Jacoby's pick-up, so it's going to be a little crowded on the way back." Jacqueline grinned, "We are going to have a lot to discuss."

"Lieutenant Colonel Lisco," a voice resonated from the crowd.

All three turned to locate the person yelling at Jon.

"Sir, it's Captain Huang," A short, stocky middle-aged man yelled from about ten meters away. He was wearing a short-sleeved khaki shirt that embellished his large biceps.

"I'll be damn. Irving Huang," Jon said. The captain was a soldier he had thought about on several occasions since his retirement. "What are you doing here?"

"My parents and I left Arvada for my aunt's home in Nashville. We were about three kilometers east of here on Interstate 70 when we were hit by an EMP. It completely fried the engine." He shook his head, "I thought you were in Texas?"

"It's a long story. We came here to watch a football game and were stranded too." Jon motioned with his arm toward the two women. "Irving, this is my sister-in-law Jacqueline Lisco and a neighbor of hers, Linda Jones."

The captain was a small man in stature but the confidence he exhumed gave him a large presence. Both women could tell that Jon considered him to be someone special.

"Irving was captain of Company K, which was part of my battalion before I retired," stated Jon.

"How long have you been at this compound?" Irving asked.

"We aren't staying here. We are at a farm about forty kilometers to the south." Jon thought for a moment, "There is plenty of room if you and your parents would like to come with us."

"My mom would definitely like to get out of this place." The captain clenched his jaw, "But our car is still on Interstate 70. I wouldn't want to leave it."

"The rebels responsible for firing the EMP weapon have to be found before the mechanics, here in town, can even begin to work on the cars. With the availability of parts and time to repair them, most vehicles will never be fixed," Jon declared. "You might be stranded here for quite some time."

"Can we pull their car to the farm with the pick-up?" Jacqueline asked. "Jerry and Terrance might be able to fix it."

"I think this would be a very good choice for you Irving." Jon turned his head as a gust of wind hit him square in the face. "I have met your parents, but I can't remember their names."

"Mom is Li Na and my dad's name is Shen." The captain took a moment to glance at trash swirling around the compound. "Why not, if you are sure there is room for us."

"There are already more than thirty people at the farm, and room for many more," said Jacqueline.

"You know my sister, Colonel Deb Lisco. The farm is her place."

"Of course, I do. I will pack up my parents and meet you back here in thirty minutes," he walked quickly away.

"We should use the restroom," said Linda to Jacqueline, pointing at a line of port-a-potty toilets. "You have to see just how disgusting it is. I promise, I won't complain about the conditions on the farm again."

***

The wind was blowing at a constant rate of over thirty kilometers an hour as Hank pulled the pick-up to the Huang's car on Interstate 70. Jacqueline, Jon and Irving were riding in the bed of the truck.

As soon as the truck stopped Irving jumped out and Jon handed him the chain. He quickly shimmied on his back under the car and attached one end to the chassis and the other to the tow bar on the bumper of the truck.

Linda rode with the Huangs in the towed car as Hank turned around on the wide Interstate and drove west for nearly fifteen hundred meters in the east bound lane. When they found an emergency vehicle road between the two lanes he crossed over to the west bound side of the highway. They were on a level which gave them a perfect view of the small town and the FEMA compound. Jon asked Hank to stop the vehicle. There was no traffic in either direction as Jon contemplated the panorama.

"This would be a perfect spot to do reconnaissance to see if we can locate the magicians who are firing the EMP weapons." He looked at both Jacqueline and Hank. "I wonder if Captain Huang will be willing to take a little hiatus from his retirement to help me do some more soldiering. If we can get the Interstate flowing again and free up most of the people at the compound, it would certainly help us at the farm."

"At the very least, keep the mass of people from increasing in size," stated Hank. "If the supply chain is cut off to this location, there will be a terrible humanitarian disaster."

Eastern Colorado Farm

Hank drove past the Jacoby's RV and parked near the garage. The warm wind of the day melted most of the snow, leaving shallow puddles of water throughout the hardened gravel of the farm grounds.

Bobby, Sherry, Emilee and Harold were just cleaning up around the site of the block tower, while Dave and his crew continued roofing the final half of the apartment. Jerry and Terrance stepped out of the door to the apartment, after a long day of working on the final phase of the electrical wiring for the first half of the large building. The Huang family stood outside their disabled car surprised at the amount of activity occurring on the farm.

"I'll get that," said Irving when he noticed Jon getting ready to climb under the car to release the chain.

Jon stepped back as Gina approached.

"You remember Captain Huang," Jon said to Gina before looking at the captain. "This is my wife, Gina."

"Of course," Gina acknowledged the captain as he bounced up from under the car. She had met the captain at several army functions over the years, as well as his parents on a couple of occasions. "And I remember your parents too."

Li Na and Shen were both smiling as they witnessed the flurry of activity happening at the rural location, in what they would have considered the middle of nowhere.

"If I remember right, you were a school principal," said Gina. "I can't recall your name."

"Yes, I was an elementary school principal." The small lady turned to her husband, "I'm Li Na and this is my husband Shen."

"I remember now, Shen is a cabinet maker," stated Gina.

"Yes," Li Na smiled, appreciating the tranquil nature of their welcome.

Bill, Maddy and Samantha came out of the office in the garage and approached Linda.

"It looks like you survived your ordeal," Samantha gave Linda a quick hug. "I figured you would be ok, but they sure made me mad how they took you."

"I could tell," Linda chuckled, "I think you might have given the one guard a black eye."

"He deserved it," Samantha showed her white teeth as she smiled.

"Where's Al?" Linda looked in the direction of the farmhouse. Riding with the Huangs on the trip to the farm, Linda remained unaware of the disagreement between Al and the others at the farm.

"Umm," Maddy moved next to Samantha and looked up at Linda, "Al has been hiding, because he called Samantha a bad name."

"Maddy," yelled Bill.

"What happened?" Linda raised her eyes from Maddy as she turned to Samantha. "What did he call you?"

"Al was upset with you not coming back with us." Samantha turned to the others for support. "Let's let bygones be bygones."

Linda leaned down to Maddy, "What did he call her?"

Maddy glanced up to Bill with both eyes wide open and whispered, "He called her a bongo."

Linda jerked her head to look at the others. Samantha

burst out laughing.

"A what?" Linda shrugged her shoulders and looked directly at Samantha.

Samantha closed her eyes and sniffled, "A bimbo," she breathed out hard as she said the word.

"Oh my God, what in the world was he thinking?" Linda sighed and placed a hand on Samantha's arm. "I am so sorry."

Jacqueline came over to stand next to her neighbor. "You and Al can discuss all this in private. I'm sure we can work everything out." She gave Bill a quick glance.

"There are some army vehicles coming," yelled Jason from the roof of the apartment.

Jon stepped to the side of the garage and looked down the driveway. The convoy was not visible. "How many?" he yelled to Jason.

"Six."

"Platoon size," he tuned to Nicole, "it has to be Ted."

Nicole followed Jon as he moved to the front of the crowd to watch the convoy come to a halt in front of the farmhouse. A tactical vehicle drove around and parked next to Jon. Bill, Maddy and Samantha moved closer to see if Ted would emerge.

"Grandpa," Maddy yelled as soon as Ted opened the door. "You're back."

Ted did not have a chance to get out of the seat before Maddy ran into his arms. She hugged him for several seconds.

"Let me get out so I can give Grandma a hug too." Ted held her so he could see her tiny face. "I really missed you," he said.

"I missed you too." Maddy grabbed his hands to help him out of the vehicle.

Nicole threw her arms around his neck. They embraced as Jon and Bill moved next to them. Bill was the first to notice Jessica sitting in the back of the tactical vehicle. He watched her as she opened the door on the opposite side of the crowd. There was a hush as she made her way around to stand next to Ted.

Jacqueline stared a hole through her as she stood with her mouth open in disbelief. Jessica turned her head to scan the property in search of her daughters.

"I understand there are going to be some problems here with the return of Jessica. But I want everyone to know she has been very cooperative in providing information about the rebel's movements." Ted was going to do all he could to help the young mother.

"What are your plans?" Jacqueline asked tersely, slighting Ted's remarks. "Reagan, Avery and Emilee are doing very well."

"They are my children," Jessica said much more aggressively than she would have liked.

"They are your children who you left," Jacqueline yelled with her face turning a bright red. Hank moved to his wife's side.

"I made a mistake, ok." She turned her head to the side.

"A mistake is when you spill a gallon of milk or burn some cookies." Jacqueline was breathing hard as she tried to make eye contact. "Leaving your children at such a dangerous time is not a mistake."

"I knew immediately after leaving that I was wrong." Jessica bit her upper lip as she tried to hold back the tears. She saw Emilee and Bobby walking in her direction. She took several steps, around Jacqueline, in their direction. Emilee stopped and folded her arms.

"I'm sorry," Jessica mouthed the words as she approached her daughter. "I missed you so much."

"Why, Mom?" Emilee looked at Bobby and then back at her mother. "How could you take off and leave us without saying anything?"

"Where are your sisters?" she ignored the question.

Emilee squinted her eyes as she stared at her mother. She was breathing from a barely open mouth as she folded her arms even tighter.

"They are coming now," Bobby pointed to the barn as he answered Jessica's inquiry. Avery and Reagan were walking with Breanna. "They must have finished with riding the horses."

The two girls walked to Emilee and stood next to their sister. They looked vacantly at Jessica.

"Can we find somewhere to talk?" Jessica glanced quickly over her shoulder at the group behind her.

"There's a table in the back yard," Emilee replied. She turned to Bobby. "Come with us?"

"No, you should talk alone." Bobby was surprised Emilee would ask him. She looked tired and was still dirty from working with the masonry. "I'm going to get cleaned up and we can talk at supper."

She gave him a kiss on the cheek before turning and walking in the direction of the farmhouse without saying a word to her mother. Jessica followed her three daughters.

"What about Deb?" Hank asked Ted. "We haven't heard anything from her."

"She sustained a concussion in the explosion we saw on the monitor before I left, but it is my understanding she is doing ok." Ted turned toward Irene and Ed. Ed was slumping much more than when he last saw him. "Her

Brigade is relocating to southern Utah. They might even be there already."

"Can we get her to check on the kids?" Ed asked anxiously.

"If our technicians can get communication up and running in the next hour, I'll try and contact her from here." Ted noticed Captain Huang. "My God, is that Irving Huang?" Ted walked quickly to where the Huang family were waiting patiently. "How in the world did you end up here?"

"We were stranded, and Jon helped us out." Irving shook Ted's hand. "I thought you retired."

"I did, but I believed I was needed back in the fold. But I'm not so sure about that now." Ted gritted his teeth as Jon and Hank came to his side. "Irving, it really makes me feel better that you are here at the farm."

"How long can you stay?" Jon asked Ted.

"Another two hours," Ted looked toward Nicole, and then at Bill. "I have to be back at the base this evening."

"You probably want to get caught up with Bill and Nicole," said Jon. "We can get the Huang's situated and talk with you in a bit."

Ted listened to Maddy explain all that happened since he left, while Bill, Samantha and Nicole listened and corrected her when she was blatantly wrong. It was obvious that Bill and Samantha had grown much closer over the past few days. He stared into Nicole's beautiful eyes as everyone spoke. He was about to grab her and break away when he saw Lieutenant Hanson approach.

"Colonel, the communication center is now operational."

Ted moved to the garage and waited at the office for everyone else to catch up. Irene and Ed were especially interested in seeing if he could contact Colonel Deb.

"Dad," Bill stepped in front of his father. "I forgot to tell you. We found the Browns murdered at their farm."

"When?"

"The night of the missile attacks," answered Nicole. She could see the distress in his face. "It was absolutely horrible."

The technician from his platoon who revived the system was still sitting at the desk in front of the screen. When the specialist noticed Ted approaching, he stood up and saluted. "The problem was the setting was wrong for the satellite position. Everything else is functional, it was really a very minor glitch."

"Sit back down," said Ted. "I want you to locate and connect with Colonel Deb Lisco with 4th Infantry, 2nd Brigade."

"Yes sir."

"This news about the Browns, really worries me." Ted's left eye twitched and his charmed expression faded. "We ran into a roadblock on the way here this afternoon. There were nearly forty rebels."

"There were another thirty to forty of the insurgents hiding about five hundred meters off the road in the field," said Lieutenant Hanson emphatically.

"They were well armed," Ted shook his head. "We need to have a meeting with everyone before I leave."

"Sir, I have Colonel Lisco on the radio. We won't be able to bring her up on the monitor," said the specialist as he relinquished the seat at the radio.

"Ted," Deb's voice was loud and clear. "Where are you?"

"I'm at the farm." Ted hesitated, then looked at Samantha, "Could you run and get Jon and Hank?"

"Is everything ok?" Deb asked.

"Everything is good here." Ted wanted to wait to discuss the issue of the murder of the Browns. "Where are you?"

"We are just south of Richfield, Utah on Interstate 15. Trying to get around a blown bridge. It is the second one we have had to deal with today."

"I'm glad to hear you sounding so good," said Ted, noticing Jon and Hank at his side.

"You had us worried to death," said Hank.

"Is Jon there?" Deb asked.

"I'm here."

"You need to continue to fortify the farm. This war is not going to be over for a long time." Deb's voice cracked. "This is just the beginning."

"Everything is coming along well," Hank assured her. "Did they tell you about the Browns?"

"No," Deb said softly.

"We found them murdered at their farm."

"Oh, good Lord," Deb yelled before lowering her voice. "Jon and Ted, you need to make sure to set up adequate security measures."

"Colonel, this is Ed Jacoby," Ed leaned closer to the radio. "You are close to our farm outside of Parowan. If I can have Ted send you a map with the location of our grandchildren, will you check on them for us?"

"Ed, send the map, but there is no guarantee I will have the time to find them," Deb's voice was forceful. "Most of the citizens have already departed from the towns we passed through. I'm hearing more and more rumblings that all civilians will be ordered to relocate."

"We are worried sick about them," said Irene pleadingly. "Please check on them."

"Get me the map." Clamoring filled the radio and Colonel Deb could be heard shouting to others in the distance.

"Deb," Ted yelled into the receiver, "are you there?"

"I'll get back in touch as soon as I can." The radio went silent.

It was quiet enough in the garage to hear the battery-operated clock on the wall ticking. After a few seconds of silence Hank locked eyes with Ted. "Things are about to get a lot worse, aren't they?" he asked.

Ted rubbed the grey hair at his right temple. His mind was churning as he reached around Nicole's waist and pulled her close. Most of the people important to his existence were in the cold garage, staring at him like a group of Sunday morning parishioners waiting to hear a positive message of hope and salvation. He smiled at Maddy.

"Grandpa," Maddy moved next to him, "can you stay here tonight?"

Ted reached down and picked her up in his arms. He stared at her as she leaned in and placed her forehead on his.

"We can play some games," she said.

He hankered for a moment with her head gently pressing on his. It all hit him like a ton of bricks, for the first time he realized he was better situated at the base in Fort Carson where he held the power of the United States Army at his calling. He was going to make sure his son, his wife and his brothers had a direct line to him twenty-four hours a day. The farm was going to be protected by the full force of the Army.

"I'm sorry Maddy. I have to go back to the base tonight."

Parowan, Utah

A cold November wind blew into Tommy's face as he walked nearly four hundred meters past the convoy of 1st Battalion's vehicles to where Colonel Deb was riding, with twelve soldiers, in an Oshkosh R-ATV assault vehicle. It had already been a strenuous fifteen-hour journey from Great Falls, and they were still nearly a hundred kilometers north of their destination of St. George, Utah. Deb stepped out of the vehicle onto the concrete of Interstate 15 to address the command sergeant major.

"Colonel, I just received a message from Corps that they want us to secure Interstate 15 between Cedar City and Interstate 70 for a shipment that will be passing through at approximately 2200. They want us to inspect all bridges," stated Tommy. "I already dispatched Company B forward to Cedar City and Company A about ten kilometers south of here between Parowan and Cedar City. 3rd Battalion will have to backtrack about thirty kilometers to the Interstate 70 interchange."

"Are we removing nuclear warheads?"

"That's my assumption."

"It's real nice of them to give us some warning," Deb looked at Tommy with concern. "Make sure all search and reconnaissance is conducted by platoon sized units. This is where Ted said he witnessed the landing of several odd aircraft. I have a bad feeling about this place."

"They were going to move the nukes north of Las Vegas through the countryside but changed routes at the last moment."

"Where's Lieutenant Colonel Barnet?"

"He is with Company D at Parowan."

The humming of the MQ-30T Reaper broke the silence as it flew quietly over the top of the convoy. The drumming of chopper blades became louder and louder as helicopters approached from the south. Five M200 Guardian vehicles passed swiftly by, traveling north bound in the south bound lanes, causing Deb and Tommy to reconsider standing so close to the highway. Several more assault and fighter vehicles passed by before fifteen large semi-trucks slowly threaded their way down the freeway. It took nearly thirty minutes for the entire convoy of military might to pass.

"What is going on here Tommy? Where are they moving these weapons?"

"I have no idea where they are going," Tommy wrung his hands. "They must feel they are unsafe here."

"Colonel," a specialist approached and saluted. "General Lauer wants to speak with you."

"Jesus, it's almost midnight at Fort Carson." Deb shot Tommy a look of unease, "This can't be good."

Tommy followed her into the back of the command vehicle. The full face of General Lauer was visible on the largest screen.

"Sir," Deb said as she sat down in the seat at the monitor.

"Colonel, there will be a helicopter arriving for you in St George for a departure of 0500 to deliver you back to the base here at Fort Carson."

"What is this all about General?"

"It is all I am at liberty to disclose at this time. Just be ready to leave," stated General Lauer.

Fort Carson Army Base

After arriving on base, Colonel Deb rushed to the briefing room. She was one of the last to arrive. Besides General McClinton and General Lauer all the big brass for the 4th and 99th Divisions were present, as were all the Colonels from within the Divisions. She acknowledged Colonel Tyler from Stryker as she sat down a couple of seats to the right of him. She noticed Ted walking up the incline toward her. He took the seats next to her as General McClinton began to speak at the podium.

"The reason we summoned everyone here today can be explained in one word, security." General McClinton looked over the large group of soldiers. "It is a terrible state-of-affairs that we cannot be confident in the refuge of our own communication system from the Chinese and Russian hacking technologies. What we know for certain is that we are in a fight for our lives. The enemy is vicious, they are shrewd, and they are not going to negotiate. With information we have gleaned from our operatives entrenched with the enemy forces along the Mexican border, and with prisoners we have captured on our own soil, we have been able to better understand their tactics and possibly their blueprint for defeating us. We now have a strategy with which each soldier in this room will have a specific part in implementing. General Lauer at your leisure, sir."

General McClinton stepped back from the podium, and General Lauer moved to the microphone. He turned toward a large map of the United States on a screen behind him.

"As you can see on this map there is a dark line from Corpus Christi, Texas to the Continental Divide of the Rocky Mountains, that proceeds to northern Montana. On the western portion of the map is a line from Los Angeles, California to Reno, Nevada proceeding to the Oregon and Washington state borders. It is our intention to evacuate all American citizens from this area between the Sierra Nevada's all the way to the Rocky Mountains. Civilians from Phoenix on a line north to Las Vegas and northward to Washington state will migrate to the west coast, with everyone east of this line moving east. Sixteen bridges on the Interstate system have been destroyed and many others have been compromised." General Lauer turned from the map as another map became visible. The map displayed four areas with the names of brigades of the 4th Infantry, and two areas designated for brigades of the 99th Infantry.

Deb could see an area shaded in blue designated for the 2nd Infantry Brigade, 4th Division, which included the entire state of Utah, the eastern third of Idaho, the western half of Wyoming and the eastern third of Colorado. Of the six shaded areas, hers was by far the largest.

"Aircraft will be used from the Salt Lake City and Albuquerque locations. Otherwise, evacuation will be through land transport. FEMA has halted all deliveries of food and supplies to these areas and will now assist in the transporting of civilians." General McClinton stepped next to General Lauer, indicating he wanted to address the troops.

"It must be made perfectly clear that the enemy entrenched in the cities and small towns are just that, enemies. The rebels are engrained deep within the fabric of the neighborhoods. Some will remain imbedded, and others will leave with the citizens. The process to vet them will take place after they have evacuated. By executive order just signed by President Weller, leaving the area is not a request and anyone staying behind will be considered a combatant." General Lauer took a deep breath, "We have a short time period, so, it is imperative that you do your jobs quickly and efficiently. Each of you have general orders in your secure systems. The timetable for the evacuation is three days, so get back to your soldiers and take care of business."

"Sir," Colonel Taylor of 1st Stryker Brigade yelled from the center of the auditorium.

"Yes, Colonel," General Lauer pointed at him.

"Why, sir, can you tell us why we are evacuating all these civilians?"

General Lauer glanced at Chief of Staff McClinton. General McClinton motioned to a man dressed in a suit coat to take the podium. He was the same undetectable man who warned President Weller and his Cabinet of the dangers the country faced.

"Every model we have run with us committing hundreds of thousands of soldiers to protect our soil north of the Mexico border, indicates us losing more than two hundred thousand soldiers and a million civilians. Every one of these models shows us eventually losing the war. By removing the noncombatants and using nonhuman forces we can reposition troops that the enemy supposes us to use to protect this sector."

"Sir, do your models show us winning the war if we do this?" Colonel Tyler yelled.

"Not in all scenarios." The man breathed through his nose before continuing, "But we don't lose in all circumstances."

"So, we are going to have pimple faced technicians on the east coast fighting the invading forces across an area from San Antonio to Phoenix using their computers to control weaponized robots."

"I will allow the brass to answer that question for you." The man moved away from the podium.

"Colonel," Chief of Staff McClinton stepped to the podium, "our land-based forces will be involved with all the combat we can handle as the enemy adjusts to the situation. We will leave it there."

After the generals stepped away from the platform and others began to clamor about the room, Colonel Taylor edged his way to stand in the aisle next to Ted and Deb as they remained seated. Tyler was the type of soldier who was serious as hell, who could never possibly look at something from the sunny side. Yet there was something soothing about his cocky smile that always intrigued Deb.

"Three days to move millions of people." Colonel Tyler gave an acknowledging glance to Ted as he spoke directly to Deb.

"We just traveled south on Interstate 15, and most of the citizens have already fled," Deb remained seated. There had always been an unofficial competition between the two commanders to be the most knowledgeable about any circumstance they encountered.

"Stryker is going to be to the west of your location, and it might suit us both if we coordinate missions." The colonel moved back from Deb so she could better look him in the eyes. "Have you thought about how you are going to direct your battalions to cover the area?"

Deb glanced up at him and took in a deep breath. His eyes were flat with no cheek bones visible on his round face. "I have some ideas but will hash it over with my commanders before making any solid decisions," she said.

"Keep me informed, I'm out of here in about an hour." He surveyed the room before turning and walking quickly out the door.

Deb shot Ted a smile.

"When are you scheduled to leave?" Ted asked.

"1300 mountain time. I have about thirty minutes before I should go."

"You need to be careful with the area around Cedar City. I know for a fact; insurgents are there in great force." The muscles in Ted's jaw clenched, "I'm sure you realize the danger."

"After what I witnessed in Great Falls, I will never underestimate the threat. In order to cover the entire sector, I will have to spread the troops pretty thin."

"The main threat you will face will be along the Interstate 15 corridor." Ted leaned back in his chair. "Captain Hendersen has full knowledge of the area of eastern Utah. There are a lot of stranded people in that section, but I have a feeling the locals have taken care of the resistance from the insurgents. I don't know how they expect you to move everyone in three days, not just because of the number of people, but because it will be difficult to locate them over the vast area."

"I'll do the best I can."

Ted leaned forward and removed his wallet. He pulled out a piece of paper and handed it to his sister. "Here is the map Irene made showing the location of her grandkids."

"I'll find them," Deb said firmly, using a tone he knew she used only when she meant something. "It's as good a place as any to start."

"The Jacobys will be happy to hear that."

"What about you Ted?" Deb checked her watch. "Have they told you anything about where you will be during all of this?"

"Nothing," Ted hated the feeling of uselessness. He also despised the portrayal of selfishness he was showing to Deb by complaining about his situation. Their father would not approve of moaning about oneself, especially during a time of crisis. It was against everything the Army embodied. "I'm going to suggest to General Lopez that I take over a company sized unit to work on getting rid of the insurgents along the front range."

She looked at him for a long moment with a quizzical expression on her face. He was a terrific soldier, yet his strategic and analytical talents would never be used from a desk in Fort Carson. The Department of Defense made all the decisions and most likely any of his suggestions would be taken with a grain of salt.

"I need to go," said Deb, taking a step toward the door before turning back and stating, "You are absolutely correct in wanting to take care of the problems here. Make sure to speak with the general in private. Too many ears might help him find reasons to deny the request."

***

The view from the third floor of the concrete block tower was stunning as the sun began to set over the wide-open landscape. The farm was located on top of a hill which provided a vantage to see for many kilometers in all directions. The tower provided a perfect perch for surveillance. Harold planned to set the trusses for the roof in the morning and then place the plywood sheeting later in the afternoon. He made it clear he would be doing the dangerous job by himself. Bobby, Emilee and Sherry made room for Dave and Caroline to join them in the small room at the top of the structure. No more carrying concrete blocks and buckets of mortar up the stairs.

Deep down in his soul Bobby was sad that working with the two beautiful ladies was over. Being covered in cement and so exhausted he could hardly move seemed like an odd thing to pine for, yet the hard work brought a sense of allegiance between the three of them that could never be emulated.

Sherry stared out the open-air window with the breeze blowing her blond hair onto her neck, shutting out the entire surroundings inside, as she viewed the world below. She moved closer and placed her hands on the concrete filled block that made the sill of the window and looked straight down to the ground below. A sense of vertigo caused her to lean back. It seemed much higher inside the tower than it looked from below.

Emilee locked her arms around Bobby's waist, feeling the hidden pistol holstered on his hip, as they moved next to Sherry at the edge of the window and scanned the farm. Dave and Caroline tried to acclimate being in the structure and remained back from the openings.

"I can't believe we helped build this tower. I did learn that this is a bond beam." Sherry showed her bright smile as she tapped her index finger on the block.

"The tips of my fingers are so cracked; I don't know if they will ever heal." Emilee held her hands palms up out the window in front of her.

"You'll be just fine." Bobby playfully nudged her with his elbow. He had not discussed with her about how the meeting with her mother had gone earlier. A heavy smell of dinner being cook filled his nostrils as the wind blew lightly from the southwest, he noticed his mother and father gathering with a group of people by the garage.

"There's a van coming down the driveway." Dave leaned between Bobby and Sherry and pointed in the direction of a light blue van entering the parking area in front of the farmhouse. There was a blind spot for observation from the tower directly in front of the house, so as the van moved closer, they lost sight of it. The vehicle came back into sight as it slowly moved past the house, in front of the Jacoby's RV, toward the group at the garage. Hank and Jon moved forward to receive the vehicle as it approached.

Four young men stepped out of the van, and from their actions seemed very cordial as they were greeted by Hank and Jon.

"Look over there," Emilee's voice was rushed as she held her hand out the window in the direction of the county road about three kilometers to the south. "Are those people?"

The tiny silhouettes of people were visible, spread out on a hill nearly eight hundred meters south of the gravel road. A large box truck was parked on the road in front of the threatening figures.

Caroline brushed Bobby as she stuck her head out the window. Her large almond shaped eyes squinted as she scrutinized the four strangers talking below, where Jon and Hank were now joined by Jacqueline, Nicole and Gina. She ground her teeth and raised her hand to her mouth. She lurched back from the window."

"Two of those guys are the ones who attacked me." She thought back to lying, barely conscious, in the bar ditch before she was found by the Hamiltons.

"Are you sure?" Bobby jerked his head to look at her.

"The one with the blond hair and the guy with the

gray cap." She swallowed hard and leaned her head back on the cold block wall. She never thought she would have to relive the horrible experience. "They attacked me. They are both bad, but the guy with the cap is… he's cruel."

Bobby glanced quickly at the massive assemblage of people to the south and then gazed toward the garage where Terrance and Jerry were standing next to Breanna, Irene and Ed. Samantha and Maddy lingered at the utility door to the garage.

"I'll go down and warn them. With Maddy and Samantha at the door Bill must be inside with the radio," Bobby spoke quickly, when he noticed the man in the cap glance toward the tower. Although Caroline was away from the window, he used the back of his arm to nudge her deeper into the corner, further away from the openings. "Don't let them see you."

Bobby leaped down the stairs but slowed when he exited the door of the tower. He gave a wider than usual swath as he made his way to the garage. He used his peripheral vision to keep an eye on the perpetrators as he approached Terrance and Jerry. Ed, Irene and Breanna were slowly making their way to the RV.

"Can I speak with you two inside?" Bobby asked softly, giving Terrance a serious look as he moved to the garage door and prodded Samantha and Maddy to step inside. Bill's voice could be heard in the distance from the back office. Bobby shut the door and turned to Terrance.

"We have a problem. The guys outside are not friendly." Bobby grabbed Maddy's hand and rushed to the office where Bill was talking to Scotty and Irving Huang. Bill stopped in mid-sentence as Bobby quickly moved to his side.

"Caroline just identified two of the guys outside as

her attackers," Bobby spoke rapidly.

"What guys?" Bill looked at his cousin confusedly.

"Listen," he slowed and gained his breath. "Four guys just arrived outside. Mom and Dad, along with Uncle Jon, Aunt Gina and Aunt Nicole are speaking with them right now. There are a massive group of people on the road to the south, who are obviously with them. It's a set up."

Terrance glanced at Jerry. He took a step toward the exit.

"Terrance, wait a minute," yelled Bill. "We need to make sure we are all armed before you confront them."

"Where do you keep the weapons?" Irving asked.

"They are in a safe room in the basement of the main house." Bill looked directly at Bobby, "Only seven of us have our eyes scanned for access."

"And five of them are talking to the guys outside," stated Bobby.

"And you are the remaining two." Irving brought his right hand to his chin and looked directly at Bobby.

"I take it that if Colonel Lisco stockpiled the arms, they will be military quality. How proficient are you and your friends with firing the weapons?"

"Aunt Deb's soldiers gave us a crash course. We know how to load and fire them." Bobby did not seem overly confident in the abilities of his friends with handling the guns.

"Terrance and I both have AK-47s here in the garage," stated Jerry. "There are five .50 Caliber rifles in the gun vault."

Irving shot Jerry a surprised look before asking the general question, "Do all of you know how to fire the fifty?"

"Dave, Sherry, Emilee and I all know how," said Bobby. "There are a lot of other weapons in the vault besides those."

"These are your friends who are in the tower?" Captain Huang inquired.

"Yeah."

"Besides the two AKs, what do we have for weapons here?"

"Bill and I both have pistols." Bobby hesitated for a moment, "Uncle Jon always carries his handgun."

"We both have pistols, too," stated Jerry.

"Can I use one of your weapons?"

"Of course, but what is the plan? It is going to be dark before long."

"We have to surprise them, before they do it to us." Irving looked out the window. He could see Ed, Irene and Breanna, in the distance, walking slowly toward the RV past the car, which was a good fifty meters from the garage. Everyone at the car seemed to be talking amiably. Sherry and Emilee were noticeable in the window of the block tower. "I can't tell if the strangers have any weapons on them."

"Samantha, I want you to take Maddy and Scotty to the farmhouse." Bill rose from his chair.

"Bill," Irving stepped away from the window and placed his left hand on his shoulder. "I want you to go with them."

"Irving are you sure that's what you want me to do?" he scoffed.

"As soon as we see you are safely in the house, I will go out and join the conversation at the car. I can warn Lieutenant Colonel Lisco about the danger without being detected. When you get to the house, open the gun safe and arm everyone capable of firing a weapon."

"What about us?" Jerry asked, glancing at Terrance.

"Give me thirty seconds after I engage the group, and then quickly come to my side."

"And me?" Bobby asked.

"Are any of your friends in the tower armed?"

"Sherry still has the pistol she used when she went to the Brown's farm."

"Walk back to the tower as if nothing has happened." The captain's tone was calm and confident.

"Watch to make sure none of the people on the road are advancing. As soon as you see me unholster my weapon, then, and only then do you and Sherry come to our side."

"Ok," Bobby was not about to question the captain's judgement.

"You can leave now." He looked at Bill, Samantha, Maddy and Scotty, "I won't go until I see you safely in the house."

Eastern Colorado Farm

Although the temperature was rapidly falling and the sun was beginning to set, Jon continued talking with the four strangers. They were making such a good impression, that all five of the Liscos considered asking them to stay at the farm. The two youngest strangers were leaning on the hood of their van while the other two stood in the center of the group, laughing and joking, as Irving entered the assemblage and paused at the back side of Jon.

"This is Irving Huang," Jon said, stepping to the side to allow Irving a chance to advance closer. "He was a captain in the Army, who I served with."

The men smiled and acknowledged him. The man with the cap blatantly stared at the concrete tower, although quite a distance away, Sherry and Emilee were still perched in the window. Hank, Jacqueline, Nicole and Gina were all calm and completely unsuspecting of any danger from the four intruders.

"Hello," Irving nodded, glancing at the strangers, before turning to Jon and giving him a serious look. "I was just telling Terrance a great story about the time Sergeant Spencer met the group outside the bar in Bamako."

Jon momentarily let Irving's comment pass as general conversation before suddenly taking in a deep breath. His heart flipped in his chest as he twisted his neck in the direction of the retired captain, hard enough for it to pop. Nearly ten years earlier, a good friend of theirs, Sergeant Spencer, was murdered by acquaintances he thought were friendly, in a trap set by a group in Mali.

"Are you telling me these guys remind you of the ones in Bamako?"

Irving clapped Jon on his muscular shoulder and said, "It's about to happen here."

Jon slid in front of Gina, reached to his back and flipped the latch to his holster. Irving drew his pistol out and leveled it in the direction of the two men leaning on the hood of the car. Hank jerked back as his brother moved in front of him and aimed his weapon at the two closest perpetrators. Terrance and Jerry rushed past Gina, Jacqueline and Nicole with their AKs at the ready. Bobby and Sherry were running across the gravel driveway, with Caroline right behind them.

"What is going on?" Jacqueline yelled, shuffling her feet as she moved back quick enough to bump into Nicole.

"Place your hands straight up," ordered Irving. "Now."

All four men remained frozen in place with their arms slightly raised. Bill hurried from the house carrying a M16 A2 battle rifle with Breanna and Aaron Jacoby joining him as he passed their RV.

"Why are you doing this?" asked the blond man, holding his muscular arms barely over his head.

"Uncle Jon, there is a large group assembled at our driveway on the dirt road south of here," Bobby yelled.

"Ok," Jon swallowed hard. "Let's sort this all out."

"We are just trying to find a place to stay." The guy with the cap had a long, skinny nose and an oblong face. He put his hands out in a questioning manner and raised his upper lip. "You seem like nice people."

"Like everyone else, we have been having a hard time over the past few weeks," said the man with blond hair. His head was on a swivel as he checked out the growing crowd of people. He gasped when he noticed Caroline step next to Jon.

"Do you remember me? My name is Caroline Sanchez." Her dark eyes raged, and her high cheek bones quivered as she untucked her blouse and pulled it up high enough to show half her bra. Both sides of her ribcage were dark black and blue, and there was a small cut under her left breast. She turned so they could see the large welts on her back. "I am still having a hard time breathing after you beat and raped me."

"It wasn't us," the man with the cap lowered his eyes.

"It was you. I remember every little detail about you. You are an animal." Her nostrils flared as she stared at him. "There were four of you, but you were the most vicious."

"They will pay for this." Jon put his left hand on Caroline's shoulder and patted her gently. He licked his lips as he remembered her lying in the ditch, like garbage discarded to the side of the road. The more he thought about it, the more furious he became. "All right, all four of you face down. Put your noses in the gravel."

The four men slowly fell to their knees and folded over onto their stomachs. Hank reached down to the man with blond hair and removed a pistol from the back of his pants. He lifted the shirt of the man with the cap and removed his concealed firearm. Neither of the two younger men were armed.

"Check their pant legs," said Jon.

Both armed men had ankle holsters. Hank removed their weapons.

Caroline leaped at the man with the cap and kicked, she aimed for his head but missed and booted him on his right shoulder. The man swiped at her foot with his right hand. Jon smacked him hard on the side of his ear with the butt of his Beretta.

"Jon," Hank moved between his brother and the perpetrator on the ground, just as Jon was about to kick him. "Let the sheriff handle this."

Jon backed away to stand next to Gina, trying to catch his breath. "I can't stand bullies who use their strength to abuse people." He smacked his lips and shook his head. "I never could stand them."

"What about the people on the road?" asked Bobby.

"Who are they?" Hank realized he was standing less than a meter away from the men, so he took a large step in the direction of Terrance. He continued to look down at them. "Are they a threat to us?"

"You are going to find out how big of a threat they are to you." The man with the blond hair raised his chin off the cold ground and smirked.

"Can I take a look inside the gun safe?" Irving took the man's warning seriously. "I'd feel a hell of a lot better with a M16 in my hand right now."

"I'll show you," Bobby was shoulder to shoulder with Sherry with his pistol directed at the men on the ground. He holstered his weapon and looked to the tower where Emilee and Dave were watching from the window. Irving followed as he headed to the farmhouse.

"Where are we going to put these guys?" Jacqueline asked.

Jon moved to the two younger men who were not privy to Caroline's attack. He nudged the young man closest to him with the side of his foot. "Stand up," he ordered.

He pushed himself from the ground. Terrance and Jerry continued to aim their weapons. Bill held his rifle pointed down away from the intruders. Jon holstered his pistol and motioned for Sherry to do the same. He turned to the frightened young man.

"How do you know these men?" Jon was calm, while breathing through his nose as he moved directly in front of the frightened man and looked him directly in the eyes. He looked to be about sixteen years old.

"My brother, father and I came across them the day before yesterday." He lowered his eyes to the other boy still prone on the ground at his feet. "We left the city on Thursday with the idea of walking to Kansas City."

"Who are the people on the road?" Jon asked.

"Mostly friends of theirs."

"Are these men the leaders of the group?" Jon glanced toward the man in the cap.

"Ummm, I don't think so."

"Do they have weapons."

"A lot of them do."

"What's your name?"

"Tyrone."

"Can I trust you, Tyrone?" Jon put his chin straight out in front of the young man. "Don't tell me I can, if I can't."

Irving and Bobby returned to the group, both carrying heavy rifles. Bobby took a double take at the boy on the ground as he moved next to his dad.

"You can," he stated barely loud enough to hear. He pointed to Bobby and spoke louder, "Von played football against you this fall."

"Von is your brother?" Jon prodded the boy on the ground with the toe of his shoe. "You can get up."

"I thought I recognized you. You were a linebacker for Arvada." Bobby watched the young man pull himself from the ground, then turned to Hank. "Remember him Dad? He's the guy who intercepted me in the endzone during the last game of the regular season."

"I remember," Hank looked at Jon. "I think we can trust these kids."

"I want you two to take a message from us to the people at the road. Tell them that this farm is a place they should leave alone. We are very capable of protecting ourselves and we want them at least ten kilometers away from this area." Jon took in a deep breath. "We want them gone immediately. If they stay, we will consider it an act of hostility."

"Are they coming with us?" Tyrone looked toward the two on the ground.

"They are going to stay here. They will have to answer to the sheriff in Limon for attacking Caroline." Jon glanced at Caroline. He opened the front door of the van. "You can go now."

"I'll have Dave take some plywood and board up a horse stall to hold these guys." Hank stepped next to Jacqueline. "It looks like it will be a long night."

Hank, Bill, Terrance and Jerry marched the two attackers to the barn. The van drove down the driveway and disappeared into the darkness. Caroline made eye contact with Sherry before staring at the backside of her attackers. Her chest heaved as she remembered the monstrous things the men did to her.

PART TWO

Jacoby Ranch

The area was much more rugged than Colonel Deb anticipated as she stood outside her Humvee parked on the side of the county road, nearly five kilometers from the Jacoby ranch in central Utah. A steady wind of thirty kilometers an hour blew from the north as she inspected the overwhelming vastness of the desolate area.

Captain Hendersen with F Company spent most of the morning executing the tedious task of directing the troops to check for civilians occupying farmhouses. Drones sped up the process but many of the inhabitants refused to leave and hid out until the armed forces passed by their homes. FEMA vehicles transported the few civilians willing to leave to a staging area at the I-70 and I-15 junction near Beaver, Utah. Larger modes of transportation were ready to convey the citizens eastward across the Rockies and beyond.

Deb scrutinized the handwritten map Ted gave her for the location of the Jacoby's farm before opening the door of the Humvee and placing it on the seat to keep it from blowing away. After examining the diagram, she stepped into the middle of the road and looked to the east, attempting to locate a red barn. It was not in sight.

Lt. Col. Woodworth was planning to take G Company and H Company to Parowan to vacate the tiny municipality of any remaining civilians and dispatch all the residual subversives. Having lingered behind to finish cleaning up the attack at the warehouse in Great Falls, the convoy of the 2nd Battalion traveled south on Interstate 15, past the little town less than twelve hours prior without encountering any sign of the enemy. Colonel Deb made the decision to bring Josh to the Southern Utah location and send Lt. Col Barnet north. She felt more comfortable around Josh, so, it was a personal decision with little strategic value.

"Colonel," Captain Hendersen joined her at the side of the Humvee. Dirt was blowing across the road. "We located the farm with the red barn. First squad with 2d platoon are on the outskirts of the location."

"Is there anyone on the premises."

"It is occupied."

"Have 2nd platoon wait to engage with the occupants until we arrive." Deb hesitated for a moment before asking, "Is the rest of the Company close?"

"All but 3d platoon." Captain Hendersen always portrayed a sense of being under control. "They are about twenty kilometers to the north."

"Dispatch them to our location." During the past two days the small city of St. George was overtaken by United States Military Forces, as was most of Cedar City. Ted warned her that enemy soldiers were in the area before he fled with the Jacobys. So, they had to be somewhere. The whole damn ordeal felt like a large sudoku puzzle, where, finding one aspect of the dilemma would lead to the next step in solving the problem.

Deb's Humvee was at the back of the convoy as they drove down the long driveway to the ranch where they parked behind the tactical vehicles in front of the farmhouse. The Jacoby ranch was immaculate. From the white fence around the front yard to the perfectly laid stone sidewalk going in a straight line to the porch in front of the farmhouse.

A dark-haired man, holding a cup of coffee, watched from the porch while soldiers flooded the farm grounds. He was soon joined by a small lady who walked down the sidewalk to the gate. Sergeant Collins of 2d Platoon was the first to approach her with his entire platoon spread out across the fence line.

Colonel Deb observed the encounter from the front seat of her Humvee, nearly fifty meters away. The small lady turned toward the man on the porch and yelled indiscernibly. He opened the screen door and spoke to others inside. Soon several men and women were standing on the porch. Deb exited and made her way toward the sergeant at the gate.

"Ma'am," said Sergeant Collins, "she says they are friends of the rancher." The sergeant nodded toward the small lady. There were four men and three women on the porch.

"Where are the Jacobys now?" Deb kept her eyes on the group at the entryway as she spoke.

"They left a couple of weeks ago. We came by to check on them and decided to watch over their home until they return."

"Are any of their kids or grandchildren here?"

"No, we haven't seen any of them."

Had Deb not known better, the woman aired a confidence and calmness in her mannerisms that radiated a sense of honesty. That all passed in an instant when Deb noticed she was wearing Giveh shoes, footwear common in rural and mountainous parts of Iran. Besides being durable, the shoes were soft and comfortable, perfect for the Utah terrain. Deb brought her eyes back up to gaze into the woman's emerald-green eyes. A corporal from the communication vehicle approached.

"Ma'am, Command Sergeant Major Talfoya wants to speak with you." The corporal seemed confused about his task. "He wants you to come to communication but not to speak or appear on screen."

"I'm not following you here." Deb abruptly turned from the woman and began walking in the direction of the communication vehicle.

"Captain Hendersen will explain, ma'am," the corporal hurried to walk by her side.

Captain Hendersen stopped them at the door to the large communication truck. Standing next to him, speaking into her Pulsnet wrist radio, was Specialist Sophia Grant.

"Colonel, this may seem out of the ordinary, but we have a specialist who is communicating for Command Sergeant Major Talfoya. They are requesting that you personally cease all forms of exchange transmitted by way of our communication system." Captain Hendersen looked directly at the colonel before turning to Specialist Grant. "Tell Command Sergeant Major Talfoya that Colonel Lisco is here."

"Ma'am, the Command Sergeant Major, via the specialist, wants me to repeat verbatim his words to you." Specialist Grant's voice was clear and steady as she repeated the message. "Colonel, cyber security has sent a warning that the enemy has figured a way to intercept and encrypt data, using voice and visual acknowledgement of all commanding officers, colonel and higher. They are homing in on radio-frequency emissions to track targets. The identifying information is being used to locate and eliminate our upper command, whether they are moving or not."

Deb listened with her heart rate increasing, letting the information soak in. "Ask if the enemy has been successful."

Specialist Grant grimaced as she replied, "They have been very successful."

"Let him know I understand and will reveal further directives as our situation mandates."

"Yes ma'am." The specialist relayed the message and turned toward Captain Hendersen. "Is that all, sir?"

"That's all." The captain turned to Colonel Deb, "Ma'am, something doesn't feel right about this place."

Deb breathed through her nose as she stared at the white sideburns poking out from beneath the captain's cap. His once salt and pepper hair was now almost all white. She concurred with his observation and was about to acknowledge her agreement when Sergeant Chamberland 2d Platoon approached from the north.

"Captain," the sergeant was out of breath. "We came across two civilians about three klicks north of here who say they are members of the family from this ranch. They claim the people in the farmhouse are not who they claim to be."

"Where are they now?" Captain Hendersen asked.

"On the other side of the barn. I didn't want to bring them into this setting."

"Sergeant, load the two civilians into your Humvee and follow us out of here." Captain Hendersen turned to Deb. "I'm going to pull everyone back and re-evaluate this location."

"Let's go," the captain stepped in front of her. "Ma'am. Command advised that you transport in the

Cougar XR MRAP. It's best you travel with 1st Platoon."

Master Sergeant Herrera was waiting at the side of the combat vehicle. It was the first time she came face to face with him since the incident at her farm in Colorado where she asked the Master Sergeant to beat the living hell out of a squatter. There was no soldier she would rather have by her side. She took a couple steps in the direction of the combat vehicle before turning to look back at the Jacoby's home. The woman was still at the fence calmly watching.

Eastern Colorado Farm

Bill felt more invigorated than he would have imagined after catching only two hours of sleep for the entire night. The kitchen table was already surrounded by people having coffee. He pulled out a chair for Samantha and retrieved one from the living room for himself. They spent the night, along with Bobby, Emilee, Terrance and Jerry, watching over the two attackers being held in the horse stall at the barn. Nicole poured two cups of coffee and placed them in front her son and Samantha.

"Is Maddy still asleep?" Bill asked his mother.

"She was just getting around a few minutes ago." Nicole took a seat at the table. "She's in the basement playing with Avery and Reagan. I told her to come up for breakfast."

"I'll go down and check on her." Bill placed his left hand on Samantha's right shoulder as he stood up. She patted his hand and smiled.

He could hear the girls talking as he walked past the first bedroom toward the room the girls used as a play area at the far back of the large basement. It was dark and the musky smell of steam from a shower filled his nostrils. He could feel the moisture as he came closer to the second bedroom where Avery, Reagan, Emilee and now Jessica slept. When he reached the open door to the bedroom, he hesitated and looked through the mist. Standing at the edge of the bed was Jessica wrapped in a large white towel, wringing her wet hair to the side of her head with both hands. Dark circles were apparent under her eyes as she straightened her head and gazed in his direction.

"I'm sorry," Bill turned quickly and began to walk away.

"Wait," she yelled loudly, then lowered her voice, "please, can we talk."

Bill grimaced before taking a full step inside the room. Blood rushed to his head as he remembered the intimacy, he and the beautiful mother experienced only a short time ago.

The previous night had been spent cuddling and holding Samantha, who he now had a promising connection, which he hoped would lead to a meaningful relationship. If being honest with himself, he had the same feelings for Jessica only days earlier.

"I'm not sure we have anything to talk about," he sighed.

"I know I screwed up," she spoke softly. "I made a split-second decision to leave with Christian that I wish I could take back. I truly regret losing what we had together."

He took in a sharp breath when he smelled the mixture of shampoo and lotion as she moved around the bed to stand in front of him. The top half of her breasts were exposed.

"But I'm sure I can make it up to you," she said with an exaggerated accent.

He gasped when she dropped the towel and reached over with her right hand and placed it on his elbow. She held her head steady and stared into his eyes with her lower lip pushing out as if she were pouting.

"It's not going to be that easy Jessica. I have to get Maddy and get her some breakfast." Bill felt a sense of redemption as he turned and walked out the bedroom.

"Here comes Maddy," said Irene when she saw Bill and Maddy coming up the stairs. She hurried to the kitchen counter and filled a small bowl half full of oatmeal.

Maddy went to her side and placed an open hand to her mouth and whispered," do we have our secret ingredient?"

"Shhh…" Irene placed a finger to her mouth and reached into the cabinet and pulled out a plastic bag from behind the boxes. She scooped a tablespoon full of brown sugar and put it on top of the oatmeal, before pouring in the hot water. "Our secret."

Samantha was cradling her cup of coffee as Bill sat back down. He blatantly stared at her sun beaten face and frazzled hair. He had held her close only hours earlier while she told him how worried she was for the safety of her parents. With wetness filling her eyes, she reiterated how worried they must feel not knowing of her wellbeing.

"Do I have something on my face?" Samantha placed a hand to the side of her face as she stared at Bill.

"No, no, just like looking at you," he said before turning toward Maddy. "Do you want to sit here with us?"

"I'll sit with Grandma," Nicole moved to the edge of her seat as Maddy sat on a corner of her chair.

Nicole looked directly across the table to where Shen and Li Na were sitting between Gina and Jacqueline and asked, "Is Irving your only child?"

"Yes," said Li Na, "we had him a little later in life."

"Jon and Irving have known each other for over twenty years." Gina looked sideways at Shen. "I met you two a couple nights before they were deployed to Africa."

"Yes, in Texas," said Li Na. "That was a scary time. Having loved one's in the military teaches us priorities in worrying."

"It certainly does," stated Gina, noticing Bobby and Emilee entering the kitchen.

"There has been a lot of chatter taking place on the radio about activity on the southern border," Bobby said, looking directly at Bill. "We lost the signal and wonder if you might see if you can help."

"Where's your dad and Uncle Jon?" Bill rose from his chair.

"They took off with Irving in the car about thirty minutes ago to check and see where the group of people from last night went." Bobby took in a deep breath. "I think they want to try and take the two guys who attacked Caroline into Limon this afternoon."

"Why didn't they use the drone to follow the group?"

"They sent it in a three-kilometer radius but didn't see anything. They were worried about it getting shot out of the air."

"What are you hearing on the radio?" Nicole asked.

"It sounds like there is a lot of fighting taking place at the border," Bobby hesitated. "Al and Linda are there with Kori trying to get the radio back to working."

"Have you tried to contact Ted?" Nicole moved off her chair to give Maddy the full seat.

"Not this morning."

Nicole took in a heavy breath and looked at Bill. She never mentioned how hard Ted tried to get her to go back with him to stay on the base at Fort Carson before he left. When she told him that she would rather stay at the farm with her son and granddaughter he never tried to pressure her to change her mind. "Let's go and see if we can get in touch with him."

"Are you finished?" Bill asked Maddy.

"Yes," Maddy walked to the sink and washed her

bowl and placed it in the drainer. She walked to Samantha and took her hand as they all walked out the door.

Although it was still cold outside, activity throughout the farm was bustling. Harold and Jason were high on top of the tower, precariously building the hip roof. Dave and Sherry were visible at the second-floor window with the .50 Caliber rifle perched on the ledge pointed to the bright blue sky, safe from any falling debris by the floor of the third tier of the structure above them. The Jacobys were busy at the barn and corrals taking care of the cattle.

Linda and Kori were seated at Ted's desk in the garage fidgeting with the instruments of the radio, as Al watched, standing slightly to the side of his wife. Al had avoided Bill and Samantha since the incident where Samantha was called a bimbo. Bill tried to make eye contact with the dentist but was unsuccessful as Al continued to ogle the radio.

"We lost the connection," said Linda, twisting her head to look at both Bill and Nicole. "There was a major push north across the Mexican border by the enemy early this morning."

"We've been following it since about five, but now we can't get access or a signal," stated Kori.

"Can I try and see if I can contact Ted?" Nicole leaned against the back of Linda's chair. Kori pushed back and stepped out to let Nicole slide into the seat.

Nicole typed in the entrance information given to her by the communication specialist and waited to be connected. In small red letters at the bottom of the screen appeared the words "access denied". She tried again with the same results, this time with a small FBI icon visible at the lower righthand corner of the screen.

"Something major has happened," said Nicole. "If

they are stopping all communication, then there must be a reason."

"Let's keep trying," replied Bill, noticing Al finally making eye contact with him. "Maybe it is only a temporary glitch."

"Bill and Samantha," Al moved next to them with Linda watching closely, "can I have a word with you two?" He took a couple steps back.

Bill stared at Al for a moment before looking at Samantha, who was standing with both hands on Maddy's shoulders. Samantha removed her hands and shifted toward Bill. They followed Al out the side door of the office to the west side of the garage. The wind was blowing from the northwest, directly through the corrals, bringing about a pungent smell of manure.

"I've been meaning to speak with you." Al shuffled his feet as he resisted looking either of them in the eyes. "I've lost a lot of sleep over my behavior."

Neither Bill nor Samantha replied.

"I'm sorry Samantha. Sometimes I speak before I think. I'm one of those guys who thinks out loud," Bill looked her directly in the eye. "I am such an idiot. I hope you will accept my apology."

"Of course, I will," Samantha laughed softly. "I was hoping we could talk. It would have been really uncomfortable having to come to you if I would have had a toothache."

"Believe me I would take good care of you," Al stated. He reached his hand out in the direction of Bill. "Are we good?"

"We are good Al," Bill took the smaller hand in his large hand and firmly shook. He knew Al was sincere in the apology and now they could move beyond the entire incident.

"Here comes Hank," said Al, pointing in the direction of the driveway.

The three of them moved to the front of the garage as the car sped down the driveway. Bobby, Emilee, Sherry and Caroline joined them just as the vehicle came to a stop. Jon, Hank and Irving quickly hopped out.

"Did you find the people?" Bobby asked.

"Yep," Jon nodded his head. "They are about forty-five kilometers south of here."

"We believe they took our threat seriously," said Hank.

"Can we take the guys to the sheriff now?" Caroline came to stand close enough to Jon that she brushed his shoulder.

"Yes," he never faltered in his answer. "If you and Sherry want to go with me, we can take them there as soon as I get back from taking a break.

Bobby was caught completely by surprise that his Uncle Jon requested the two women to assist him in transporting the dangerous men to Limon. He knew Jon respected Sherry's ability to come through in a hostile situation, but still, there was a chance that the two men might overpower them.

"Do you want me to come with you?" Bobby asked.

"No," Jon answered emphatically. "Caroline can drive, and Sherry and I will watch them."

"We need to make sure they are restrained tight enough that they can't get loose," said Hank, looking with concern at his brother.

"Take care of it. We'll leave in fifteen minutes."

Limon, Colorado

The concrete blockade on the road to the FEMA camp was nearly two kilometers further west than it was when Jon was there only a few days before. It was his understanding, at that time, the camp was expected to have fewer inhabitants, not expand in such a drastic manner.

Jon decided to have Caroline take the entrance ramp to Interstate 70 and drive eastward toward the town. It would be difficult to walk through the camp dragging the criminals. The hands of both men were bound tightly behind their backs, and neither caused any problems during the ride from the farm. Having Caroline drive was a thoughtful strategy in that she didn't have an opportunity to shoot the men. Sherry kept a keen eye to the back seat and retained her pistol at the ready, but at no time pointed it directly at the prisoners as she rode in the front seat between Caroline and Jon.

The hotel which housed the FEMA director was visible from the highway but at the bottom of the exit ramp was a roadblock with several guards visible. They parked on the Interstate nearly a kilometer from the blockade.

"Wait here, I'll see if one of these guards will find the sheriff for us," Jon spoke through the door before closing it. He walked down the exit ramp to the sentries, who seemed indifferent to his arrival.

"Can we help you?" asked a muscular man.

"Yes sir, I believe you can. I'm Lieutenant Colonel Jon

Lisco." Jon stood as straight as his arthritic back would allow him. "I was wondering if one of you could retrieve the sheriff for me. I have two men who attacked a young lady that I would like for him to take into custody."

"Are you serious?" the man looked at him with his forehead crinkled. "We've had, like eight murders in the area over the past week."

"Bob is still sitting in his cruiser by the Holiday Inn." An older lady joined the conversation as she moved next to the muscular man. "I can run over and see if he will talk to this gentleman."

"I would appreciate that," said Jon. As the lady scurried off, he noticed a massive amount of people in the FEMA camp. "Why are there so many people in the camp?"

"There are going to be a hell of a lot more real soon," said a young kid who looked to be about sixteen years old. "They are going to bring a whole lot of people from the west side of the mountains now that the Russians and Chinese have attacked from Mexico."

"When did all this happen?" Jon looked away from the kid toward the muscular man.

"They started evacuating a couple of days ago. They attacked across the border last night."

Jon swallowed hard. He could see the sheriff pulling up to the backside of the roadblock. He looked like a character out of the old west as he exited his cruiser. The old lawman rubbed his right knee as he struggled to walk to the concrete barricade.

"What can I help you with?" his cowboy hat was tipped as he spoke slowly.

"I have two men who attacked a young lady that I would like to place in your custody." Jon noticed the sheriff's worn blue jeans and cowboy boots as he stood bow-legged in front of him.

"I told him about all the murders we've had," stated the muscular man.

"Honestly, what do you want me to do with these guys?" the sheriff scoffed. He rubbed the white stubble on his chin. "There is no place to put them. We expect another twenty thousand people to arrive here over the next week. The whole damn town is overwhelmed. I would have to set them free the second you left."

"We are just trying to do the right thing here," said Jon.

"Listen, if you haven't noticed, it's the wild west out there. If you don't believe me, take a look at the bullet holes in my cruiser over there." He pointed at the police vehicle.

"We know times are dangerous. Our neighbor Clint Brown was murdered a few days ago." Jon looked at the ground and shook his head.

"Oh, good Lord," the sheriff sighed. "I know the Browns. What about Peg?"

"Her too, and the hired hand."

"God have mercy on all of us. We are doing all we can, but things are going to get worse." His eyes were puffy as he shook his head. "Are you one of the Liscos?"

"Lieutenant Colonel Jon Lisco, retired."

"I've met your sister," the sheriff grimaced. "She is one of the few people I would never cross."

"We are all staying at her farm." Jon glanced up the hill. Caroline was staring out the open window of the car. "Now, I have to figure out what to do with these two men."

"You look like a moral man. Do whatever you think is just and right." He removed his hat, swallowed hard, then turned around and limped back to his cruiser.

Jon thought for a moment as he watched the sheriff leave. He planned to speak to him about helping find the infiltrators in the little town who fired the EMP weapon. But now with all the chaos and the massive invasion of people to the location, it really didn't matter. Both men had more pressing issues to deal with.

Southern Utah

Sergeant Chamberland was standing outside a Humvee with his back to the howling wind. Next to him were Adam and Megan Jacoby's sons, Seth and Arthur. Colonel Deb stepped down from the Cougar into the menacing wind.

"Are you Irene Jacoby's grandsons?" she spoke loudly as she moved right in front of the disheveled boys.

"Yes ma'am. I'm Seth and this is my brother Arthur." Seth noticed the name tag on Deb's uniform. "Are you Ted's sister."

"Yes, he gave me the map to find your grandma's house." Deb held her hand to the side of her face to block some of the wind. "Where is the rest of your family?"

"They are outside a mountain resort about thirty kilometers from here."

"I'm going to send a squad with you to locate them and we will get you transportation east to Colorado." Deb looked at the tattoos and ring in Arthur's nose. He was completely different from his clean-cut brother. "I'll give you a map to find my farm on the plains. It's where your family is now."

"They made it to Colorado without any problems?" Seth asked.

"They had a few problems." Deb did not want to get into the details about his Aunt Ashley's head injury. "But they are all safe at the farm now."

"Colonel, this place is full of enemy troops." Seth looked at the convoy that made up most of F Company, strung out along the dirt road. "They are hidden in the hills and farms all across this area."

"Do you have any idea how many there are?"

"Thousands," stated Seth. "it seems like they are everywhere."

"How have you been able to keep from being detected? Were you in the military?"

"Marines," Seth adjusted his rifle at his shoulder. "I know every valley and canyon in this area."

"So, you can help the squad we send with you to find your family?"

"The enemy are located almost entirely along the ridge lines. There are several routes we can use to get back."

"Are there still civilians in the farms around this area?" Captain Hendersen asked.

"There are some, but you will never convince them to leave. The one's willing to leave already took off around the same time our parents left."

"We don't have time to search for those unwilling to leave," stated Deb.

"Let's get going," said Captain Hendersen.

Deb clutched tightly to the piece of paper with the map to the farm to keep the whistling wind from blowing it away. She handed it to Seth. Captain Hendersen was briefing the squad from 2d Platoon on the mission of having the Jacoby brothers help with identifying locals in the area as they escorted them to their hidden family, when Corporal Dobbs rushed between the captain and the colonel.

"Colonel Lisco, Corp is sending a helicopter to extradite you from this location." Corporal Dobbs hesitated in front of Deb and then turned to Captain

Hendersen. “The transport is twenty mikes out.”

“Did they say what location I will be transported too?”

“No, ma’am.”

Deb watched as Seth and Arthur entered the Humvee and the platoon drove north on the county road.

Eastern plains of Colorado

Caroline and Sherry were as baffled as Jon was by the dilemma of deciding what to do with the two men, created when the sheriff refused to take them into custody. They drove west bound in the east bound lanes of Interstate 70, then back down the entrance ramp to the county road. Both women were surprised when Jon told Caroline to turn north, rather than south at the junction under the overpass of the highway.

"What are you planning?" Sherry focused her eyes on the back seat where the two prisoners were both slumped, one to the right door and the other to the left.

"We can't take them back to the farm," Jon spoke forcefully with an ominous tone.

They quietly drove for more than twenty minutes down a desolate dirt road, when Jon pointed at a tree on the left side of the road. "Turn around and pull over next to that cottonwood."

Caroline slowed the car and made a U-turn and parked on the side of the road. Jon exited and opened the door to the back seat. He grabbed the man still wearing the cap and yanked him out onto the ground. His hands remained bound as he rolled a couple meters into the ditch. He pulled the blond man out from the opposite side, dragged him on his butt behind the car and pushed him into the bar ditch, next to his friend.

Sherry stood about ten meters behind the car with her pistol directed at the men. Caroline slowly walked around to the back edge of the vehicle and leaned on the trunk.

"Caroline," Jon aimed his revolver at the two men. "This is going to be your call."

Both men were laying in a fetal position in the moist dirt and weeds, gritting their teeth so hard that the muscles of their jaws were protruding out. They looked down and away so as not to make eye contact with their once victim.

"What are you saying?" Caroline asked.

"We have two options. We let them go." Jon smacked his lips and looked into her dark eyes. "Or we don't."

The vivid memory of the brutality of the attack pounded in Caroline's head as she took a step into the ditch with her shoe sinking about two centimeters into the semi-frozen dirt. Jon followed behind her. She held out her hand. He gave her the pistol.

"Why did you hit me so many times? All I wanted was a ride to see my family." She knelt over the man wearing the cap, remembering the pain of her ribs cracking as he continued to pound her with his fists. "Tell me why."

"I'm sorry," he murmured, closing his eyes. A smell of wet dirt rose into his nose as he breathed into the ground.

"Why?" She pointed the pistol only a centimeter from his head. Her hand was shaking.

"I don't know."

"Open your eyes."

He opened his eyes and looked at her twisted face. The cheeks on his oblong face were white and drooping as if they were melting off the bone. Dirt surrounded his nostrils.

"What you did to me wasn't human. You are an evil, evil person." The gun continued to quiver in her hand.

"You are lucky that I am not. God will take care of you."

She handed the firearm back to Jon and stepped out of the ditch, back onto the gravel road. Sherry came to Jon's side.

"We can't let them go," Sherry yelled. "We will be watching over our shoulders from now on. They are going to come back in the dead of night and kill us."

"Do you want to be the one to finish them?" Jon asked. He was sure she would back away.

"Hell, yes I will." She moved over the top of the man wearing the cap and pointed the pistol. He rolled onto his back. His eyes were the size of saucers as he leaned back into the dirt.

"Hold it. Hold it." Jon stepped between the man and Sherry. He placed his hand on her muscular shoulder. "I think they know not to come anywhere near the farm again."

Sherry lowered the handgun and backed away. Jon breathed through his open mouth as he watched her stride up the embankment. In all his years as a soldier he never met a person as perplexing as the innocent looking young lady. He rotated to the men.

"You know we will fire first and ask questions later if you come near our home again? You need to point your asses that way." He kicked the man wearing the cap with the point of his shoe, then pointed northwest. "Right."

"We won't be back," the blond man said loudly, spinning his head to look at Jon.

Sherry moved next to Caroline by the car.

"Lean forward," Jon looked up to Sherry as the men slumped forward. "Keep your pistol on them."

Sherry stood with both hands on the weapon as he proceeded to unwind the tie wire from around each of their wrists. He purposefully showed his back to the men as he scrambled out of the ditch, onto the road. He had complete confidence Sherry would not hesitate to fire on the men should they try to overtake him. His trust was something he as a military man gave to very few people.

"Get in ladies." Jon walked to the driver's side and entered the car. Caroline never looked at the men as she climbed into the back seat. Sherry on the other hand stared at them as she backed to the car door. They understood, she wanted them to give her a chance to finish the situation.

Jon could see the men clambering out of the ditch in the rearview mirror as they sped away.

South central Utah

The clapping blades of the helicopter could be heard coming in from the east as the sun rapidly set, bringing about a stinging chill to the diminishing wind. Captain Hendersen waited next to Deb as her ride came closer. Out of the corner of her eye she saw a flash race across the sky. A rocket hit the tail rotor of the low flying aircraft, causing it to flail about in the sky and finally hit hard into a field about five hundred meters north of their location.

Before anyone from F Company could react to the downing of the helicopter, rockets began to strike all around them, destroying several vehicles. Chaos ensued as small arms fire swept the area. Master Sergeant Herrera rushed to Colonel Debs side and returned fire at the clearly identifiable enemy on the eastern edge of the convoy. He shielded the colonel as they backed out of the opening between trucks to cover next to the Cougar. The clanging of shells hitting the metal of the combat vehicles and the sound of the weapons being fired in response to the attack was almost deafening. The attack lasted only a couple minutes.

"Are you ok, ma'am?" Sergeant Herrera asked.

"Yes," Deb looked at smoke rising from many vehicles along the skirmish line. She moved out from the side of the Cougar. "I need to procure a rifle."

"Yes ma'am," he moved quickly as Captain Hendersen came to the colonel's side in a crouched position.

"Colonel, you need to stay as concealed as possible."

The captain remained slumped over. “We have to move from this location.

“Are you able to assist the crew in the helicopter?” With darkness setting in, she could see dust rising from the area of the helicopter crash.

“3rd Squad is at the scene.”

Before Deb could reply, an explosion from a rocket shook the ground. Sergeant Herrera with a large ammunition bag on his shoulder ran to her side carrying a M-16 and a Barrett M210 50 Caliber rifle, another rocket hit the Cougar behind them. Several small splinters from the shell hit Deb squarely on the right calf of her leg. She grimaced as she accepted the M-16 from the sergeant.

“Are you ok Colonel?” Sergeant Herrera asked.

“I’ll live,” she answered just as she saw a soldier in front of her hit by a bullet directly in the chest. She saw the form of the enemy who claimed the lieutenant’s life retreating from the eastern edge of the convoy. She leveled the M-16 and fired.

“We have to move off the road,” yelled Captain Hendersen, turning to Specialist Grant. “Redirect everyone to the ravine.” He pointed to the south.

“Sir, they jammed communication,” yelled the specialist frantically. “Everything is dead.”

Captain Hendersen did a double take at the soldier before yelling, “Let’s move out.”

Deb limped noticeably as she followed closely behind the captain. Sergeant Herrera, carrying the heavy rifle and ammunition bag, grabbed her under the right arm and all but carried her away from the dirt road. Soldiers abandoned their vehicles and jumped into the deep ravine.

Captain Hendersen noticed the blood soaking the back of her pant leg while they leaned into the red clay on the side of the gully. Soldiers all along the line popped out and set their weapons, checking for the enemy with the veil of darkness quickly covering the area.

"Do you need medical?" The captain crawled up the bank of dirt as he spoke. He looked at the burning vehicles on the road.

"I don't know." Deb placed the M-16 to her side and pulled the torn pant leg up and twisted her leg to look at the back of her calf. She began pulling out small shards of metal.

"I'll send for a medic," said Captain Hendersen, glancing back down at her.

"No, I'm good." She picked at the bloody wound, took her handkerchief and poured a small portion of water on it. She wiped away much of the blood, then looked up at the captain. "What do you think our best options are?"

"Even if we can't drive out, we need to obtain our supplies and ammunition from the trucks," stated the captain. "Hopefully, we can get communication up."

"Captain," Sergeant Herrera was looking through the telescope of his rifle, "there is a hell of a lot of activity taking place on the hill northeast of here."

"How far out are they?"

"A little more than a kilometer."

"Within range then."

"Yes sir. Even in the dark." The sergeant worked on adjusting the sights as he looked through the telescope. "There are manpads visible."

"Let us bring in more snipers before you fire. We might as well take out as many as we can before they go into hiding."

"Sir," a private shuffled next to the captain. "3rd

squad extracted the helicopter crew and have taken them to medical."

"Is medical west of here?"

"Yes sir," the private stood up with half his body out of the ravine.

Captain Hendersen grabbed his shirt at the back of the neck and pulled him down. "You can't expose yourself like that son. There are people out there that want you dead."

"Yes sir."

"Private, I want you to escort me to medical." Deb slid about a meter deeper to a level spot at the bottom of the chasm. She limped behind the private down the wash line.

Medical was situated at the end of the ravine where the steep walls flared out into a meadow. 2nd Platoon was located at the area with two M6 Bradley fighting vehicles positioned safely in the pasture. Condoleezza was busy rendering aid to one of the pilots when she observed Colonel Lisco limping her way.

"How are the pilots?" Deb noticed several soldiers with severe injuries receiving medical aid from the other medics. All the medics were functioning under dim light as they worked at a hectic pace to care for the wounded.

"The pilots suffered bumps and bruises." Condoleezza had an excessive amount of blood on her blouse as she stepped closer to the colonel. "What's wrong with your leg?"

Deb pulled up her trouser leg and turned around. She could feel the blood running down to her ankle.

"It will need to be cleaned and wrapped."

Condoleezza supported Deb's right arm as she led her to sit next to the pilot. The sound of intermittent gunfire could be heard. An RG 75 NYLA and a Humvee appeared nearly 400 meters past the other combat vehicles in the fallow pasture. All the vehicles moved north in the direction of the attacking forces.

"Private," Deb motioned to the soldier who arrived with her at the medical area. She pointed to the pasture. "Go to where the Bradley just left and ask 1st Lieutenant James if any of the drones are operational."

"Yes ma'am," the private took off in a full sprint.

"Turn over on your stomach." Condoleezza placed a small mat on the dirt.

Deb felt the back of her pant leg being cut as she placed her nose into a hard, plastic mat. The temperature dropped below freezing, making the frosty fluid being poured over her leg seem even colder. She shivered as the medic worked quickly on the lacerations. Her thoughts were on Tommy and the other soldiers in the 2nd Brigade.

"Ma'am," the private was breathing hard as he lowered his face to be only a couple centimeters from Colonel Deb's nose. "Lieutenant James said the drone is up and working. We also have communication back."

"Dammit private, move back a bit." Deb shifted her chin on the hard mat, to give some relief to her neck, before turning back to the side. The private was now on one knee. "Find Specialist Grant in communications and have her come here."

"Yes ma'am," the private hopped up and left in a full sprint.

"Lucky you didn't have further orders for him," Condoleezza chuckled. "I just need to wrap this, and I'll be done."

The humming sound of a squadron of MQ 7T Reapers could be heard flying overhead to the north. Soon the sound of explosions filled the air. Flashes of light lit up the horizon through the cloud covered darkness.

"Ok," Condoleezza finished the wrap and released her leg. "Just keep an eye on it."

Deb turned to sit on her butt, before standing. She was surprised how far away the blasts were taking place. F Company had pushed the enemy back.

"Colonel," Specialist Grant stood at full attention, "your new ride should be here by 2200." She turned to Condoleezza. "Helicopters are in route to evacuate the wounded."

"What is their ETA?" Condoleezza asked.

"Within fifteen mikes, ma'am." The specialist turned back to Deb. "We received a message from Command Sergeant Major Talfoya that G Company is in route to this location. The remainder of 2nd Battalion is moving headquarters to the civilian conveyance location north of Beaver."

"Did he say why they are moving?"

"No, ma'am, but that is where you are scheduled to be transported." Specialist Grant hesitated for a moment, before continuing, "Command Sergeant Major Talfoya didn't specify, ma'am, but the enemy has broken through and there is continuous fighting about a hundred and fifty klicks south of our location. It's quickly moving northward."

***

Deb was whisked away in the new generation AH-102 long range attack helicopter which allowed for the crew of two plus room for two passengers. Perfect for the scenario where the colonel found herself in need of a ride in the war zone.

As the helicopter ascended rapidly, she could see

fires filling the valley. A column of lights making up G Company was momentarily visible snaking along a dirt road rushing toward F Company's position. Her head was aching, and her leg hurt as she looked out the window at the dark landscape. She gasped when she saw the Jacoby home burning and several big holes blown into the side of the red barn.

"How long to my destination?" Deb asked with a humming noise in her ear, causing her discomfort.

"About fifty minutes, ma'am."

She leaned back in the seat and closed her eyes. The battle happened so quickly she was glad to have a moment to reflect on how she handled her duties, and the performance of the soldiers under her command. The distinct, unwavering commands shouted by Captain Hendersen filled her thoughts. One of her dad's oft used quotes was "If you cannot do great things, do small things in a great way". The captain processed situations quickly and made solid decisions while under distress. He handled all the small details greatly. She dozed off.

"Ma'am, we are here," said the pilot, waking her from the light sleep.

Her stomach rose to her throat as the chopper plummeted quickly to the ground. Once she was out of the helicopter and standing next to Tommy, it ascended and sped away, causing her to turn away from the wind caused by the blades.

"We have your quarters all set." Tommy had his arm around her waist, pulling her close to shield her from the force of the wind.

"I need an update," she leaned back, slipping out of his arms.

"We can do it in your tent." He noticed she was

limping. "What happened to your leg?"

"Shrapnel." She was surprised at the amount of activity happening in the middle of the night. There were hundreds of large buses lined for kilometers along the Interstate highway. Crowds of people were in lines, roped off, leading them to tables where each would stop and speak to a soldier before climbing on to a bus.

"Do you want to go to the medical tent?"

"No," she allowed him to place his hand around her back to help her walk. "How well are we vetting these people before they are transported?"

"We don't have anything to say about the process. Families are taken on certain buses and individuals are on others. They will be evaluated by Homeland Security when they reach the FEMA encampments."

"Where are Lloyd and Teresa?" she was still chilled by the cold breeze. Tommy released her waist. She held his arm to keep the weight off her leg.

"3rd Battalion is at Salt Lake City and 1st has made it to Grand Junction."

"Did they encounter any problems?"

"Nothing significant. Here are your quarters."

Tommy held open the canvas door to the tent. Deb stepped inside and he followed. She sat on the bed.

"What is going on with communication?" she asked, placing her injured leg onto the bed, but keeping the other on the floor while continuing to sit upright.

"They are using voice patterns to identify and locate our commanding officers. They have been successful in eliminating some of our upper command."

"Who?" Her eyes widened in anticipation of the update.

Tommy hesitated and swallowed. "Colonel Tyler

with Stryker. Among others."

"Is he KIA?" she asked.

"Yes." Tommy knew Deb's relationship with Colonel Tyler was tight. "You and I are scheduled to leave here tomorrow morning at 1100."

"Where are we going?"

"Catch a chopper to Toole, then fly to Peterson, and onto Fort Carson." Tommy stared at her, obviously wanting to talk.

Deb brought up her hanging leg and leaned her head back, stretching the skin under her chin. She took in a deep breath and asked, "Can you give me a little time? If I'm not out by 0500 have someone wake me."

Eastern Colorado Farm

Bill rubbed the three-day old stubble on his chin, watching the clouds overhead accumulate from the third floor of the concrete tower, knowing snow would be flying soon. Although everyone was trying to work together to make the place better, there was still an underlying sentiment that everything would soon change, and everyone would be able to go home to their normal lives. The progress, especially the building of the block tower and apartment was spectacular. His mind wandered to when he and Aunt Deb deliberated on the best ways to supply and organize the farm, how everything was more a fantasy, a game they played to prepare for the worse, without real human emotions.

Finding someone like Samantha amongst the chaos and confusion was another thing he never envisioned. She was becoming more than just a girlfriend; she was the one he wanted to spend the rest of his life with. Seeing Harold and Jason carrying pieces of plywood from the garage in his direction brought him from his thoughts.

"We are coming up to place the folding windows," Harold set the plywood down as he yelled to Bill. "I'd like to get them built today to keep snow out."

"Do you need me to help carry the plywood up," Bill yelled down.

"No, I measure and cut it down here." Jason pulled the collar of his coat tight around his neck to block the cold wind.

"We will need help getting the flat iron pieces up,"

said Harold. "It's going to take more than two of us to carry them."

Deb insisted on having the one-inch-thick pieces of iron placed at the bottom of the windows in the tower. She realized many bullets could pierce the grout filled concrete blocks, but not through both the reinforced concrete block and the iron. The problem was the iron was two meters long by a hundred and ten centimeters high, making them extremely heavy.

"The front-end loader on the tractor can lift them high enough to get to the second-floor window," stated Bill.

"We can figure all that out later. I need to get the window shuttered," yelled Harold as a gust of wind blew hard enough to lift the plywood in his grasp. Jason grabbed hold and helped push the wood level to the ground.

Bill looked to the southwest, over the top of the house. An old car, a 1957 Chevy was slowly coming down the driveway. He watched until they were no longer visible behind the house. Breanna and Irene scurried out of the RV and made their way in the direction of the new vehicle.

"Looks like we have a visitor," Bill yelled down.

Jason took several steps backwards to find a vantage point to look in front of the house. "It's a family," he yelled. "Irene must know them."

By the time Bill found his way to the car, some of the Jacobys and most of the people from inside were greeting the people. Maddy was holding onto Irene's hand, with Scotty standing next to her.

"Daddy," Maddy rushed to his side and pulled him in front of the man. "This is Travis, he was the pilot who wrecked our airplane."

"He didn't wreck it Maddy," Irene scoffed, laughing

softly. "He landed it."

"It wasn't wrecked?" Maddy turned to Irene and pulled on the neckline of her sweater. "Then why did we have to walk to your house?"

"She has a point there Irene." Travis chuckled before motioning toward his family. "This is my wife Sue and our two girls Willow and Aubrey."

"Nice to meet you," said Bill, noticing how handsome the pilot was as he stood next to his petite wife with their two children holding onto his legs. The younger girl looked to be about Maddy's age and the other slightly older.

"I was becoming a little concerned I wasn't going to be able to find this place. Ted's map was good, but the dirt roads aren't marked very well." Travis looked at Irene. "I figured Ed would like his car back."

"Believe me he will." Irene looked to the RV where Megan and Ashley were sauntering in their direction.

"Thank God," Travis looked to Ashley, "how is Carol?"

"She passed," Breanna answered quickly, glancing at Scotty with her lower lip covering her upper. "We couldn't save her."

"Ummm," Travis looked directly at Scotty, "I'm terribly sorry to hear that."

Scotty's big round face turned bright red. Maddy went to his side. "Grandpa is going to take us to California to find Scotty's mom. And then we are going to get my mom and bring them back to the farm."

Irene moved closer to the two children, smiling she reinforced Maddy's thoughts. "It may take a while, but we have confidence Ted is going to do all he can to help us."

"We are adapting to the changes we have to face each day." Breanna redirected the conversation, "Our family, Terrance, Jerry and of course Samantha seems to be getting along better each day."

Bill noticed Samantha remained at the edge of the crowd, making no attempt to interact with the pilot. She was looking off into space. Her mind was on something besides greeting Travis and his family.

"Is everything alright?" Bill stepped to her side.

"Fine," her smile tried to portray her feelings as being content, but her drooping eyes told him otherwise.

Bill was sure there was something major bothering Samantha concerning the arrival of Travis. Remembering how Jessica disappeared unexpectedly with Christian after creating a union with him, caused him to question his ability to understand the new woman in his life. He had a strange feeling he was being set up to be betrayed again.

He could hear Travis telling Hank and Jon how much they looked like Ted. Jacqueline and Gina were gushing over how cute the little girls were. Samantha slowly turned and walked into the house.

Littleton, Colorado

Christian and Tim could see their breath as they waited in the morning cold for the food line to move forward so they could receive breakfast. It was easier than expected for the entire group of insurgents to blend in with the locals at the encampment located at the Denver Seminary off Santa Fe Drive in Littleton. The military sweep of the area was successful in that it kept them from overtaking the new police station and pushed them into hiding. Food was now an issue. They left their large weapons at a small house in old town Littleton that they used for a rendezvous spot. Several of the rebels slipped handguns thru the minimally secure checkpoint at the entry gate.

After receiving their plate of food, eight confederates joined Christian and Tim at a table. The rest of the rebels scattered across the large open space park where more than a hundred tables covered the frigid landscape. Armed security patrolled the grounds, keeping an eye on the crowd partaking in breakfast. Most looked like police but several were armed civilians.

"I don't feel very good about this place," Christian surveyed the surroundings. "We better locate some other areas for food."

"All the other camps in the Denver area are north or east of here. We have to go way east, or way north, to find them." Tim placed a frayed map of Colorado, with several areas circled in red pen, on the table before taking in a large mouthful of powdered eggs. "Yuk. This is awful."

"You better eat a lot; it might be a while before we eat again." Christian ate quickly. He took note of an older man in a khaki shirt who seemed to be keeping close tabs on the group.

"There are a lot of police around here." Tim sensed there was something bothering Christian. "What's wrong?"

"This guy," he said lightly, smiling at the man in the khaki shirt positioning himself next to their table. He stopped and stood right behind Tim's chair.

"How are ya all doing? I'm Thomas Westmoreland, the director of the camp," the man spoke pleasantly. His face was freshly shaven with noticeable blood marks from nicks on his sunken chin. "I haven't seen you here before."

"We literally arrived an hour ago." Christian noticed several of the security personnel assembling closer to the table. "We left the encampment near red rocks this morning."

"Why here?" the man rested his hand on the back of Tim's metal chair.

"Just stopping to get something to eat as we pass through." Christian took a large bite of food.

"And where are you heading?"

"We are going to Fort Carson to enlist."

"Are you walking there? We are expecting cold temperatures and snow." The man was surprised and a little confused with the response of enlisting. He was not sure if he was dealing with rebels or patriots. All FEMA personnel were required to report large, unknown groups who suddenly arrive at a camp without previous notification or approval from regional headquarters. It was obvious some of the people at separate tables were part of Christian's group, making them fit the criteria to be reported. "It's nearly a hundred kilometers to the base."

"That's the plan." Christian leaned back in his chair. "Unless you want to give us a ride."

"All of you planning to enlist?" He measured the looks from the five women eating at the table.

"All of us," stated a large woman with a scar on her forehead. "I'll probably be infantry."

"I want to drive a tank," said the woman next to her, smiling with crooked, yellow teeth.

The man sensed they were having fun with him. There was no way the group of misfits were planning to travel to the Army base. "I'll tell you what. I will contact the base and have them send a truck to transport you." He took a step away from the back of Tim's chair and enjoyed the surprised expressions.

"That would be great," said Christian confidently, smiling at the others.

"I'll do it now."

The man stopped to talk with the security personnel before disappearing into one of the buildings on the edge of the field. Several more armed members joined the others to watch over the group.

"Here is the exit strategy. There is a wooded area to the south of here." Christian leaned over the table and spoke quietly. He nodded his head to the south. "If we have to leave in a hurry, run through the crowd toward the woods."

"That won't work Christian," said the large woman sitting next to him.

"What do you mean, Shira, it won't work?" Christian scoffed.

"I walked around the perimeter when we first arrived. There is a chain length fence surrounding the entire property. It is about three meters high."

Placing his right hand to his chin, Christian stared at Shira Rosenfeld. She was an acquaintance from high school, where he thought of her as quite odd. She was an intellectual with a tendency to question everything, just like him, which caused them to draw to one another. She had a sand texture on both cheeks of her face that easily turned a bright red in the cold or when she got excited. Although she and Jessica were quasi friends, she quickly moved to take Jessica's place with him the same afternoon Jessica left.

"Nix that then." Christian felt anxious as he watched the director of the camp approach, flanked by four armed policemen in uniform. Another twenty members of the security team lined up about ten meters away. Christian looked in the direction of the other insurrectionists at the surrounding tables, who were all closely watching the actions at their leader's table.

"Ok, here is the deal. I don't believe for a second that you are going to Fort Carson to enlist." The director stood at the far end of the table away from Christian. "But…the base will send transportation here in the morning."

"What time should we be back in the morning?" Christian asked in a calm manner.

"No, no. You need to stay here tonight."

Christian folded his arms. He was sure the man informed the Army that there were rebels at the government camp. More than likely forces were on their way to the location as they spoke.

"I don't want to stay here. Half these people look diseased," said Shira.

"Everyone has had their temperature monitored and we have members keeping an eye out for sickness," stated the director.

"It will be alright." Christian squinted his eyes, giving her a cold stare.

"Here's the rules. No weapons of any kind. No political speech. No words or statements that can be perceived as disrespectful. No…"

"What the hell," Shira shouted, interrupting him. "What is wrong with you people. Why are we fighting so hard to defeat the Russians and Chinese? You are suppressing our freedoms more than they will. This is the reason the cities are burning, you authoritarian asshole."

Christian rose from his chair with his head on a swivel, looking at the rebels at the other tables." It's time for us to go," he shouted.

Director Westmoreland motioned to the security team. The four policemen pulled their weapons and leveled them in the direction of the people at Christian's table.

"I wouldn't do that if I were you." Christian signaled to the rebels eating at the other tables. More than a hundred of them popped up from their chairs and advanced toward him and the director. "You give us no other option. If you want a blood bath at your camp, you will be one of the first to go."

The multitude of armed insurrectionists swarmed to surround the security detail.

"Just go." The director stepped back next to the policemen and motioned with his right arm in the direction of the gated entrance. His hand was shaking. "Lower your weapons please, we won't try to stop you."

Christian was the first out of the gate, followed by the throng of dissidents. He jogged across an open field, over some railroad tracks and did not stop until arriving at the nearly vacant residential area of old town Littleton. Locating food in the city was going to be much harder than anticipated. His militia was recognizable and the camps that offered food were on high alert.

He had not crossed paths with the foreigners since they were thwarted by the presence of the Army after being ordered to take the police station on Colorado Boulevard. He came to the realization, after the confrontation at the FEMA camp, that the foreign rebels were the supreme threat to him and his friends. They faced being arrested by the government people, whereas confrontation with the foreign rebels would be much more deadly. Eventually either the rebels or the authorities were bound to catch up with them if they stayed in any one place for a long period of time. There was no place to hide in the city.

Beaver, Utah

Deb was up and pulling on her boots when she heard Tommy yell her name from outside the tent. She looked at her watch. It was exactly 0500. What the hell she thought, did he sit outside the entire night waiting to wake her.

"Come in Tommy."

He backed through the entrance carrying two steaming cups of coffee. He handed her a cup.

"Fighting has moved all the way to the St. George area and Corp wants us to expediate our schedule," Tommy stated.

"Are all the people evacuated?"

"FEMA ran out of buses last night, so they transferred ten bus loads to Grand Junction and let the civilians off before heading back this way. They should be finishing up with loading the final group of passengers."

"When are we leaving?"

"0700."

Deb cradled the warm cup of coffee. "This is absolutely ridiculous that I can't communicate directly with upper brass.

"Hopefully the issues with communication will be resolved by the time we get to Fort Carson," stated Tommy.

"Ma'am," a soldier yelled from outside the tent.

Tommy opened the flap to the tent and stuck his head outside. "What is it private?"

"There is a civilian who wants the colonel to come to

the extradition site to help resolve a conflict."

He turned to Deb, "Did you hear."

Give me more information," Deb yelled loud enough for the soldier to hear. "What is the conflict?"

"It's a family, ma'am. They all want to ride in one bus and not split up. The civilian asked for you personally. Sergeant Bishop told me to see if you could come and help resolve the problem."

"Do we have time?" Deb asked Tommy.

"We can take our gear and stop there on the way to our expulsion area. It's the same location you were dropped off last night."

"Tell Sergeant Bishop we will be there in ten minutes," Deb shook her head. "If it's not one thing, it's another."

Tommy carried both his and the colonel's duffle bags while Deb limped alongside to the area where two lone buses were waiting to depart. The Jacobys were standing at the open door yelling at several of the personnel from FEMA."

"Colonel Lisco," Josh stepped toward Deb, "these people want to have us split-up. They say that some of our family need to get on the other bus that is going to Casper Wyoming."

Deb looked at a man of about forty dressed in a light blue button-down shirt with FEMA written on the pocket at his breast. His eyes were drooping and there was no hint of a smile on his face.

"Are there people on the Colorado bus willing to go to the Wyoming bus?" Deb asked.

"Obviously, Colonel, I am not so incompetent to have not already tried to coax people off," the FEMA official scoffed. "Now, I have about had it with these people. Either they get on the buses, or I will arrest them, and they can ride to their destinations in handcuffs."

"Arrest them?" Deb glanced at Seth before turning to the man. "For what?"

"Failure to obey my orders," he screamed.

Deb stared at him with her nose curled and her hands palms up.

Tommy sat the bags at his feet, grabbed ahold of Deb's arm and led her back about ten meters before speaking softly, "Since Martial Law has been implemented, he most likely has the authority to arrest and detain civilians without a warrant."

"So, it is possible he has the power to arrest them?" Deb squinted her eyes as she twisted her neck to look back at the FEMA group.

"Not only possible but most likely. Executive orders go back before FEMA existed to President Kennedy where he gave powers to the government when the threat of a nuclear attack was a real possibility. Over the years the orders have been revoked and shuffled to other departments within the United States government," stated Tommy. "I don't know the specifics of the scope of his power. One thing I know is that Homeland Security has complete authority over this situation."

Deb limped in the direction of the director, knowing it would take all she had to be civil.

"Can we use some common sense here?" Deb forced a smile. Her head was beginning to throb. "These are all young people who would have no problem sitting in the aisle of the bus or doubling up on the seats."

"These buses have a capacity for fifty people. We stretched the rule to allow for a sixty person maximum, which we have followed all night long." He held his right hand in the palm of his left hand. "If this entire group goes on the Colorado bus there will be sixty-nine passengers. I won't allow the bus to be that overloaded when we have another bus leaving the area that is only half full."

Deb swallowed hard. She looked at his colleagues glaring at her with smug expressions. "What is your name?"

"I am Theodore Sutherland, Deputy Assistant of response for region 8."

"I truly sympathize with the task you have had to deal with. You have done an outstanding job." Deb smiled at him and motioned out with her left hand. "But can we be reasonable here? Use a little foresight? In this time of complete chaos none of us would want to separate from our families. Having an afternoon of being crowded on a bus would save a lot of suffering and worry for this family down the road."

"Not going to happen." The deputy shook his head. He turned his back on Deb and stepped nearer to Seth. "Pick nine to ride on the other bus."

"Ok, listen here Deputy Sutherland. We are going to put this entire family on the Colorado bound bus." Deb positioned next to Seth. "All of you, go ahead and get on."

"Hold it," the deputy moved closer to the bus as the Jacobys boarded.

Deb hobbled forward and put the index finger of her left hand about a centimeter from his nose, stopping him in his tracks.

"Oh Jesus," Tommy shuffled next to her. "Colonel, please."

The entire Jacoby family climbed on the bus. The door closed.

"If you," she shook her finger, "or anyone else from FEMA detains this family, I will take it as a personal affront to me."

"Are you crazy? I have complete authority of this base, given to me by the Department of Homeland Security." The deputy jerked his head straight back and stared at the tip of her finger with his mouth wide open. "Are you threatening me?"

"Sergeant Bishop," Deb never floundered as she yelled, "see these buses off."

"Colonel, your career in the Army is over." He recoiled back to the safety of the other personnel from FEMA.

"Just shut up," Deb's dark eyebrows folded over her eyes. She started to walk away before stopping and pointing at the cowering man. "Just remember what I told you Deputy Sutherland. Leave that family alone or I'll knock the living hell out of you."

"Oh, Lord," Tommy shuddered while placing his left hand to the top of his head. He stared at the startled group from FEMA.

Deb waited patiently as the bus made its way to the Interstate. She turned quickly and walked away.

"Oh my God, Colonel, I wish you had handled that differently." Tommy ran to keep up with her, bouncing both duffle bags on his knees. "This is awful. I mean this is really awful."

They hurried to the open field. The hacking sound of the blades of the chopper became louder and louder as it neared. She turned to the command sergeant major.

"Tommy, I am who I am. I told Irene and Ed Jacoby I would watch out for their family. I will never stand by and allow stupidity to stand in the way of veracity and common sense."

They watched the helicopter land.

Eastern Colorado Farm

Maddy ran downstairs and grabbed her heavier coat while Scotty waited for her in the front yard. He was already wearing a winter jacket, albeit a size too large for his little body, but one that protected him from the dropping temperature and spitting snow.

She ran out the front door on the kitchen side, quickly past Scotty and out the side gate of the yard. She was halfway across the courtyard by the time he caught her. They both ran past the garage and around the barn to an area they discovered the day before, about five hundred meters further from the corrals on the north side of the barn. A dusty concrete foundation from the remnants of an old farmhouse poked from the ground covered with dirt and weeds. Deteriorated wood siding and two by fours were scattered on top and to the side of the structure.

"Be careful," Maddy removed her heavy mitten from her right hand and pulled a rusty nail from a piece of wood. She held it out for Scotty to see with her dark eyes wide open. "This could go right through your shoes."

"Look at this." He held up an old mason jar with a small band of metal around the threaded neck of the container. "We should keep this."

"Look at this," Maddy kicked a wasp nest off a pile of red brick from the chimney laying at the side of the structure. The nest turned to powder in the cold wind.

Scotty stepped onto a floor of eight pieces of wood with an opening of about two centimeters between each of them. He went to a knee and tried to look through a gap.

"Look," he yelled, raising onto his feet, allowing Maddy to get closer.

Maddy stepped onto the sagging structure. Just as she was preparing to go to her knees to look through the cracks, the wood floor collapsed. They fell straight down with Maddy landing feet first before falling backwards into the brick wall, partially breaking the fall with her arm. Scotty landed on his feet and fell backward onto his butt.

"Ohh…," Scotty moaned loudly as he lay on the cold dirt floor. He could see up sheer walls of brick to a circular opening about four meters above.

Maddy gasped for air as she struggled to gain her breath. She grabbed her left wrist with her right hand and continued struggling to breath.

"Are you ok Maddy?" Scotty moved to her side, scattering fragments of the wood floor which followed them down into the old well. He put a hand on her shoulder.

Maddy caught a deep breath and tears flowed from her eyes.

"I hurt my arm," she gasped.

Scotty placed a hand on the cold brick and stretched upward. His reach was not even close to the opening. His big round face was rosy.

"We can't get out of here Maddy." He could feel a sharp pain at his left hip. "We're trapped."

"I want my daddy," Maddy sniffled, "and mommy."

Scotty sat down next to her and placed his arm around her. His lower lip pushed out and he cried.

Maddy quieted and stared at Scotty through wet eyes. She leaned her head to the cold fabric of the coat on his shoulder. She looked up at small snowflakes floating above, evaporating before they reached her.

***

Immediately after lunch, Nicole sat down at the kitchen table with Jacqueline and Gina to contemplate a list of food items still left in the large pantry in the basement. It was becoming ever apparent they would be living at the farm for an extended period. The three women were taking it upon themselves to organize and delegate different tasks important to keep the farm operational.

One concern Nicole confronted was the consideration of taking care of the children that were arriving. As a grandmother she feared that Maddy and the other children were unsupervised on too many occasions while adults tended to other tasks. She wanted to bring some structure to their lives by organizing care for the children. Bill, along with Travis' wife Sue and Glenda Hernandez were all more than willing to take their turns tending to the kids. Travis and Victor were recruited to help drywall the southern rooms at the apartment in anticipation of having them ready for occupancy within a day, so they were going to be too busy hanging drywall to help care for the kids.

Nicole was hesitant to ask Jessica if she was willing to spend time with the children. It was an awful thing to think, but she was not sure she could trust her. Avery and Reagan were probably old enough to wander on their own. Since she arrived back at the farm Jessica was either working in the greenhouse or hiding in the basement, with Emilee keeping track of her little sisters most of the time.

Irene was around Maddy on many occasions during the day and Nicole wanted to leave it to the discretion of her on how often she wanted to be involved. Samantha on the other hand was someone who should be offered the opportunity to be immersed with the kids.

Nicole rose from her chair and walked to the kitchen window and looked outside. Maddy and Scotty were nowhere in sight.

"I'm going to go check on Maddy." Nicole put on her coat and walked outside. Light snow dampened her hair before she pulled the hood up and tightened the draw strings tight around her chin. She walked through the yard, across the driveway to the Jacoby's RV. She knocked and Breanna opened the door.

"Are Maddy or Scotty here?"

"No, I'll ask Mom if she has seen them." She turned but Irene had heard the inquiry and was already nudging her way to the door.

"We are planning on baking some cornbread this afternoon. I will help you look," Irene grabbed her coat from the hanger.

"No, that's okay. Let me check with Bill and Samantha. I'm sure they are with them." Nicole stepped back from the RV.

Bill and Samantha were at the apartment watching Jason and his crew place electrical switch plates and finish wiring for the electrical heat on the first set of apartments. The room smelled of caulking and fresh paint. Samantha decided she wanted the single bedroom on the southeast corner of the structure. It would still be a couple of days before the first of three community bathrooms would be ready to use, but she was still excited to have a room for herself. Finding themselves alone in the room, Bill decided it would be a good time to find out why she was so distant around Travis.

"Can I ask you a personal question?" Bill asked.

She twisted her mouth which signaled to him she was waiting to have the inevitable conversation.

"What's going on with Travis?" he waited for an answer as she peered out the window at the back pasture. He continued when she didn't answer, "I'm surprised you never acknowledged him or his family when they arrived."

Bill was wondering if maybe they were lovers. The more she remained silent the more he conjectured.

"I spoke with your dad about part of this on our way back to Colorado," she remembered Ted asking if Travis was her lover. She imagined Bill was pondering the same visions in his mind. She looked him directly in the eyes. "Travis and I were friends who worked together for the same airline."

"Why are you so distant?"

"His wife Sue thinks we were having an affair. She still does." Her breathing was increasing as she positioned herself directly in front of him. "I was about to lose my job for an alcohol related issue, that was false. Travis and I were in a compromising situation at a hotel in Los Angeles that Sue found out about. I lied to her about certain things that she was able to confirm as being a lie. She and Travis have been working through the issues ever since. She thinks of me, not only as a liar, but someone who was sleeping with her husband."

Bill was having trouble following her conversation. Her whole explanation was vague and so unclear, he didn't know how to reply. He struggled with understanding what she meant by both a compromising situation and an alcohol related issue? He decided not to pursue the questions because she was vulnerable to believing everyone would consider her a liar.

"Is it something that might be resolved by sitting down with Travis and his wife?" Bill heard his mother yelling for him outside the apartment, but he waited to hear Samantha's reply.

"I don't want to face her just quite yet." Samantha raised her eyebrow over her right eye and then looked away.

He tried to look her in the eyes, but she refused to make eye contact. He could hear his mother continue to call his name from outside. He stepped out of the apartment into the cold.

"Have you seen Maddy or Scotty?" Nicole was holding the collar of her coat tight around her neck.

"Not for a while. Did you check with Irene?"

"Yes, she hasn't seen her."

"Maddy, Scotty," Bill yelled loudly. He walked nearer the garage and yelled again. Jon and Hank, followed by Irving, Terrance and Jerry stepped out the door of the garage.

"What's wrong, Bill?" Hank yelled.

"We are trying to locate Maddy and Scotty."

"Well, they can't be very far." Jon walked to the west edge of the garage and yelled in the direction of the barn, "Maddy."

Soon, the sound of people yelling the kids names could be heard from all directions. After nearly thirty minutes of searching everyone on the farm gathered in front of the Jacoby's RV.

"Oh God, where could they be?" Nicole inhaled deeply.

"This is not like her," Irene claimed, folding her arms in front of her.

The door to the RV opened and Breanna helped her

dad down the steps. Ed was wearing a patched coat with an original Kromer cap. He hobbled to the middle of the pack of anxious people.

"When was the last time anyone saw them?" Ed asked.

"It was around lunch time," stated Nicole.

"We have to open and check all the freezers and refrigerators. Look in all the corrals and under all the machinery," Ed's eyes were watery. "Look in all the closets and rooms in the house. Check any old wells or cellars on the property."

"Mom, would you, Aunt Gina and Aunt Jacqueline organize a group to search the house?" Bill felt nauseous.

Heavy snow began to cover the ground. The sun was barely visible as it sat low on the horizon.

"Oh Lord, I hope the snow doesn't get any worse," Nicole covered her mouth with her hand.

"The snow might not be bad. If they are outside the cloud cover will keep the temperature from falling," stated Ed. "But darkness will be a problem with the sun setting so early this time of year."

"We will check all the farm equipment and around the barn," said Aaron, motioning to Adam, Ashley and Megan.

"Maddy is afraid of the horses, but I'll check the stalls." Breanna walked quickly toward the barn.

"Let's set this up systematically. Break into four equal groups." Jon pointed at Hank, Irving and Terrance. "I'll go north, Hank west, Terrance east and Irving south."

Bill wandered aimlessly from farm building to farm building. Everything imaginable, from being attacked by a wild animal, to someone coming to the farm and taking Maddy, began to cram his mind. It was nearly time to eat supper and darkness covered the landscape. He sat down in the snow outside the garage and grabbed tightly to the hair on top of his head.

"Come on Bill," Bobby placed his hand on his cousin's shoulder. "Let's keep looking. We are going to find them."

Fort Carson Army Base

Operation Lumberjack was grounded on three independent movements. First was the placement of forces in Northern Africa; Second was American Special Forces, along with the Mexican Army, to systematically begin taking back the occupied cities of northern Mexico; Third was to use mostly nonhuman weaponry to engage the enemy moving through the area of the western United States from the Rockies west to the Sierra Nevada mountains.

Army Chief of Staff General Ron McClinton, General Lopez and General Prost sat at a table in the Army base mess hall. They were taking a lunch break after a long morning of coordinating the movements and strategic placement of the nonhuman weaponry. They were preparing for the attack on embedded insurrectionists and advancing enemy troops in the evacuation area.

According to the information formulated over the past several days, everything the enemy was doing was predicted within the models. The process of putting into motion the United States Military machine was slow, but, cutting off the supply chains to the embedded enemy and giving them no options but to move northward into the non-human forces of the United States was already beginning to develop. The massive size of the enemy forces at the border would eventually be their undoing. General Lauer was summoned to a call immediately after leaving the strategy session. He rejoined them at the table.

"I just got off the horn with the Chief Security Officer

from Homeland Security," General Lauer sat his plate of food on the table. "He was all up in arms. Apparently, Colonel Lisco threatened the FEMA Director for Section 8 this morning at the civilian dispersion site in Utah."

"Ha, ha, does that surprise any of us?" General McClinton laughed while leaning back in his chair.

"He was genuinely upset," General Lauer scoffed. "I told him I would discipline her appropriately."

"Ted met her this morning at Peterson, and they went straight to the base hospital," stated General Lopez. "She has a wound to her leg."

"Is it serious?" General Prost asked.

"Ted indicated it was for precaution," General Lopez looked at General Lauer. "Looks like you might be pinning a medal on her at the same time you are chastening her."

"I have to respond to her behavior." General Lauer took a bite of mashed potatoes. His right eye twitched as he swallowed.

General Prost glanced at Chief of Staff General McClinton. He was still smiling while General Lauer grimaced.

"Did Colonel Lisco physically strike the man?" General McClinton asked. He tossed a napkin onto his half empty plate.

"No, it never reached that point."

"We all know who Colonel Lisco is," stated General McClinton. "Let's get her version of what happened before we make any decisions."

"Without structure and discipline, mostly from our commanding officers, our whole chain of command will collapse." General Lauer placed his fork down. "I have to address her conduct."

"I agree, we could not exist without discipline within the ranks. But Colonel Deb Lisco is a whole different animal," stated General Prost.

"Ann," General McClinton pushed out his barrel chest, "as contentious as the encounter was between you and the colonel a couple of years ago, I am surprised you would come to her defense."

"I understand her better after our meeting in Great Falls. Besides, she was correct in almost all aspects she raised at our conference two years ago." General Prost decided not to mention the bonding over a bottle of Scotch. "The information we collected at the warehouse outside Great Falls gave me a different perspective on the colonel. Besides being incredibly discerning, she is someone we need on our side."

"We have an Army full of hardnosed leaders who are perceptive and dedicated. How is Colonel Lisco different?" General Lauer looked at the determined eyes of the petite general staring at him across the table. He took a sip of coffee.

"The warehouse in Great Falls has been a location used by enemy insurgents for over fifteen years. Since the structure was built, there have been twenty-six different inspections by county officials, and sixteen calls handled by the local sheriff at the location. Last year there was a walk through by an FBI agent in response to complaints from local farmers, claiming they witnessed flying objects traveling from the location into Canada," stated General Prost. "Not one thing was found to be out of the ordinary during any of these visits. It was simply a store providing jobs for the community. A factory and warehouse for building and selling custom wheels, much like thousands of others in the United States."

"It was a warehouse," General Lauer held his cup out in front of him. "I'm not following your point about Colonel Lisco."

"She blew the damn thing to smithereens," shouted General Prost, motioning across the table with her hand. "What other commander in our forces would have the gumption to take the initiative to use the power of the United States Army to blow up a factory, in a city, in the middle of America?"

"I'm pretty sure none," stated General McClinton.

"I can guarantee the Chinese and Russian models never predicted it either," stated General Prost. "There was a crater thirty meters deep in the center of the building, and we had to excavate down another twenty meters to find the fuel and weapons. It was a massive structure. The information and documents we found made it clear our enemies were confident none of it would ever be discovered. It is so significant. Being a World War II buff, it reminds me of the secret bunkers Hitler built so the German army could hide fuel and weapons from the Americans and their allies. If the supplies would have been above ground, they would have been noticed and easily destroyed by American forces."

"With information from that factory alone we have been able to locate and destroy five other strongholds across the country. This all should be taken into consideration with handling Colonel Lisco," stated General McClinton, turning to look at General Lauer.

"I have a meeting with staff this afternoon. I'll have her and Command Sergeant Major Talfoya come to my office before the briefing," said General Lauer.

"Would you mind if Ted and I also attend?" General Lopez asked. "Maybe I can clear some of the air with him at the same time."

"Did you discuss with Ted about the possibility of him leading the effort to search and destroy the local rebels?" General McClinton asked.

"Actually, it was his idea," General Lopez grinned. "It is almost uncanny how accurate the behavior model has been in-regards-to his duty and commitment.

"It is absolutely imperative we diminish the threat of the imbedded rebels along the front range," stated General McClinton. "This will be a topic discussed at the Chief of Staff meeting this afternoon. Ted Lisco is the perfect soldier to figure out the complexities of separating the external threats from the domestic revolutionary fighters and dealing with them accordingly. When this is all over, we, as well as our enemies will find these two groups to be total opposites."

"I am thinking Ted could take a platoon size force and work from his base at Colonel Lisco's farm. Most new data suggest the majority of rebels moving eastward." General Lopez looked to General Lauer, "We had no problems when he worked remotely during training."

"Let's meet at 1400."

"Everything else is on schedule," stated General McClinton. "Ann and I are leaving for Virginia in two hours."

"I wish I was going to be here to speak with Colonel Lisco," said General Prost.

"Why don't you send Colonel Lisco to her farm with Ted for a week?" General McClinton pushed his chair back. "With the missions planned and scheduled for next week it would be a good time and place for her to recuperate and take leave. Knowing Colonel Lisco, she will consider it punitive."

***

Colonel Deb waited with Command Sergeant Major Talfoya to be summoned into General Lauer's office. The command sergeant major was constantly shuffling his feet, having a hard time sitting still.

"Jesus, Tommy, why are you so nervous?" Deb chuckled. "You would think we are about to go on trial for murdering someone."

"This isn't a laughing matter colonel. It really could be the end of your career."

"If this is the end of my career for putting an overreaching bureaucrat in his place, then so be it." Deb relaxed back in her chair.

"Was there anything new with Ted?" Tommy asked.

"He had just talked with Nicole at the farm, so he was in a good mood."

"Colonel, the general will see you and the command sergeant major." A soldier stepped in front of her and pointed to the open door.

"I thought Ted was going to be here." Tommy waited to let Deb go in first.

"He is supposed to be," she glanced toward the entrance to the waiting area before stepping through the door into General Lauer's office.

"Sit," General Lauer said gruffly, pointing to two chairs opposite his desk.

The skin on his face was sagging, with light gray patches under both eyes. He stared at Deb and Tommy as they parked themselves into the cushy chairs.

"Colonel," he yelled, "do you understand that military discipline applies to you, as well as others.

"Yes sir," she sat with her back washer board straight. "I do understand it does apply to me."

"So, you do recognize your actions are a reflection on every other member of the United States Army and every other branch of service."

"Yes sir."

"Members of 2nd Brigade were called upon to assist the Department of Homeland Security in transporting civilians out of central Utah. You were supporting them, not in charge of the movements," stated General Lauer.

"Yes sir, I understood our role."

"Do you disagree with the functions Homeland Security was performing?"

"No sir, I wish the situation in our country would never have reached this point, but I understand the purpose of FEMA is necessary and honorable. I have absolutely no problem with the agency."

"Then why in hell did you threaten the administrator from FEMA?" General Lauer spoke loudly and pronounced his words clearly.

"Sir, he was acting in an un-American manner."

"An un-American manner." The general curled his lip. He almost burst out laughing, wishing General McClinton were there to listen in on the interview. "An un-American manner," he repeated.

"Yes sir," Deb's head never moved as she continued, "I often ask soldiers within our ranks to recite the Articles of the Code of Conduct."

"Explain how you were following the Code of Conduct when you threatened the FEMA official?" General Lauer remained calm as he stared at the bruise above the Colonel's eye, to the side of her thick eyebrow.

"The deputy was being unreasonable in his actions to the Americans he was charged with helping. We, in the military, are fighting for the rights of our citizens to live in a free country where officials use common sense when making decisions that affect their lives. I understand the Code of Conduct is for members of the Armed Forces to fulfill their responsibilities and survive captivity with honor. But Article 6 of the Code is a way I justify my role in the Army with the idea of eventually becoming a citizen." She could see Tommy peripherally staring at her with squinted eyes while she prepared to recite the Article. "I will never forget I am an American, fighting for freedom, responsible for my actions, and dedicated to the principles which made my Country free. I will trust in my God and the United States of America."

General Lauer inhaled deeply. He stared at her for a few seconds and then let the breath out loudly.

Tommy opened his mouth as though he were going to speak, before leaning back in the chair. He thought that this meeting must have been like the same one where General Patton was brought before the brass for slapping a soldier more than a hundred years earlier.

"Sir, I take full responsibility for my actions. I will always stand for what makes this country great." Deb held her head high with her chin straight out.

"Well Colonel, you have some very powerful people in your corner," he scoffed. He looked at Tommy and shook his head before looking back at her. "What did the doctor tell you about your physical condition?"

"I'm a little beat up. Nothing that will affect me long term."

"Here's what is going to happen. Tomorrow you will go to your farm on the eastern plains and take leave, for a week."

"Sir, with the enemy advancing I can't leave 2nd Brigade." She glanced at Tommy.

"Not only can you, but you will. The commanders for all three Battalions of 2nd Brigade are capable soldiers." General Lauer smiled, remembering General McClinton stating she would consider the leave as punishment. "The Battalions are repositioning eastward while nonhuman infantry Divisions and aerial squadrons are preparing to confront the enemy."

"Sir, please, with communications being unreliable, I can't be disconnected from them." Deb was sitting on the edge of her chair.

"All communications to this facility are secure. You will have a secure system to communicate with the Battalion headquarters from your farm."

"Sir, am I to travel with the colonel?" Tommy was trying to figure out the strategy of casting Colonel Lisco away from the action.

"Yes," the general moved to the side of his desk and sat on the edge. "Also, Ted is going to join you with a platoon of soldiers from the 99th.

Deb's mouth was partly open. She licked her lips while staring at the general's name plaque on the desk. She folded her arms and sat back in the chair.

The general's aide opened the door and announced, "General Lopez and Colonel Lisco have arrived."

Eastern Colorado Farm

"It's past midnight." Nicole leaned back into the cushions of the sofa, rubbing her temples. "Oh Lord. I don't know what to do with myself right now."

Jacqueline sat on the edge of the couch, unsure of what to say to comfort her sister-in-law. She glanced at Gina who was sitting in a lounge chair. They were exhausted from looking through every nook and cranny in the house. She could only imagine how tired the others were as they searched in the dark and cold.

"I think I will go back out and look," said Irene, barely able to stand.

"No, please Irene, stay here with us." Nicole put up her hand. "Everyone is looking as hard as they can."

"Maybe we should say a prayer." Irene took hold of Nicole's hand and sat down beside her. She prayed for the two children.

Nicole smiled and then sniffled. She did feel better after listening to the plea from the country woman to God to help her granddaughter and Scotty. Jon burst through the door causing her heart to jump. She looked in anticipation for good news.

"Nothing," Jon looked at them and shook his head. "We have looked everywhere."

There was a collective moan from the women.

"Are there any old water wells around here?" Irene gritted her teeth. It was something Ed brought up earlier, but everyone seemed to dismiss. "A lot of old farmsteads have hand dug wells that were never filled after the new water wells were drilled."

"I don't know enough about the property to know," Jon swallowed hard.

"Ted told me this morning that he was planning to take Deb to the hospital on base at Fort Carson." Nicole jumped from the sofa. "We have to get in touch with her and see if there is something we are missing."

"Wait here, I'll try and get hold of her."

Jon was out the door, running to the communication area in the garage before Nicole could say another word.

Nicole's heart was pounding in her chest as she looked at the clock on the kitchen wall. It showed 12:20. She tried to make small talk with the other women. When the clock showed 12:30 she grabbed her coat and rushed out the door.

The utility door to the garage burst open and Jon, Hank, Irving, Bobby and Bill rushed out and sprinted to the south, past the garage. Terrance, Jerry and Breanna dashed through the door behind them before it had a chance to close.

"What happened?" Nicole screamed.

"Colonel Deb said there was an old house south of the property that was torn down before the Liscos owned the property. If there is an abandoned well it would be there," Jerry stopped to inform her. He was carrying a rope. "Come on."

Nicole and Breanna followed Jerry as he shined the flashlight ahead of them. The frozen grass under the snow crackled as they walked in the direction of the voices in the distance. Beams of light were shooting into the frozen air from the rescuers frantically searching. Nicole turned and saw the form of Samantha following behind them in the pitch darkness.

"Here," Bobby yelled, "it's a concrete footer of some sort."

Jon shined his flashlight on the remains of the old house. Plywood on the floor joists was rotted to the point that the dirt below them was visible. "The place didn't have a cellar," he said.

"Be careful," yelled Hank, "it's so dark out here it's impossible to see without a light."

Bobby noticed some pieces of one-by-six wood sticking in the air. He shined his light on a piece of jagged lumber sticking up about twenty centimeters above the snow on the ground. He heard a noise he thought might be from an animal as his light caught the top of the brick well, nearly concealed by dirt, weeds and snow. He leaned precariously over the opening and shined the light down. "They're here," he yelled. The light flickered off the wall of the well where Maddy and Scotty were holding on to each other. "It's ok we are here."

Bill rushed to the edge and looked down. "Are you hurt," he yelled.

"Yes," Maddy's voice was hardly audible.

"Secure the end of the rope and I'll go down." Irving's muscles were noticeable through the down jacket he was wearing. "You will have to pull me up."

Irving tied the rope around his waist and easily shimmied down the side of the brick well while the others held tight to the opposite end. When he reached the bottom, he straddled the two children. He reached down and easily picked Scotty up.

"Grab ahold of my neck, real tight."

Scotty held tight as Irving rappelled up the wall as the others pulled. When he was at the top, he allowed Scotty to place his feet on the ground at the edge of the well, Breanna stepped forward and grabbed him. As soon as he was out of his arms Irving hurried back down. He placed his feet in the soft dirt on each side of Maddy. He easily picked her up.

"Grab my neck."

"I hurted my arm," Maddy sobbed, letting her arm fall limp.

"Ok, I'm going to grab tight, and you lean over my shoulder."

Maddy leaned over his shoulder as he climbed out of the well. Bill reached down and lifted her off his shoulder.

"Let's get them to the house," yelled Hank.

***

Maddy was so tired she could barely keep her eyes open while Julia wrapped her arm. She sat on Bill's lap covered with a blanket with her face buried in his chest. Scotty sat on the exam table with Breanna standing next to him.

"You are going to be ok," Julia secured the wrap and patted her gently on the shoulder. "Nothing broke."

Maddy closed her eyes and dug her head deeper into her dad's chest.

"Keep an eye on them tonight. Tomorrow we can check to make sure I haven't missed anything." Julia wiped her hand with a towel.

"Ok, let's get you two to bed," Nicole placed her hand onto Scotty's shoulder.

Maddy sat forward in Bill's lap. She looked past Nicole.

"Irene," she was so tired her head was wobbling.

"Yes Maddy," Irene moved closer and placed her hand out. Maddy took hold of it.

"Did you make cornbread without me?"

"No, I waited," Irene smiled, her face was pale. "We can make it another time."

"Come on Mom. The sun is going to come up in a couple hours, we might as well try and get some sleep." Breanna placed her hand on the back of Irene's arm. They slowly walked out of the clinic.

"All right you two," Bill scooted Maddy off his lap. He reached for Scotty's hand, "Let's go to bed."

Nicole followed them to the basement. Samantha hesitated at the top of the stairs before proceeding after them.

Jon, Gina, Jacqueline and Hank were so wound up from the activities they decided to remain awake and talk. Jon waited for Nicole to come back upstairs before mentioning that Deb told him, in the hectic call, she was going to arrive that afternoon to spend a week at the farm. Also, Ted and a platoon of soldiers would be arriving with her.

Nicole was taken by surprise of the news that her husband would be coming back to the farm. He must have just found out or he would have told her so in their conversation earlier the previous morning. She sensed the news might mean Ted would be at the farm much more often than they anticipated.

Samantha waited by Maddy's bed, with her hand on Bill's shoulder, as they both watched the little girl fall asleep.

"Can we talk?" Samantha moved back away from the bed.

"Let's go to my room," Bill moved off the bed.

The door to Jessica and her daughter's room was slightly open with a light shining from a table lamp. Bill placed his hand on Samantha's lower back and nudged her quickly past and into his small room. He quietly closed his door.

He collapsed into the soft bed and fell back with his legs dangling over the end. Samantha slithered onto the bed and turned toward him on her side. She placed a hand on his stomach and rested her head on his chest, breathing in the smell of his musky shirt.

"I'm sorry Bill," she whispered, "I never expected Travis to come here."

He remained still as he felt his heart beating next to her head. The warmth of her breath could be felt through his shirt.

"All I want you to do is tell me the truth," he whispered. The walls between his room and Jessica's were thin.

"Ok," she lifted her head slightly and swallowed. "I did sleep with Travis in Los Angeles. But it was a onetime thing, that I regretted immediately after it happened."

He moved up, readjusting his position to cause her to sit on the end of the bed. They turned toward each other. "Was it really just a one-time thing?"

"Yes, I have lied about this incident on so many occasions that I sometimes think it never happened. I was about to lie to you yesterday in the apartment."

He heard the toilet flush, through the thin wall, in Jessica's room.

"Are you in love with Travis?" he lowered his voice.

"No," she noticed he was speaking softly and followed suit by whispering, "it was never love. I was intrigued with him being a pilot."

"Travis said there is a lot of chaos still in town, but the police are gaining more and more control. If you had a chance to go to Littleton to be with your parents, would you go?" Bill asked.

She waited to answer while they listened to Jessica's muffled voice conversing with her daughters on the other side of the wall.

"I don't know," she answered, before turning her head away. "I care for you and Maddy, but with Travis and Sue arriving here, it might make it unbearable for me to stay."

"You are strong enough to handle these circumstances." He placed his hand onto her lap. "If you stay you will have to be straightforward with Travis and his wife."

"I don't want to ruin his marriage. I don't know if he ever told Sue the truth about what happened that night."

"Then ask him," he swallowed hard. "Decide how to handle it from there."

He felt her stop breathing and swallow. She placed her lips to the side of his mouth and asked, "Do you trust me, Bill?"

He flinched, thinking how odd a question to ask at that point of their conversation. He was glad her head was not still positioned over his heart as it thumped his chest. He leaned in and kissed her, keeping his lip next to her as he whispered, "Of course I do."

Watkins, Colorado

Christian hunched his shoulders, trying to avert the piercing wind from drumming the back of his naked neck. After a night of walking, they arrived at a hill west of the small town of Watkins on the eastern plains. Tim and Shira looked over his shoulder as he deliberated over a tattered paper map of Colorado. Waiting nearly two hundred meters to the east, the remnants of his rebels who agreed to leave the city with him, clustered together along a stone wall in a grove of Colorado blue spruce, unnaturally placed as part of the landscape entrance to a housing development.

"It shows the government camp to be right around here." Tim looked to the east in the direction of the small town. "These places are supposed to have thousands of people. How can we not see it?"

"The map shows it being east of the little town," stated Shira, "just north of Interstate 70."

"Let's follow the highway and cross over on the other side of the town." Christian wiped his nose with his fingers and sniffled. "If a camp is there, we have to run into it sooner or later."

"Wonder if it isn't? We can't go on without food." Tim looked to the north at several high-end homes. He pointed. "I think we should check some of those houses for food."

"Take five people with you and check it out."

Tim ran down the hill to the group in the trees. Soon he and five others were advancing in the direction of the large houses. Christian and Shira continued to study the map for the locations of the other encampments. According to the markings on the map, the next camp was nearly 90 kilometers further east in Limon.

A column of eight large buses appeared on the interstate and zipped by them at a high rate of speed. The buses turned off at the interchange from Interstate 70 and Watkins. They continued through the small town and turned onto highway 40 east bound. They disappeared over a hill, before reappearing on a ridge traveling north several kilometers away.

"Those buses have to be taking people to the camp," stated Christian. "This map can't be correct. It's not next to the Interstate."

"We are going to be in trouble if we stay here much longer." Shira thought how small the big man seemed as he slouched in the wind. "You have to make a decision."

Christian shielded his face from the blowing snow while considering the circumstances. There was no sign of human activity in the small town. The area to the east, where the buses traveled, seemed to be rolling hills of fallow fields, with kilometers of emptiness. The homes to the north where Tim was scouting were the best option for the group in the immediate future.

"Christian," Shira yelled from nearly three meters away with large flakes of snow falling between them. "What are we doing? Without food and water, we can't stay here any longer."

"We are going to that house." He pointed at the first house in the development.

The group of insurrectionists covered the entire gravel road as they walked up a slight incline in the direction of the large home. The front door flew open and a man of about fifty stepped out onto the small porch. He held his hand up in a greeting manner.

"Hello, can I help you?" his voice was high pitched and soft.

"We are trying to find the government camp," Christian spoke with a non-threatening tone. He stepped closer to the porch.

"It's at the old airport northeast of here." The man looked at the large mass of rebels gathered across his driveway and on his snow-covered lawn, all shouldering rifles.

"How far away is that?" asked Shira, moving next to Christian.

"Oh gosh, I'd say between ten and fifteen kilometers." He was forcing a smile.

Christian let out a heavy breath. He could see movement through the partially opened door inside the house. "Here comes Tim," resonated a voice, causing Christian to turn and step away. The man moved back inside his house and shut the door.

Christian rambled down the driveway, past his group, in the direction of Tim who was jogging, all alone.

"You aren't going to believe this." Tim bent his neck to look up at Christian as he leaned over at his waist to catch his breath. "There is a farm on the outskirts of this development being used by Angela Wolf as her base. She said she will give us a place to stay."

"Angela, her area is Aurora and eastern Denver," stated Christian. "I'm surprised she would be out this far.

"She has had this base for a long time," said Tim. "It's just over the crest of this hill.

Christian was not overly enthused about interacting with Angela. Of all the rebels in the Denver metropolitan area, she was by far the most radicalized. She was the offspring of long enduring anarchists who came from California about five years earlier to organize and stabilize the homegrown groups in Colorado.

***

Smoke was rising from the chimney sitting on the sharply pitched roof of the small farmhouse. Snow catching on the rooftop gave the place a serene aura. The round roof of a barn was visible over the top of three large Quonset buildings, spaced about thirty meters apart from one another, north of the house.

Several people watched from a vantage point at the first Quonset as the mass of new rebels arrived at the property. A small woman with very thick hips, who Christian recognized as Angela Wolf, was waiting on the small concrete porch, right outside the door of the main house. She motioned with her arm when she saw him.

"Christian, come inside, Tim can help your people get settled," she yelled loudly.

Shira followed behind, through a small hall and into the kitchen. Sitting at a table were two men wearing black biker jackets and a woman dressed in a green synthetically made parka jacket. There were four empty coffee cups on the table.

"This is Christian and…." Angela pointed at Shira.

"Shira." Shira scrutinized the lady who was dressed in a dark blue blazer over a tan turtleneck sweater. She had shoulder length sandy colored hair that was receding at the hairline. Her tan pants were stretched to the limit by her large legs which were out of proportion to her small upper body. The image she portrayed was far more retro than any of the other women rebels she had come across.

"Why are you here?" Angela remained standing, not offering a place for the two to sit.

"We need food."

"Is it why you left the city?"

"For the most part." Christian looked past the table to the small living room. There was an old piano resting on worn carpet, but no indication of others in the house.

"Why didn't you blend in at the shelters?"

"We tried, we stuck out like a sore thumb, and they called the authorities on us." Christian noticed the three sitting at the table were much older than Angela.

"You have to go in small groups?" Angela placed her hand on the back of a chair but continued to stand. "None of this is anything we didn't anticipate. You were forewarned that the authorities in the cities would fight us."

"I never realized how much of a danger the foreign fighters would be." Melting water was dripping from his shoulders onto the linoleum floor. "They seem more threatening than the police or Military."

Angela twisted to look at her three friends. She turned back to make eye contact with Christian, intertwined her fingers and lowered her hands. One of the men rose from his chair, towering over her.

"What in the hell do you think this is?" Angela scoffed. "Without the foreign revolutionaries we would still be whining and complaining to a group of hypocritical politicians and elite managers of corporations. Blindly following them while they grew richer, and we simply tried to exist."

"What's our place going to be when everything is settled?" Christian raised his voice, "What do you think your place will be in a new world."

"To build a place where we all count and have an opportunity to reach our full potential," she never faltered in her reply.

"I'm not seeing any cooperation with the foreigners. They don't have any inclination of working together with us." Christian felt water drip on the back of his hand from the sleeve of his coat. "What will be the difference when all of this is over. Will they expect us to follow their orders?"

"The Army chased us out of the houses we were staying in," interjected Shira, crowding closer to Christian.

"I know you, Christian, you are bright." Angela disregarded Shira. "This is not just disruption of life in Colorado. Chaos is taking place over the entire world. When we win there will be a place for all of us at the table."

"I want to ask you straight out Angela. Have you got an agreement with the foreign insurgents that will sell all of us out?"

"Christian," she swallowed hard and glanced at the large man at her shoulder. "I don't have to discuss this with you right now."

The second large man pushed his chair back and stood. He was nearly as large as the man standing.

Christian pressed his lips together, wetting them as he took in a deep breath through his nose. He stared at a Howard Miller wrought-iron pendulum clock with black Roman numerals hanging on the wall next to the door going into the living room. The house had the same furnishings from forty years ago. He was tired and hungry and needed time to think before making any more decisions.

"Can we stay here," he asked.

"One night," Angela turned her back and sat in the

chair. She looked across the table to the old lady who seemed completely detached from the conversation. “Then you need to prepare to go to Colorado Springs and complete the duties you agreed to when you began receiving money from the foreigners.”

“They plan to attack NORAD. You know as well as we do it is an underground fortress. There is no way we can invade the place successfully.” He could see the old lady breathing easy as she listened while he spoke to the back of Angela’s head. “We are going east from here tomorrow.”

After a moment of silence with no discussion from Angela, Christian and Shira turned and were out the door into the darkness.

Eastern Colorado Farm

Tommy and Deb caught a ride to the farm with Ted and the Platoon from the 99th. Ted had met Command Sergeant Major Talfoya on several occasions, but never really got to know him. The short ride from Fort Carson made it apparent to Ted that his sister and Tommy were more than soldiers to one another. It gave him a peaceful feeling knowing Deb had someone completely devoted to her well-being. Jon radioed earlier, before they left the base, to inform them that Maddy had been found.

Nicole and Bill were up by ten o'clock, but Maddy slept until noon. Although Maddy's arm was sore, she was managing ordinary tasks without any problems. She sat with Nicole on the porch watching the road in anticipation of the convoy. The sun was falling quickly when the rumble of trucks emanated from the distance.

"Here they come," yelled Nicole, pointing to the six vehicles moving quickly down the driveway. They rushed to the front gate where Nicole placed her hand over Maddy's chest to keep her from running in front of the procession.

The moment the Humvee transporting Deb came to a stop, she was out the door. "That is just spectacular." She motioned toward the tower before turning to the apartment where the large silhouettes of Jason and Dave Jenson were visible placing outdoor lights next to an entry door. "They have almost finished the outside of the apartments."

"Wow, I never imagined your farm would be like

this." Tommy inspected the surroundings as he joined her on the wet driveway.

Ted scanned the property for Nicole as everyone began to gather around the convoy. Out of nowhere Maddy sprinted at full speed right toward him. He leaned down and she ran into his arms. He held her at arms-length and surveyed the wrap on her arm.

"What is this?" he put her tiny wrist in his hand.

She bobbed her head up and down and declared, "I fell into a well."

"I heard about that, but I didn't know you hurt your arm." Ted felt Nicole's hand on his shoulder. He rose and placed a hand around her waist and lifted her. He gave her a quick kiss on the lips. "You will have to catch me up on all the action that happened here yesterday."

"It was something I hope we never have to go through again," stated Bill, picking Maddy up so she was eye level with Ted. Samantha moved next to him.

Ted noticed the 57 Chevy sitting in front of the garage with frosted windows and a layer of snow on the roof. "Is Travis here?"

"Yeah, he along with his wife and two children." Bill left it there. "How long will you be here?"

"My duties keep changing, so I suppose it all depends on what happens over the next week," stated Ted. "With the foreign insurgents creating more strongholds east of the city, there is a possibility of using the farm as a base."

Deb took in a deep breath when she noticed Breanna and Irene walking slowly in her direction. By the time Irene arrived at her side, the entire Jacoby family were standing next to her.

"Were you able to find the kids?" Irene asked with a raspy voice. She had her hands clasped together as if in prayer.

"I did," Deb glanced at Tommy. "They were placed on a bus the night before last outside of Beaver, headed to the Denver area."

"Do they know we are here?" Breanna asked with moistness showing in her eyes.

"Seth has a map with directions to the farm." Deb felt blood rushing to her head.

"Are you hurt?" Irene noticed she was dragging her leg.

"I took some shrapnel in my calf during fighting west of Parowan." She glanced at Jon and Hank, "It's a superficial wound."

"Is there a lot of destruction around our place?" Aaron asked.

"I don't know if you heard but the citizens of Utah have been relocated," Deb turned to Irene and stared directly into her eyes. "Irene, I need to be straightforward with you. Your farmhouse was destroyed. I witnessed it myself as I was being evacuated from the area."

"Oh God," yelled Breanna.

Irene clenched her teeth, then sighed. She reached over and placed a hand on Ed's shoulder.

"We have to look on the bright side Mom." Breanna rubbed the back of Irene's neck. "The kids are safe."

"I know this news is devastating," Deb stepped closer to Tommy. "But war is occurring in the region around your ranch and the combat is only going to escalate. I'm glad you and your family fled the area when you did."

Irene looked at Ted.

"Is there a way we can go to the camp in the city and pick up the kids?" Breanna asked.

"We aren't sure where they ended up." Deb twisted

her neck to look at Tommy. "Do you know?

"All I heard was that Homeland Security was opening several encampments at golf courses and shopping malls from Denver, north to Casper. The people evacuated from the Beaver location were transported to one of those camps," Tommy answered. "Most will be vetted and sent east."

"Do you know what is happening in the cities east of here?" Irving asked.

"There is chaos, with different amounts of severity, occurring in most cities across the country. But there are some localities that have experienced little or no affect from the insurgents. Northern Ohio, much of the area around the Shenandoah Valley, most of Missouri and Arkansas have hardly been impacted." "Tommy answered, glancing at Deb. "I learned most of this before you arrived at the transfer location in Beaver."

"Ted, is there anything you can do to find out where they transported the kids?" Irene asked. "Can you get in touch with the FEMA people?"

"I'll see what I can do tomorrow. I can speak with Colonel Myer and see if she has any suggestions about locating Seth and the others. With the large number of people being processed, it will take time to have updated records," Ted answered.

"I want to get settled in," said Deb. "Is there an empty room ready for Tommy in the apartment."

"There is, but we will need to move a bed," stated Bill. "The restroom isn't finished yet so he will have to use one in the main house or garage."

"You can use the one in my room," Deb looked at Tommy.

"Everyone looks so tired," stated Nicole. "Why don't

we all get settled and meet in the living room later."

***

With the three Battalions from 2nd Brigade located on the western slope of the Rocky Mountains it was a high priority for Deb to keep in contact and follow their movements in real time. Tommy was the one who communicated almost hourly with the commanders, and then relayed all activities to her. His diligence allowed her to relax and enjoy the farm and her family.

Imagining people together talking and having fun was a huge part in her aspirations when she first decided to build the haven. It was meant to be much more than a fortification for protection during the war she hoped would never happen. She remembered telling her father, nearly two months before he passed, about her ambitions of turning the farm into a special place to survive an attack or disaster should it ever occur. He told her that if anyone could find paradise amidst the chaos, it would be her.

She was in front of the fireplace mantle staring at the picture of her grandfather standing outside a stone building in Dattenburg, Germany. She took a sip of scotch as she felt Tommy brush her shoulder.

"You look like you are lost in thought," Tommy moved right in front of her. The living room was packed with people.

"Just thinking," Deb smiled at him. "I really like seeing my family safe and together."

"If you don't mind, I'm going to take a quick shower in your room and then retire for the night."

"Of course," she placed her hand on the side of his arm. "I'm going to go to bed early too."

She had an extraordinary amount of saliva build up in her mouth as she watched him walk away. Just as she was taking the final swallow from her drink, Jacqueline moved to her side.

"Are you doing ok?" Jacqueline noticed the dark bruising around the raspberry to the side of her head.

"I'm doing great," Deb assured her.

"Thank you, Deb."

"You know Jacqueline, this is everything I envisioned when I began preparing the farm."

"I wish we were back home with our boring lives," Jacqueline took in a deep breath. "But, since we can't, I thank God, you gave us this place."

"Thank you for saying that," Deb gazed into her eyes and smiled. "I am really tired. I think I will go to bed early."

"Of course, Let me take your glass." Jacqueline took the glass and watched as Deb limped her way thru the crowd and down the hallway to her bedroom.

The door to the bathroom was open with steam filling the bedroom. Tommy's clothes were neatly folded and placed on the chair in the corner of the room. His shoes were sitting together, tucked under the chair.

Deb went to her dresser and opened a drawer. A white, satin negligee sat on top of her warmer nightgowns. She hesitated for a moment before removing her clothes and slipping on the negligee. The water in the shower quieted as she pulled the comforter from the bed.

Tommy was momentarily startled when he came to the door of the bathroom with a white towel wrapped around his waist. A large smile filled his bronze face when he saw Deb slinking at the edge of the bed dressed in the short nighty with her large breasts barely concealed by the fabric.

She paused before moving closer, never bringing her eyes above his muscular chest. He placed his thumbs to the edge of the towel and released it. She tried to catch her breath as he moved his left arm to allow her to embrace him. His muscular back felt hard as steel as he slowly walked her back to the bed.

Once on the bed she rolled over on top of him and sat up. She reached down and pulled the negligee over her head. Tommy completely relaxed as they made love.

Watkins Colorado

The inside of the Quonset was ice cold with no heat source, making for a restless night. Dinner the previous night was a bowl of rice with cinnamon and sugar. Breakfast was a small bowl of oatmeal. There were only twenty-five rebels from Angela's force housed at the farm, far fewer than anticipated when they arrived the night before.

Angela saying, she expected he and his rebels to honor their duties because they had been paid by the insurrectionists over the past several years, triggered Christian to contemplate his role in the revolution. The further he analyzed the future of his rebels, in the scheme of things, at the end of the war, no matter who won, he could configure no other outcome than his fighters being discarded, arrested or killed. Something Coach Lisco tried to beat into his head when he helped the teacher and his family escape from the city.

"I was talking to Angela's people last night," said Tim. "There were hundreds of foreign fighters at this location yesterday. Apparently with all the military activity in the city they are moving eastward."

"Just like we are," Shira shivered as she took a bite of oatmeal. She noticed Christian turn away after hearing Tim mention that many foreign fighters were recently at the location.

"Apparently, there are hundreds of thousands of new people being evacuated from the west." Tim put the empty bowl of rolled oats on the concrete floor. He wanted to share all the information he gleaned from the other rebels. "All the golf courses in the city are being used as camps for the evacuees."

"It seems the Military is more focused on the south side of the city. Maybe it's because Fort Carson is closer." Shira focused on Christian standing in a trance, staring out the open door of the building, paying no attention to the conversation. She moved next to him and asked, "What's wrong?"

"I'm thinking we are a bunch of fools," Christian spoke loudly. "What in the world are we thinking, letting someone like Angela Wolf decide our destiny?"

"She's been a leader of the movement for years. What's different now?" Shira asked.

"She has made a different deal with these people than we have. I'm not exactly sure what, but she has a much better relationship with them than we do."

"Most everything that has happened so far is what we were told would occur," Shira spoke confidently. "She isn't coming up with anything new."

"You and I are always implying how intelligent we are." Christian looked at her choppy Bob haircut. "But if we are so damn smart, why are we freezing our asses off, eating stale oatmeal and being commanded to follow orders as if we haven't a living brain cell in our heads?"

"You are overthinking all of this."

"The hell I am, we are pawns in this insurgency." The skin on his large forehead creased as he stood up tall and narrowed his eyes. "We have been betrayed."

"Christian, what are we planning to do?" Tim's hands were shaking as he spoke.

"Shira, are you with me?" Christian yelled, aggressively placing his face close enough in front of hers for his breath to hit her eyes.

"One hundred percent," she yelled.

"We are taking all the food, water and clothing we can carry, and getting as far away from these people as possible." Christian let out a breath of relief. "Tim, start packing the supplies. let everyone know that the plan is to leave in an hour."

"What if Angela's rebels try to stop us?" Tim asked.

"We outnumber them. Make it clear to them not to interfere." He stepped out the Quonset door into the snow and glanced back. "Shira, let's have another talk with Angela and that big son of a bitch who tried to intimidate us last night."

They marched through the snow, onto the concrete porch and opened the unlocked door. Christian rushed in first, past the hall and into the kitchen. The large man who stood up and the woman from the previous night, along with Angela were sitting at the table. All three of them jerked their heads and watched as Christian moved right over the top of Angela.

"What is wrong with you?" Angela yelled, reaching her arm up to put pressure on the rifle as Christian pinned her head.

The big man rose from his chair. Christian popped him on the nose with the butt of the rifle. He dropped like a fly to the floor. The old woman pulled her hands up and held them slightly above the table. She sat calmly and watched, making no attempt to help Angela.

"Alright, alright," moaned Angela, unable to move as Christian used his knee to push her chair tight to the table. "Why are you doing this?"

"Keep an eye on the living room." Christian eased up on the pressure from his knee as he motioned to Shira with his head. "The other guy is somewhere in there."

The man on the linoleum gasped but remained on the floor.

"You are double crossing us," Christian nudged the chair with his thigh. "There is no way all the revolutionaries are part of the grand scheme when the war is over. I think we will be disposed of at the end."

"That's not true," her voice cracked.

"I don't care what kind of deal you made with the foreigners. But I want you to know we are on to you and will never be used as your pawns again."

"Christian," Shira motioned toward the door to the living room. "There is someone in there."

"Move back," Christian leveled his AK-47 toward the door as Shira stepped back, shielding herself behind Christian's large body just as a shirtless man, holding a pistol with both hands, rushed into the room. He positioned himself right under the kitchen clock.

Angela raised up from the chair with her powerful legs, pushing Christian's rifle into the air. The shirtless man fired his pistol trying to pick off Christian over the top of Angela. The bullet flew well over their heads. Shira fired four rapid shots into his chest. Christian pushed Angela hard to the opposite side of the table.

"We are going to leave now." He leveled his rifle squarely at the head of Angela. "If you take a shot at any of my people when we leave, we will burn this place to the ground."

"Wait Christian, I have to know this for my own sanity." Shira pointed her pistol at the lady sitting at the table. The woman's pale face was smooth with deep wrinkles meandering from the corners of her eyes. "Tell us what the plans are for all the homegrown rebels if the

Americans lose this war?"

The woman took in several shallow breaths and folded her arms across her chest. "None of you will survive," she answered matter-of-factly, staring straight at Shira.

"Is she your daughter?" Shira motioned with the pistol in the direction of Angela as she focused her eyes on the older woman.

She shrugged her skinny shoulders, leaned back in the chair and said, "You are making the correct decision. Let's just leave it at that."

They backed out of front door. Tim and the others were waiting. The sky was bright blue as they began to walk through the snow down the driveway.

Eastern Colorado farm

The forty-person platoon positioned tents in the field northeast of the apartment. Bivouacs used for living quarters were placed the night before but there was still work for the mess tent and communications.

Corporal Mary Pint took a liking to the colonel's granddaughter and offered to have Maddy work with her to supervise the digging of a trench from the garage to the communication tent. Having the platoon at the farm was a perfect time to give Maddy a chance to learn the discipline and work ethic of the soldiers.

"Just remember you have an eight-year-old in your presence." Ted stood alongside Corporal Pint, addressing Private Tiger and Private Sinclair while they stood at attention with picks in their hands, preparing to break the frozen dirt.

"Yes sir," both men barked at the same time, holding their chests out in front of them.

"Corporal, are you good with having Maddy follow you?" Ted stared at the corporal's chubby cheeks with strands of brown hair escaping from under her cap while she stood at attention. She didn't look to be a day over fourteen.

"Yes sir, it will be a pleasure having her help," she showed her large front teeth as she smiled.

"You need to listen to everything the corporal tells you." Ted placed a hand on Maddy's shoulder. She pulled away while glancing at Corporal Pint.

"Grandpa," she tipped her head. "Remember…."

"You are not a baby," Ted smiled and looked at the corporal. "If you need me to take her at any time I will understand.

"I'm sure that won't be necessary, sir. Come on Maddy let's make sure this trench is being dug correctly."

Ted observed for a moment while Maddy joined the soldiers as they began digging. He spotted Deb and Tommy wandering from the concrete tower in the direction of Hank and Jon, who were talking to Jason Jensen at the far end of the apartment.

Jason was towering over the others as Deb commended him on his work with the apartment. Tommy seemed to be getting along exceptionally well with Hank and Jon.

"Ted, we were just discussing what we think should be the next project as soon as Jason finishes the apartment," Deb was relaxed and smiling.

"You are thinking of building more?" Ted grinned at Jon and Hank.

"A community building to meet, where we could watch films and play games. It would relieve all the congestion at the main house. We could build it in the opening on the east side of the house." Deb turned to Tommy, "I want the farm to be more than just a place to survive. As long as people live here it should be treated as a home."

"We have some lumber left but not nearly enough to build the kind of structure you are talking about," stated Jason. "I can come up with a design and then do some figuring on how much more we will need."

"We also need to check how much cement would be needed to pour the foundation. I'll run this by Bill this evening," said Deb.

"Where would you get the lumber?" Hank asked.

"We could go into Limon. I bought so much lumber from Ben Stewart at the lumber yard over the years, I'm sure if he has it, he will sell it to us. The guy is a go getter, who drilled the water wells, put in the septic tank and helped with the wind cones on the farm."

"I ran into the sheriff the other day," stated Jon.

"Old Bob Wilkins, he's a pretty good fella. Did you tell him about Clint and Peg?"

"He seemed pretty upset."

"Bob and his wife Judy played cards with the Brown's, so I imagine it was hard news to take."

"I would think all the lumber and other supplies would be gone by now. What are you thinking Deb?" Jon asked. "Are you planning on going to Limon and check?"

"Yeah, even if the lumber is gone, it won't hurt to keep in touch with the locals. I know these people well enough that they will give me straight answers about what is happening around here." Deb looked at Tommy, who was looking back at her with a smile on his face. "Let's go in the morning."

Nicole walked up and placed her hand on Ted's lower back and said, "We are going to have the kids do some art projects. Could you have Maddy come inside in about thirty minutes?"

"I'll go get her now."

Private Tiger leaned on the pick as Corporal Pint, with Maddy at her side, secured a string line pulled from the electrical box at the garage. Private Sinclair was helping a sergeant near the communication tent.

"How is everything going?" Ted asked, moving between Maddy and Corporal Pint.

"Fine sir," stated the corporal, smiling hard enough

to have her pink cheeks puff out. "Maddy and I have kept things going pretty well and we are almost ready to start pulling lines."

"If the f-ing sergeant over there would get his head out of his a-s-s, we'd have had this thing done a long time ago," Maddy took in a deep breath and nodded toward the men digging near the tents.

Ted's jaw dropped. Corporal Pint rose to full attention with her smile turning into clenched teeth. Private Tiger began to slowly walk away.

"Grandpa, this ground is hard as h-e-l-l."

"Private Tiger," Ted yelled. "Have you been using inappropriate language in front of my granddaughter?"

"Sir," Private Tiger stopped and did an about-face. He stood at attention, slightly hunched over, with his shirt half out from his pants. "I might have inadvertently said some words I now regret to have used. I never realized your granddaughter was such a good speller."

"The latrines are now your responsibility," Ted yelled. "If I go inside one of them at any time during our stay, they better smell like a fresh pine tree blowing in the breeze. Do you understand me soldier?"

"Yes sir."

"Maddy," he motioned to her, then turned to Corporal Pint. "As you were Corporal, continue with your work.

"Yes sir," she ran in the direction of the sergeant.

Maddy came to him as he knelt on one knee. He held out his hand. She put her small hand in his.

"Those words you used are really, really bad." He thought for a moment with her looking at him with tears developing in her eyes. "I'm not mad at you. You didn't know they were bad. If your grandma heard you say them, she would be so mad at you, and even more mad at me."

"I'm sorry."

"We have to be careful using words we don't know, even if we are spelling them."

"Ok."

Ted placed his hand on her cheek.

"Grandpa, is the latrine a bathroom?"

"Yes."

"Don't make Private Tiger clean the latrine," she lowered her chin. "He and Corporal Pint are really nice."

"He'll only have to clean them his share of the time," Ted winked at her. "I just wanted to let him know not to use bad words around you."

Maddy smiled and placed her arms around his neck.

"Your grandma wants you to go inside to work on art projects." Ted let her slide off his chest and rose to his feet. "We'll forget about using the bad words. Deal?"

"Deal."

***

One of Deb's objectives was becoming better acquainted with Bobby. Being partners with Bill in the farm, as well as other businesses, created a special bond with her oldest nephew. Before the war started, she made plans to spend an extra week in Colorado, after attending the state championship football game, to discuss with Bobby some business opportunities for him during his time in college. Although Bill was partners with her on certain endeavors, making him wealthy in his own right, her two nephews were equal beneficiaries of all her possessions.

Bobby spent much of his time on the highest floor of the tower with Emilee, Sherry, Caroline and Dave. They furnished the observation area with several chairs. A solar heater kept the room warm enough to keep the shutters open during the coldest night.

"We have hot cocoa," Bobby held up two thermoses.

Caroline and Sherry placed two chairs about a meter from the window and situated the remaining chairs in a semi-circle around the two.

Tommy glanced out the window onto the moon covered landscape. He noticed two grooves about five centimeters deep in the block at the bottom of the window to be used to rest the barrel of a rifle. The warmth radiating from the heater was comfortable, countering the cold air blowing lightly thru the window. He sat down in the chair next to Deb.

Deb watched Emilee as she held the two cups for Bobby to pour the hot chocolate. Her beautiful facial features blossomed as she smiled at her nephew and giggled while he poured the hot chocolate. Her approach was one of appreciating the small things in life that could have only come from experiencing the hardest of times.

"We helped build this," Emilee stated, handing the steaming cups of cocoa to Tommy and Deb. "I have never worked so hard in my life."

"You did?" Deb was surprised. Jon bragged endlessly about Harold's hard work but never mentioned his helpers.

"Oh yeah, Bobby and I carried block, mortar and grout while Sherry mixed the cement," stated Emilee.

"I actually miss the workout from lifting the bags of cement." Sherry showed her white teeth as she smiled.

"I'll admit it was much harder than lifting weights during football," stated Bobby, smiling. "How are you doing Aunt Deb. Everyone around here was really worried about you when the explosion happened during your conference call."

"I'm doing good," she glanced at Tommy.

"Do you two work together?" Sherry leaned forward as she asked. "What is a Command Sergeant?"

Deb looked at Sherry with her blond hair ruffled, giving her a wild appearance. Jon was impressed with the young woman who he said was a true soldier at heart. Her hardened character was different from Emilee, although it was obvious, she too never had an easy life. She was ready to fight.

"I'm a Command Sergeant Major. I give Colonel Lisco feedback and perspective on issues and concerns she faces while commanding the 2nd Brigade." Tommy also noticed the fighting spirit in the young woman.

"Colonel Lisco is going to help me and Caroline get to basic training." Sherry remarked, "We have already joined but are having difficulty finding out where to go."

"Everything is in total chaos right now with everyone displaced. It's hard to locate individuals to give them specific orders." Tommy looked at Deb, "I'll speak with Ted. I'm sure we can have you an order to report and transportation before we leave."

"Why are you so adamant about joining the Army?" Deb had been briefed by Hank about the past Sherry had with the homegrown rebel group.

"They lied."

"Who lied?" Deb asked.

"The foreigners who paid us," Sherry glanced at Bobby. "They recruited us hard in high school and I fell for their lies. These people are beyond ruthless."

"How much did they pay you?"

"I got $2400.00 a month."

"Right out of high school?"

"Payments actually started during the spring of my senior year."

"Bobby, did they try to recruit you too?" Deb asked.

"Our sophomore year, and a little bit our junior year, we were aware of the gangs offering kids money." Bobby glanced at Emilee and then at Dave. "We never heard of anyone this year being contacted. There was a buzz about the FBI cracking down on the gangs."

"There were a few kids approached," Emilee swallowed as she stared at Bobby.

"Coach Lisco talked a lot about not being influenced by the recruiters," stated Dave. "He and his assistants did a good job of warning about the danger."

"I wish I would have listened to the counselors at school," said Sherry. "We were trained with weapons but never expected we would need to use them. When the war started to take over the city, we were asked to kill people in our neighborhoods."

"Did you?" Deb asked.

"Never, I didn't fire my weapon." Tears were welling up in her eyes. "I stayed back and tried to find a way to escape the situation while the others fought the police. The foreigners who paid us were in total control of our orders. I am positive if we didn't follow their commands, we would all be dead."

Emilee was sitting on the edge of her chair. She was having a hard time catching her breath as she listened to Sherry speak about the group of pawns her father was leading, something they had kept out of previous conversations.

"Did my dad shoot at the police?" Emilee asked.

"No, none of the six of us who rode the bikes to the farm shot anyone," Sherry declared. "It was something we discussed on our way here."

"Why did he leave to go back?" Emilee was asking the question to not only understand Christian, but her mother also.

"Probably because his mantra has always been live free or die. He couldn't fathom conforming to working with everyone at the farm." Sherry twisted her head to look into Emilee's eyes. "He's not an evil person."

Although having all of Bobby's friends present was stifling her getting to speak with him about the future, Deb found the conversation intriguing. After the discussion with the foreign rebel in Grand Junction she was well-aware of the tactics employed by the insurgents against the homegrown revolutionaries. Sherry's rendition of her experience with the enemy was heartening in that it gave hope for the many young people already caught up in the trap set by them to fight against their own country.

"Bobby," Deb changed the subject, "how are you adapting?"

"Everything is different, especially not having electronics. But when I really think about it, most of the time was communicating with Emilee. Now we are always together." Bobby looked to Dave, "Not having football is a bummer."

"We only had one game left anyway," stated Dave.

"Aunt Deb, is this war going to last a long time?"

Deb turned to Tommy.

"It's not going to be resolved quickly," answered Tommy. "There is constant fighting at the southern border but neither side is advancing or retreating. We are waiting to figure the best way to root them out of the cities in Mexico. I believe they are biding their time while the entrenched warriors within our borders continue to disrupt."

"We are going to be eighteen here shortly," Dave looked at Bobby and Emilee, "so, we most likely will be in the fight."

"Yes," Deb replied. Captain Jensen in communication came to her mind as she looked at Dave dwarfing the small chair, he was sitting in. "It's not going to be over quickly."

"What about supplies and food?" Bobby was worried about the others on the farm. "There isn't enough to last past spring."

"It is why everyone needs to realize they have to adapt and replenish," stated Deb. "I plan to go into Limon tomorrow morning and see about getting more supplies to help with the greenhouse. It was the one part of the farm I was still working on."

"Dad said you are going to get some more lumber so we can build a recreational building," said Dave.

"I'm going the first thing in the morning to check if there is any to buy."

"Thank you, Colonel, for doing all this," said Dave.

"Yes, thanks. I would be dead right now if your place wasn't here," Caroline professed.

Deb felt blood rush to her head as she listened to Bobby's friends take turns in thanking her for creating the farm. Their acknowledgement of her vision was much more significant to her than anyone of them would have imagined. They were young and supposedly naïve to the ways of the world, but they were all intelligent enough to recognize opportunity. Not only identify it but were willing to fight for it.

Deb realized she would need to find a different time

and place to speak with Bobby about his inheritance. She decided to sit back and relax while enjoying the company of the young people and Tommy. Sitting in the block tower that she dreamt about building for many years, now allotted her the chance to witness the farm as she imagined it would be. All the hard decisions and expenditures she made over the years were well worth the effort.

Agate, Colorado

Christian and his rebel followers were exhausted from the long, cold march across the plains to Limon. They traveled all day and thru the night, taking only short pauses to sleep as they walked parallel with Interstate 70. They made a large swath around the small towns on the journey in order to avoid any form of conflict. Each hill they crested brought disappointment of only more pasture and unplanted fields as far as the eye could see. The morning sun was shining into their eyes as they came upon a small town.

The settlement was smaller than the others they passed, yet it was bustling with people. Christian directed the group to move in a southernly direction away from the town.

After traveling for about fifteen minutes Tim noticed people on the rim of a hill hardly noticeable in the bright sun. He looked thru the binoculars at the figures.

"Oh crap," he handed the binoculars to Christian, "look."

Christian viewed the group of approximately fifteen fighters, all dressed in black, carrying rifles. He directed the field glasses slightly to the right and further back where he focused in on an accumulation of enough soldiers to cover a field. Three Jeep Wranglers were positioned on the backside of the militia of insurgents.

"We have to move quickly," Christian lowered the binoculars. "They have an army."

"Who are they?" Shira asked.

"Foreign rebels," Christian stated. "I bet Angela informed them of our decision to leave. I never should have mentioned we were going east."

"I'll go talk with them," Shira took a step.

"No, let's go around and see if they follow." Christian waved for everyone to start walking.

As they trekked in a south easterly direction, the group of dissidents stalked, moving parallel with them. After traveling nearly three kilometers, they were edging closer to the three Jeep Wranglers slowly moving along the road with the large army following behind.

"Stop," Christian held up his hand. They were in a flat snow-covered field with no gullies or hills. He gazed at the insurgents. "There must be three hundred of them. They aren't going to let us pass without a confrontation."

"Now do you want me to go and talk with them?" Shira asked.

"I'll go," Tim took two steps in the direction of the road.

"Wait," Christian yelled. "Maybe we should move west, out of this area, where they can't use the road to follow. We need to be in a better location for cover should this escalate."

"If we run now, they will attack us." Tim was moving as he spoke. "I'll get a feel as to what they want."

"Tell them we are still on the same side."

Tim nodded and began jogging over the crusted snow.

Christian moved back to his assemblage, who were huddled together.

"Spread out," he motioned with his hands to direct some of them to move to the south. He pulled his AK-47 off his shoulder, knowing they were too far away for their weapons to be efficient. "Prepare your weapons."

"Don't be confrontational," Shira held up a hand. "Give Tim a chance to let them know we are not a threat."

The sun was high enough to no longer be a factor in watching the movements of the large army of foreign insurgents as they formed a line, shoulder to shoulder, along the road, stretching out on both sides of the Jeeps. All of them held their weapons leveled toward the field of homegrown rebels.

Tim was about fifty meters from the Jeeps when he stopped jogging and began walking with his right hand up in the air. Several loud pops materialized simultaneously with Tim jerking to the left and then falling face first into the field.

Christian grabbed the collar of Shira's coat and pulled her back. They fell into the snow with the sound of bullets whizzing all around them. He turned on his stomach and began returning fire until the magazine was emptied. Bullets were hitting close enough in front of him to have pellets of frozen ground and snow splatter his face. Whatever weapons they were using had a better range than those of the AK-47.

"We can't stay here," he yelled. The sound from the weapons firing behind him drowned out his warning.

"There is no place to go," screamed Shira.

"We have to run," he yelled.

They crawled to the edge of the skirmish line his followers were fighting from. He hesitated as he looked down the long row where many of them were slumped over dead, with only about a quarter of his people still shooting. Shira's mouth was wide open while she stared at their friends. He grabbed her coat at the shoulder and pulled.

"Run, get out of here," he yelled as loud as he could.

With no cover to fight from, he dashed past the decimated fighters from his group. Bullets struck the ground with a zing and hit his friends with a thud as they tried to retreat with him.

Shira sprinted step for step with him as they ran more than two kilometers before stopping and looking back. None of his rebels were following.

Still breathing heavily, she removed the binoculars from her backpack and raised them to her eyes. In the distance a lone person was jogging across the field.

"Someone's coming," she yelled.

Christian was slightly bent at the waist as he caught his breath. He ejected the magazine to his AK and replaced it with a full one.

"We have to keep moving." He glanced to the west where the sun was reflecting off the hard snow covering the flat prairie land. To the south, he could see hilly terrain with bushes popping out of the landscape. "This way," he said.

Jogging until they came to a ravine where they stopped next to a Four wing Saltbush shrub sticking nearly a meter up from the ground. Several more shrubs dotted the area surrounding the small gulley. The man behind them in chase was still nearly seven hundred meters away, relentlessly following their tracks. He was slowly catching up.

Christian slid into the gully with Shira jumping in behind him. It was less than a meter deep but low enough to shield them from the man.

"I'm going to try and surprise him." He pointed to a bush nearly twenty meters nearer to the pursuer. "When he gets close enough don't show yourself until you hear me fire."

Shira nodded her head in agreement as she set the rifle and aimed. Christian belly crawled to the shrub and hid with his rifle leveled at the rebel. The man stopped when he was two hundred meters out and surveyed the area.

When the pursuer hesitated, Shira slid into the ditch, completely out of sight. Christian watched him thru the branches of the dense plant. The man waited for about thirty seconds before leveling his weapon directly at him. He fell to his stomach at the base of the shrub as three bullets shattered the small limbs exiting only centimeters over the top of him.

He kept his head level with the ground and looked around the base of the plant. The man, dressed in black with a kerchief around his neck, was cautiously treading on their footprints, crouching as he held his rifle straight out in front, meticulously checking left and right as he walked.

When he was within thirty meters, and fifty meters away from Shira, Christian adjusted his position to the side of the bush. The hunter was looking past his location in the direction of the gulley shielding Shira.

Christian was laying at an awkward angle as he leaned around the backside of the bush and aimed the rifle. He fired two shots. The first bullet hit high and right, causing the stuffing from the tracker's jacket to fly into the air. The second one caught him in the right hip.

Shira raised up as the assailant turned in the direction of Christian. She opened fire, striking him twice in the right side of his lower torso. He dropped his rifle as he fell into the snow.

"We have to keep moving," yelled Christian,

standing up on the back side of the shrub.

Shira scrambled out of the ditch and ran toward him. They scurried across the prairie for nearly two hours, stopping only long enough to catch their breath and check the massive fields behind them for any pursuers. When they came to a dirt road going east and west, they contemplated for a moment, before jogging on the wet road to the east.

Limon, Colorado

Ted insisted on taking two squads for security to escort himself along with Jon, Hank, Deb and Tommy to Limon. They arrived in two Oshkosh R-ATV assault vehicles at the outskirts, which was now a good four kilometers from the original downtown. Traffic was bumper to bumper with large buses and military vehicles bottlenecking as they made their way past the town on the way to destinations east of the Mississippi. After moving at a snail's pace for nearly forty-five minutes they turned off the exit ramp from the Interstate and were waved thru the barricade blocking the entrance to the town.

Hardly a soul was to be seen anywhere on the main streets within the city limits. On the outskirts, a constant chatter could be heard from the encampment as thousands of people endured the discomfiture of being crammed together like cattle in a corral. The sheriff was standing outside his vehicle parked in front of the hotel utilized as headquarters for the FEMA team. He watched as the assault vehicle pulled up and stopped next to the high metal fencing separating the town from the government encampment. Deb climbed down from the vehicle, followed by her brothers and Tommy. Deb, Tommy and Ted were dressed in army fatigues.

"Colonel Deb Lisco," the sheriff's cowboy hat was cocked back on his head. He smiled as he limped across the wet pavement. "Did you come to pay your tickets?"

"Hell no, I tossed them damn things away a long time ago." Deb smiled while extending her hand. "How are you doing Bob."

"I'm trying to figure out this upside-down world we are living in." He slapped his hand into hers and squeezed before letting go. "It gets worse by the day."

"Things aren't going to get better anytime soon."

"I guess your brother told you about Clint and Peg." The Sheriff grimaced as he looked at Jon.

"It was terrible what happened to them, Bob," stated Deb.

"They are not the only ones. We have had so much crime and killings over the last two weeks that half the time I can only keep myself and Judy safe." He turned his head and spit on the ground. "They opened the doors to the prison and let all the prisoners walk out scot-free."

"When did they do that?"

"It was right after your brother came to town with the guys who attacked the girl." He turned to Jon, "What did you decide to do with them?"

Jon sighed, "We let them go."

"I figured so." The sheriff lifted his hat and ran his fingers thru his thin white hair before placing it forward on his head. "Like I told you, this place is now the wild west."

"Well, you can always come out to our farm."

"Are you serious?" he asked with his mouth partially open.

"Of course, I am. Pack your stuff up and you can follow us out."

"By God, I believe I'll take you up on that. Judy is scared to death being home by herself." Bob sniffled and ran the sleeve of his coat over his nose. "This whole damn place seems to be closing in all around us."

"Do you know if Ben Stewart has any material left at

the lumber yard?" Deb asked, noticing Jon quickly move to the chain length fence.

"The inside of his store has been ransacked but I think there is still lumber. Nobody has been building anything. The FEMA people are using our offices and hotels or have canvas tents for the people they are housing."

"We'll head over to the lumber yard."

"No, you'll have to go to his house. He and Paula have locked themselves inside, like everyone else in town."

"I'll be damned," Jon yelled from the compound fence. "Hank, come here and tell me if I'm seeing things."

Hank went to the fence and looked thru the wire, trying to locate whoever Jon was pointing at. He looked for a moment and then turned to Jon with his eyebrows raised.

"I don't see what you are looking at."

"Isn't that your football player?" Jon moved closer to his brother and pointed to a table in the dining area nearly two hundred meters away.

Christian was walking away from a table with Shira at his side. Hank got a glimpse of the big man before he disappeared into the crowd.

"That was Christian," said Hank. "I wonder why he came here?"

"They were chased out of the city." Jon turned to Ted. "Wouldn't you imagine so Ted."

"Most likely. I wonder if we can get inside the camp." Ted looked to the sheriff. "He has a lot of information that would be valuable to our mission of clearing out the cities."

"I don't have a damn bit of pull in this place," stated the sheriff. "I bet with you being a colonel in the United States Army they won't have a problem with allowing you inside."

"Why don't you three go and see if you can find him. Tommy and I will see if we can talk with Ben Stewart." Deb turned to the sheriff. "Bob, would you mind helping us track down Ben.

"I'm pretty sure he is at his house. I will drive over with you and check."

FEMA compound Limon, Colorado

The camp was longer from east to west than it was wide from north to south. The congestion and pandemonium inside the fence were worse than it appeared to be from the outside. The brothers decided to syphon through the mass of people in a systematic manner by starting the search at the east border and walking to the west.

They spread out with Ted going on the south edge and Jon on the north while Hank walked down the middle. Ted never met face to face with Christian, but he was given a good enough description, from Hank, of the large man to feel confident in identifying him, should he make first contact.

The smell from the toilets and food cooking was almost unbearable as they made their way past the dining area where Christian was seen from outside the fence. The inhabitants of the camp seemed angry and defeated. Although there were times when Hank lost sight of his brothers, for the most part he was able to keep tabs on them.

They walked the entire length of the camp without a glimpse of Christian. They came together at the far west edge of the encampment.

"There are so many people in this place we could have walked right by him without noticing it was him," stated Jon.

"He might have spotted us first and hid while we walked past," replied Hank.

"This place is like a viper pit," stated Ted. "Let's head back to where we entered and get the hell out of here."

"This camp is much worse now than when we came to get Linda out," said Jon.

Hank kept a keen eye out for Christian as he continued to walk for nearly twenty minutes when he noticed a group of men about twenty meters in front of him. The oblong face of a man wearing a cap was vaguely familiar, but it did not dawn on him who he was looking at until the blond man he was talking with turned to offer his profile.

Hank tried to locate Jon but could only see a crowd of people. He focused his attention to the south in the direction of Ted. Ted was closer and noticed him waving.

Hank pointed at the two men as Ted approached. "Those are the two men who attacked Caroline."

The man in the cap glanced toward Hank and Ted. When he saw Hank with his attention fixed on him, he tapped the blond man on the shoulder. They slid into the crowd of humanity and disappeared.

Hank and Ted walked to the location. It would be futile to try and follow the two men. Jon was walking back toward them.

"We just saw the two guys who attacked Caroline." Hank swept his arm toward the swarm of people. "They're gone now."

"I can't believe they would come back. I made it clear to them that we would shoot first and ask questions later."

"They know the location of the farm," stated Hank still staring in the direction of where they ran off.

"It's another thing we have to worry about." The vision of Sherry standing over the men with her pistol zeroed in on the men entered his mind.

"Coach," an indistinct voice yelled.

Hank stopped and listened. When he didn't find anyone, he turned to his brothers to ask if either of them heard the word.

"Coach," Christian with Shira at his side emerged from the multitude of people. Dark lines were winding from the corners of his eyes. His face was pale white, making him appear to be an old man.

"Christian," Hank went to his side. "What are you doing here?"

"They killed Tim," he swallowed hard and grimaced. "We didn't have a chance."

"My God, are you sure he's dead?" Hank asked.

"He's gone. They killed everyone in our group."

"Who?" Ted stepped right next to Hank.

"The foreign rebels," The skin on his face was dark red.

"Where did you fight them?" Ted asked.

"About twenty kilometers west of here," Christian looked at Shira for verification.

"It was in a field southeast of the little town of Agate," Shira's eyes were sagging from the lack of sleep.

"How many rebels were there?" Ted stood tall as he asked the question.

"At least three hundred," answered Shira.

"Their weapons were far superior to our AKs," Christian sniffled.

"Will you come and give Ted all the information you have on the rebels?" Hank still believed in his former player and wanted to make sure he would be given a chance to atone for the many mistakes he made throughout his life.

"We'll go with you coach." Christian straightened his

shoulders and looked into Ted's eyes, "They are going after NORAD."

Ted returned the gaze but did not reply. The base for the North American Aerospace Defense Command is deep inside Cheyenne Mountain just a stone's throw away from Fort Carson, west of Colorado Springs. It is built inside solid granite and able to survive a nuclear attack.

"I know it sounds crazy. The place is a fortress." Christian took in a deep breath, noticing Ted's skepticism. "Don't underestimate these people."

"Let's go find Deb and get back to the farm." Ted took a step toward Jon, "We can sort things out there."

Limon, Colorado

Ben Stewart opened the front door after seeing the sheriff cruiser, followed by the Army attack vehicle, stop in front of his home. He waited inside the door while Deb and the sheriff approached.

"Did you finally capture her?" Ben yelled, chuckling, as the two stepped onto the small porch of his two-story cottage.

"More like she finally caught me," Bob chuckled.

"What in the hell happened to you Colonel?" Ben asked. "You're walking like you have a wooden leg."

"Just protecting your crinkled old ass from some of the nastiest people in the world." Deb could see Paula standing back and to the side of him inside the door as she stepped up to their entry.

"And I do thank-you for that," he clicked his tongue and nodded his head. "What is it that I have the pleasure of your visit for this morning."

"I need some lumber."

"Why in the hell would anyone need lumber during these times?"

Deb looked over to the sheriff and then back at Ben. "What in the hell difference does it make to you what I want it for."

"Ok, ok," Ben chuckled, holding up his hands. Paula moved around him and stepped onto the porch. "How much do you need?"

"I have a list." Deb handed him a paper with the inventory calculated by Jason Jenson.

Ben looked at the piece of paper. He rubbed his chin and stated, "I haven't been to the yard in nearly a week. But there was enough there to fill your order before we left."

"What are you building Deb?" Paula asked.

"It's an extra room for people to meet and socialize in order to free up space in the main house."

"How many people do you have at the farm now?"

"You know Paula, I'm not really sure of the number. I would guess maybe a few less than fifty."

"I'm going to see if Judy wants to go out there," Bob adjusted his hat. "It's just not safe to stay here. I feel like I have a target on my back every morning when I leave the house."

"Ben." Deb knew all she had to do was ask and Paula would jump at the chance of going to the farm. With the knowledge Ben had with the solar grid and septic system he would be invaluable to have on the premises. "You two are more than welcome to come with us."

"We've been talking about leaving for the past two days," Paula sighed. "We were thinking of going east but we don't have any family we are close enough with to show up on their doorstep."

"Do you have a car that runs?" asked Bob.

"The delivery truck starts," stated Ben. He gazed at Deb, "We can load it up and take all the lumber you need."

"We stored a lot of goods from the store when we realized we were going to have problems. We have most of it in the garage," stated Paula. "We have more coffee than we could drink in a lifetime."

Deb stared at them for a moment. She could not think of a better outcome to the visit to Limon.

"Let's load everything up and go."

Eastern Colorado Plains

Ben and Paula Stewart, driving the lumber yards twelve-ton deliver truck, overloaded with lumber and supplies, followed closely behind the two Oshkosh R-ATV assault vehicles, with Sheriff Bob and his wife Judy close behind in their brand new 2051 Chevy Sombrero. Deb, Tommy, Ted, Jon, Hank, Christian and Shira were riding in the second assault vehicle.

Nearly halfway to the farm the convoy crested a hill on the wet gravel road. The front vehicle eased to a stop. Lieutenant Rod Millet stepped out of the front vehicle and walked to the trailing assault vehicle.

"Colonel," Lieutenant Millet looked up into the open door at Ted. "There is a roadblock, about two klicks ahead. The field on both sides are full of people."

Ted stepped out, followed by Tommy and Deb. He took the lieutenant's field glasses and viewed the vehicles blocking the road. He handed them to Tommy. The Command Sergeant Major carefully observed the location.

"Sir," Lieutenant Millet stood shoulder to shoulder with Tommy and pointed to a ridge west of the roadblock. "Irregulars are accumulating to the west."

"We will need support from Fort Carson if we are going to confront them," Tommy glanced at Ted.

"We are overmatched, and I don't want to put the civilians in the middle of a battle." Ted looked at Lieutenant Millet. "Lieutenant, have the base send out a NAV to follow the rebels."

Before anyone responded several shots rang out and

bullets pinged off the front assault vehicle.

"Back up," Ted motioned with his arms to Ben and Bob. Both vehicles quickly backed-up while he jumped inside the door being held open by Deb. The assault vehicles backed down the dirt road, following the civilians, until they were a safe enough distance away to turn around.

Eastern Colorado Farm

Emily and Bobby were in the concrete tower when they saw the convoy returning down the driveway. Both the large truck carrying lumber and the brand-new car stopped between the Jacoby's RV and the garage. The Military vehicles zoomed past and parked at the far end of the apartment.

Jacqueline and Nicole approached the newcomers while Bobby and Emilee continued to watch out the window on the third floor of the tower. Emilee focused on Jacqueline and Nicole greeting the strangers, with several others, including Irene and Breanna, joining to make them welcome, when she glanced in the direction of the soldiers exiting the Military vehicles. She gasped, causing Bobby to jerk toward her.

"What is it?" Bobby asked.

"Christian," she responded, "my dad."

Bobby placed his hand on her shoulder. She never discussed, with him, her feelings about learning that Christian is her father. He remained quiet and looked at her.

"Mom guaranteed me that he is my father," she swallowed hard. "I told her, the first chance I get, I will have a paternity test. She still assured me that she is one-hundred percent certain he is my dad."

They looked out the window while Ted escorted Christian and Shira in the direction of the offices in the garage. Deb and Tommy went to the vehicles with the lumber while Jason and Harold wandered toward them.

Bobby and Emilee watched from their perch as everyone became acquainted. Jon was busy speaking with Irving, Terrance and Jerry. Deb and Tommy were back at the lumber truck with the group talking to Bob and Ben.

Out of the corner of his eye Bobby caught sight of three men running down the driveway. He leaned out the window and raised his binoculars. Tyrone and Von, the two young men who came to the farm with the men who attacked Caroline were jogging past the farmhouse with a larger man between them.

"Aunt Deb," Bobby yelled out the window. He flailed his hands. "Uncle Jon, there are men coming up the drive."

Jon and Irving walked to the side of the Jacoby RV and waited as the men jogged past the house. Deb and Tommy joined them as the men stopped next to them and leaned over to catch their breath.

"Are you running away from someone?" Jon asked.

"Yeah," the older man raised up and took in a deep breath and released it. He opened his eyes wide and said, "A lot of people."

"Are they the foreign fighters dressed in black?" Tommy moved in front of the man.

"Yeah, them plus a number of young people." The man noticed Deb and Tommy dressed in fatigues.

"We ran into the group about twenty klicks northwest of here," Tommy interjected, speaking directly to Irving. "We had to divert back north and then east to go around them."

"Not the same group, the one we were with is south of here," the man stated adamantly to Tommy. "They have a base at a ranch southeast of Colorado Springs."

"When did you last have contact with them?" Tommy asked.

"This morning, about six hours ago."

"How large a group are they?"

"I don't know." He held his hands up. "Maybe five hundred."

Tommy glanced at Deb.

"We need ariel surveillance," said Deb, pulling the collar of her jacket tight. "But it's going to be hard with this low cloud cover."

"I'll let Ted know about the additional enemy to the south. Maybe he can get a Company from the 3rd Battalion of the 99th to assist us," Tommy hesitated to see if Deb wanted to reply. She stood with her hand on her chin, so he turned and jogged in the direction of the garage.

Hank, Bobby and Emilee walked next to the young brothers.

"Where did you go after you left here?" Hank asked.

"We all went back to the original group we arrived with, but they met up with the militants," said Von.

"It sounds crazy, but we thought they were going to somewhere we would be safe to wait out this conflict. We never made it to their ranch but apparently it is a place used as the main base for several dissident groups," stated the older man. "Since we joined the militants, they have ransacked two ranches."

"Did you hear anything about why they are so far from the city?" Deb asked. "It doesn't seem worth their while to destroy farms."

"It's really confusing what is taking place." Leroy glanced at his sons. "To the best of our understanding they came to the country to establish a place to go when the authorities put too much pressure on them in the city."

"When we were here the other day, before you detained the two guys we were with, the plan was to attack this farm. After we told them how well armed you are, they decided to leave," stated Von.

"The foreign group has better weapons and is a whole lot more organized than the American rebels," Leroy said. "Even with the military presence here, they won't back down."

"The younger boy played football against Bobby," Hank told Deb. "I trust what they tell us is what they believe to be true."

"Actually Coach, I played against your team too, in 2030," stated the older man.

"What is your name?" Hank asked.

"Leroy Roberts."

Hank nodded, there were so many different players his teams competed against over the years that it was impossible to remember all of them.

"The foreign fighters are placing Americans in their ranks thinking it will protect them from being destroyed from the air," stated Deb.

"That is a pretty large force. If there are five hundred rebels south, along with the three hundred or so we came across to the north," said Hank.

"It's an army," stated Deb. "They are soldiers who eventually will have to be eliminated."

"About a third of the force are regular people like us," stated Leroy. "Some of the Americans are buying into the foreign rebel's beliefs, but there are only a few."

"Hank, you should make sure all the kids are close. Give everyone else a heads up to stay on the alert," said Deb.

"I want to take the M82 .50 Caliber rifle and set up in the tower," said Irving.

"We'll go with you." Bobby glanced at Emilee,

thinking he should not have spoken for her. "Do you want to come with me or check with your mom and sisters?"

"I'll make sure Avery and Reagan are inside the house."

"Can you help me carry ammunition and supplies to the tower?" Irving asked Bobby. "Find Dave, Sherry and Caroline and have them bring the spotter scopes to the top."

"Irving, why don't you get the sensors and set them on the perimeter," said Deb. "If the snow comes in it will be difficult to get a visual."

He looked at the colonel with his mouth open. "This is the first I have heard about any sensors."

There is a box of ten Trinity 180 camera sensors in the weapons cabinet."

"If I had known that I would have had them set."

Eastern Colorado Farm Greenhouse

Jessica was watering plants inside the greenhouse when Samantha opened the sliding door and entered. She continued to spray water with her eyes transfixed on the plants while Samantha approached.

"Bill wanted me to let you know that Ted brought Christian back with him from Limon." She moved close enough to feel the mist of the water being squirted. It was comfortably warm and humid inside the glasshouse.

Jessica swallowed hard as she tightened her grip on the hose. Her eyes never left the plants.

Samantha turned away. She had given the message and it was apparent Jessica did not want to discuss the situation with her. She took a step in the direction of the door.

"How many people are with him?" Jessica asked.

Samantha stopped and turned around.

"Just one," Samantha spoke with a soft tone, "a girl."

"Do you know where they are at now?" She finally made eye contact with Samantha.

"In the garage."

"Is Bill with them?"

"No, we have been at the barn helping the Jacobys with the cattle. Now he's with Hank and the others at the farmhouse discussing how to prepare for a threat."

"Does he want me to go to the garage?" Jessica asked lethargically. She was moving slowly and seemed to be completely distracted as she turned off the water and set the hose to the side. Her hair was in a hastily placed ponytail.

"He didn't say. He only wanted me to let you know that Christian had returned to the farm." Samantha sensed the distress the lady was experiencing. "Are you ok Jessica?"

She held her mouth closed and breathed thru her nose as she stared at Samantha. She picked up towel and dried her hands.

"I know this whole situation can't be easy for you." Samantha offered.

"God knows everything seems to be falling apart," Jessica stated. "I never thought things could get worse in my life. It's almost unbearable."

"Something tells me you are a fighter," Samantha swallowed hard. "Maybe it's time for you to start fighting."

A hint of a smile came across Jessica's lips. Samantha was the last person she would have considered to become an ally, to offer encouragement.

"It is time to fight back." She tossed the towel, "I will confront Christian right now."

Samantha followed Jessica out of the greenhouse and watched as she sauntered in the direction of the garage. She felt good about handling the conversation with the feisty mother in a cordial manner. The two of them may never be friends but coexisting at the farm would now be much easier.

Eastern Colorado Farm

The outer part of the garage was cold compared to the toasty room partitioned off for Ted's office. Christian and Shira sat next to the wall with Jon standing over them. Ted was at the monitor speaking with Colonel Myers at Fort Carson while Tommy looked over his shoulder.

"The snow and thick cloud cover will hinder the use of drones. It all should change shortly." Tommy took a step away from the back of Ted's chair. "I just checked the weather with Fort Carson. A squall of snow is about thirty kilometers to the west. It's going to pass over us quickly, leaving partly cloudy skies. Tomorrow it will be bitterly cold and remain so for the next several days."

"Then, visibility here will be no problem in a couple of hours." Deb noticed Tommy had changed into his olive drab softshell tactical M-102 field jacket. She moved closer to listen in on the conversation between Ted and Colonel Myer. The more she listened the more she realized that Colonel Myer was overwhelmed with the destruction taking place in the city. There was a huge uptick in attacks against utilities with reliable intel that cherry creek dam was to be targeted. She waited patiently as Ted terminated the call.

"I can understand Bonny's wanting to keep her troops close at hand. With significant threats against the reservoirs, she is making the correct decision. General Lopez is fully occupied at the border and is not going to deal with our problem," Ted informed them. He rose from the chair and faced Deb. "I have 2nd and 3rd squads out now to see if they can locate and track the two groups of rebels."

"Tommy, can you try and get through to Lauer. Emphasize to the general that the rebels are highly trained soldiers, not just a bunch of civilians." Deb could feel the soreness in her calf from the shrapnel she had received in Utah.

Christian was listening to the conversation when he noticed Jessica enter the room. He kept his eyes on her as she moved next to Ted.

Jessica made eye contact with Shira momentarily avoiding Christian's gaze. Although she was not friends with Shira, she was aware of the headstrong woman's fascination for Christian.

"Why did you come back?" Jessica asked.

Neither of them replied.

"Jessica," Ted stepped in front of her, "they told us their entire group has been killed."

Jessica felt her heartbeat quicken. She looked closer at Christian. His face was expressionless as if he had lost his soul. He leaned his head back and held his mouth wide open, trying to capture air. She turned to stare at Shira who was rail thin, with a redness around her neck that was rough and wrinkled.

"All of them? Tim too?" she inquired.

Shira nodded; her hands were shaking.

"You two are disgusting." Jessica leaned closer with her upper lip clenched, showing her teeth. Ted caught her with his arm while Christian never budged. "It was so obvious that you should have left when you had a chance. You are pathetic."

"We did leave," Shira shouted. "The foreigners are everywhere."

"You could have escaped if you would have left when I did. How could you be so stupid to go along with them."

"I agree," Shira rubbed the corners of her eyes where crust had accumulated, "but we didn't."

"Everything you have done is so pointless," spit shot out of Jessica's mouth. She thought how stupid it was on her part for falling for the false opportunity of being free when she joined them. She gnashed her teeth, shook her head, turned and walked out the door.

"Deb, General Lauer is unavailable. Lieutenant Delk told me that there is major enemy movement at the southern border, with a surge in rockets being fired at the troops in Texas and New Mexico. There is a major escalation taking place," Tommy cleared his throat, "all of 4th Division is heading to the Albuquerque sector."

"Including 2nd Brigade?"

"Yes."

If it wasn't for the immediate crisis at the farm Deb would be loading her gear and driving to Fort Carson.

Corporal Pint entered the garage. Her cheeks were red with snow accumulated on the top of her cap as she stood at attention in front of Ted and saluted.

"Sir, 3rd Squad has encountered the enemy force about eleven kilometers north of our location." The corporal held her arm with a Pulsenet processor out in front of her and looked at the computer on Ted's desk. "I can redirect communication to this site if you wish."

"Do it."

The corporal sat in the chair and within a minute was finished. "I have Sergeant Phillips."

"What's the situation?" Ted asked, looking at the image of the sergeant on the monitor. He was near the location where earlier in the day they encountered the insurgents.

"The force just left a farmhouse on county road 53 and is moving to the south at about four kilometers an hour." Sergeant Phillips was dressed in the Rind Impulse Operator Suit, standing on a gravel road with light snow falling. "We are eight kilometers northwest of your location, preparing to move back to a hill approximately two kilometers to the south."

"Fall back to the hill. When you get there transmit pictures of the force and gauge their speed. Then return to the base."

"Yes sir."

"Corporal Pint connect with 2nd Squad." Ted moved back from the chair in front of the monitor and glanced at Deb. "If these two forces merge and come this way we are going to have a real problem."

"If they combine, they will be a battalion size army," Deb declared.

"Sir, Sergeant Fakharzedeh is linked," Corporal Pint rose from the chair, allowing Ted to sit.

"Sergeant, have you located the rebel forces?" Ted could see the sergeant peeking out from his helmet.

"It is not one centralized army. There are eight groups of about fifty soldiers in each, spread out over a ten kilometer stretch of the road," stated the sergeant. "They are moving in a concerted manner to the north."

"How far south of our base are you now?"

"About fifteen kilometers. We are a good four kilometers north of the closest group of insurgents. It's beginning to snow hard, and visibility is becoming difficult."

"Are they on county road 53?"

"They are moving parallel with 53."

"Return to base," Ted took in a deep breath. "Make sure they don't flank you."

"They are coming our way," said Deb. "We have about four hours before they merge and hit our location."

Tommy looked back and forth between Ted and Deb. "The request made for air support has been granted. Petersen Air Base should be coordinating with your communication center for the precise location and time needed for the NAV."

"Hopefully the weather will clear off like predicted so we can use the drone effectively," stated Ted.

"I'm going to check with Jon to make sure everyone here is prepared," Deb turned to Tommy. "I'll be in the house."

***

Jon was standing on the hearth of the fireplace, holding his hand up, trying to quiet the multitude crammed into the living room. Hank stepped onto the hearth next to his brother. Jacqueline and Gina were standing to the side of their husbands.

Deb waited in the kitchen as her brothers struggled to secure control. She heard the roar of one of the assault vehicles returning from the surveillance mission as it hurried past the farmhouse. She looked out the window at the light snow falling. A rush of blood surged to her brain as she visualized enemy forces attacking the farmhouse. Her thoughts went to the children and their safety should the house be destroyed.

Bill came to her side.

"What can I do Aunt Deb?" Bill asked.

"There are several five-gallon buckets in the supply shed. I want you to get some help and bring them inside the house. Then hook the hoses up outside and pull them thru the windows and fill the buckets. Grab some insulation to wrap around the hoses and sill cocks, so they don't freeze. "

"Do you think there will be an attack, even with Dad's platoon here?"

"I don't know for sure," Deb swallowed hard. "If this army attacks, they will do so only if they think they can win."

"Is the Army base going to send help?" Bill could feel his heart beating hard.

"If the situation warrants us needing help, they will definitely get us help. Right now, we are unsure of the scope of the danger."

"I know we discussed the possibility of a threat to the farm but now that it's taking place it seems unreal." Bill shook his head, "I am really glad you and Dad are here."

"Your dad knows better than anyone how to strategically situate his soldiers. I'll direct the civilians at the farm to best support him. I want you to coordinate the effort in the house, especially the children. The safest place for them will be in the weapons closet, but we need an escape route should the house start on fire," Deb clasped her hands. "I will move the frontend loader to the east side of the house, as close to the egress window from the downstairs bedroom as possible to shield the children should they have to be moved."

"Where will we take them?"

"Bill, that will be determined by the situation. We have to be prepared to escape whether it be to the bottom of the tower or the garage," Deb cleared her throat. "All the parents need to stay either inside the house or right on the outside."

"I take that includes me also?"

"Yes, we need to make sure the house is protected. The fewer civilians outside the less chance of someone being shot accidentally by your dad's soldiers."

"Makes sense," Bill moved toward the door. "I'll get on the bucket detail."

Deb stepped outside and moved next to the Jacoby's RV. Irving was visible thru the window at the top level of the tower with Bobby and Emilee. The sound of the second assault vehicle returning with Sergeant Fakharzedeh's squad could be heard coming down the driveway. She waited for it to pass before walking to the tower and jogging up the stairs.

"Colonel Lisco," Irving rested the .50 Caliber rifle below the window before moving to the middle of the room. Bobby, holding a radio, and Emilee were working on a computer situated on a chair. "We are setting the Trinity sensors, loading them to the computer. Dave, Caroline and Sherry are finishing the positioning to give us a full 360 view."

Deb moved to the window and looked across the landscape. The sun was setting low in the southwest, shining thru the haze and light snow. Several head of cattle were visible in the corrals with Breanna leading a horse inside the barn. She contemplated quietly until Irving broke her train of thought.

"Colonel do you think the rebels will attack?" Irving stepped next to her.

"Even with Ted's forty soldier platoon, the forces advancing our way outnumber us about ten to one," she declared. "With the exception of the FEMA camp in Limon we are the only threat to them on the eastern plains. I'm almost sure they want to eliminate us."

"We will be prepared if they do launch an attack."

Deb turned to Bobby. "Could you go to the garage and ask Tommy to join us?"

Bobby ran down the stairs just as Dave and Sherry were coming up.

"We should have the Jacobys move the RV from in front of the house," said Irving.

"They can park it on the side of the garage," stated Deb.

"Dave, will you go down and ask Aaron Jacoby to move the RV to the side of the garage."

"Ok."

"Ask Jon and Hank to come back with you. Also, grab some paper and a pen." Deb slapped Irving on the shoulder and walked to the head of the stairs. "I'll be right back. I'll check with Ted to see if he can give us about ten minutes of his time to go over where we can best assist his troops."

***

"Everybody should grab a flashlight and a bottle of water before we go to the basement." Nicole took over Hank and Jon's position standing on the fireplace hearth. Maddy was holding tight to her left arm with Scotty standing next to her. "I don't want to scare the children, but we have to be prepared if the lights or water go off."

"Are we all going to spend the night in the basement?" Travis asked, sitting next to his wife in a metal chair with his daughters standing next to them.

"We want all the parents to stay in the house and all the children in the basement." Nicole glanced at Sheriff Bob who was helping Bill fill buckets of water in the kitchen. "Bill is in communication with his father to coordinate the effort to protect the farmhouse. I know Ted wants to make sure we don't place any of his soldiers at risk by shooting randomly from this position."

"Have you talked with Ted in the last couple hours," Al asked. "Is there a legitimate threat?"

"Yes, we are facing real danger Al," Nicole squinted her eyes at the dentist, "an immediate threat.

"Is Bill filling buckets in the kitchen with water because they are worried this place might burn down." Al looked around the room while holding both hands up before turning back to face Nicole. "Are you sure we want to be in the basement if there is a fire?"

Samantha opened the window in the living room and pulled out the screen causing a rush of cold air to enter. Jacqueline standing on a brick flower planter on the outside, handed her a garden hose with a thumb-controlled nozzle. Samantha pulled the twenty-five-meter hose inside before closing the window onto it, allowing for a small gap. Cold air continued to flow into the living room.

"Where do you suggest we go?" Nicole stared at the dentist.

"Not the basement."

"The weapons closet is the most secure place on the farm." Nicole pulled her arm away from Maddy and stepped off the hearth, "It's the best place for the kids."

Maddy moved next to Irene and took her hand.

"Al, this is a scary situation for all of us." Linda placed her hand on the back of her husband's arm and squeezed.

"Everything here is so ill planned. All this should have been predetermined," Al scoffed. "Why isn't there a bunker away from the house for everyone to go into?"

"My God, why are you always complaining?" Ed

asked, sitting between Breanna and Ashley on the edge of the sofa. "Complaining never makes anything better."

"Oh, shut-up," Al yelled. He leered at Ed. "There's a difference between com…."

Breanna jumped out of her seat and was nose to nose with Al before he could finish his sentence.

"You shut the fuck up," she yelled, poking him in his chest with her eyes bulging. "Don't you ever talk to my dad that way. I'll knock the living hell out of you."

Al cowered to Linda's side with his mouth wide open.

"Ok, ok, I know everyone is on edge, but we can't fight amongst ourselves." Nicole placed her hand on Breanna's shoulder. "All the children are going to the basement. We will have a plan in place for everyone else. Whether you follow it is up to you."

Maddy pulled on Irene's arm. Irene leaned down so the little girl could whisper in her ear, "Tell Breanna not to use those words in front of Grandpa. He'll make her clean the bathrooms."

"I will tell her," Irene smiled. She wasn't the least bit surprised at her daughter's reaction in protecting Ed. "I'm going to the kitchen to see if I can find some snacks for all of us while we are downstairs. You and Scotty go with your grandma and find a good place to make a bed."

Nicole's head was throbbing as she took in a deep breath. There was going to be combat taking place at the farm and everyone seemed to be unaware of the magnitude of danger they were about to face. She realized Ted was busy figuring out how to keep everyone alive, but she wished he would take a moment to come inside the house to give them an idea of what to expect.

Julia was standing in the clinic door listening to the chatter. Hopefully not, but it could end up being a busy night for the physician assistant.

Eastern Colorado Farm Tower

Deb scurried up the steps to the tower with Ted dressed in full combat gear right behind her. He was carrying headsets. Hank and Jon were standing at the north window while Irving looked through a spotter scope out the large south window. Bobby, Emilee, Dave and Sherry were huddled around the computer placed on the floor in the corner of the crowded room.

"We have visibility of nearly two kilometers," stated Irving.

"I have five headsets for the people who have the .50 Caliber rifles," Ted held up the receivers.

"That will be me, Tommy, Jon, Terrance and Irving," said Deb.

"I want Irving and Terrance in the tower with the main focus on the east flank." Ted turned to Bobby and his friends, "You four will be the spotters. You can give information of troop movement, as well as range, to either Irving or Terrance. They can relay the message to the platoon communication, or to Deb, Jon or Tommy."

"We moved a tractor to the area about two hundred meters northeast of the corner of the apartment." Deb made eye contact with Jon. "Jon, Hank, Christian, Shira, and Jerry are to locate at this position."

"It's a good location at high ground. Your main objective is to protect the four-person mortar squad on the north sector of our base." Ted could see that Jon was concerned about something.

"Are we sure Christian and Shira want to engage in

combat?" Jon asked.

"They assured me they very much want to fight," Ted answered.

"Tommy and I will go to the southeast corner of the house. The front-end loader is positioned near the back window on the east side." Deb glanced at Tommy, "Is there anything you can think of we are missing."

"Just make sure to have plenty of ammunition. Keep communication lines open so we can work as a team," said Tommy. "We should make sure everyone has night goggles."

"Another thing for the civilians," Deb looked at Bobby and his friends, "do not shoot at shadows. Make sure you identify what you are firing at before you pull the trigger."

"What weapons should we use?" Bobby asked.

"Everyone not carrying a .50 Caliber should have an M-16. We have plenty of ammunition on hand," stated Deb. "Make sure you have ear protection."

"Colonel Lisco," yelled a private from down below. "We are receiving pictures from Vocaro of a large group approaching from the southwest, about four klicks out."

"Are you sure of the distance?" Ted yelled down from the window.

"Yes sir."

"Private have communication begin calibrating the assault vehicles for remote. I will be right down."

"Look at the ridge." Irving was looking thru the scope of his .50 Caliber rifle at a group of ten rebels. "They are eighteen hundred and fifty meters out."

Deb, Tommy and Ted looked thru the spotter scope. Jon and Hank tried to see with their bare eyes but could not make out any people on the hill in the distance.

"Look at the two soldiers kneeling on the right side," said Tommy. "They are setting a mortar system."

"Irving, can you make that shot?" Deb looked at Ted for his approval. "We can't let them set up that close.

"I can make it." He had the rebel holding a shell in his cross hairs.

"Do it," said Ted.

"Cover your ears."

The loud crack of the .50 Caliber reverberated across the landscape. The rebel holding the shell flew to the ground with the others scattering.

"It's started," stated Deb. "We better get in position."

Eastern Colorado Farm

Bill stood outside the front door of the farmhouse intently surveying the countryside while Samantha remained at the threshold of the open door. He handed her his rifle and leveled his binoculars to the hills to the south and west. An assault vehicle sped in front of the house and down the driveway. It stopped about fifty meters from the county road. Every ten seconds or so the vehicle would move twenty meters in various directions.

"Do you see anything?" Samantha tried to look around his body.

"I see some people on the ridgeline, but they disappear as soon as they become visible." He lowered the field glasses and let out a deep breath. "They must be gathering on the other side of the hill."

Inside the living room the Jacobys, Sheriff Bob and Ben Stewart were staring out the picture window, with each of their rifles directed toward the carpeted floor. Jacqueline, Gina, Travis and Julia were in the kitchen.

"It's been quiet since we heard the one gunshot," stated the sheriff. "With the sun setting, things are going to get interesting."

"Look back on the hill," yelled Aaron Jacoby, pointing out the window. "Jesus, there are hundreds of people."

The side of the knoll looked like a swarm of ants moving along the landscape from west to east. Soldiers dressed in black were running along the ridge about twelve hundred meters south of the farmhouse, parallel with the county road.

A squad of ten American Soldiers dressed in combat gear sprinted up the driveway and fanned out to the west of the assault vehicle. They disappeared into the pasture. The assault vehicle raced the final few meters down the driveway to the county road and stopped. The machine gun on the turret rotated to the south and began firing. The rebels on the hillside scattered and vanished as the 32 mm shells shrouded the landscape.

Bill stepped inside the house and instinctively locked the door. Within thirty seconds of coming inside a large flash of light illuminated the area, followed by two loud explosions coming from the area near the barn. Samantha crunched down and gasped. A large blast from the back of the house, nearly shattered their eardrums, causing the entire structure to shake. The lights flickered and turned off.

Jason and Harold came running up from the downstairs and moved to the back of the house to assess the damage from the explosion. Fred lingered behind them but did not follow to the back bedrooms, instead he stepped into the kitchen and went to Travis' side to look out the window.

"Move away from the windows." Bill grabbed hold of Samantha's arm and pulled her to the enclosed area of the clinic, several of the others crowded in behind them. Travis and Fred remained in the kitchen, both holding their hands over their ears to muffle the deafening sound of gunfire being returned from the farm area.

A mortar blast hit the front door of the kitchen, causing a loud boom, followed by a whooshing sound. The detonation tossed both Travis and Fred into the air, sending bits of broken wood and tile into the living room all the way to the fireplace. Bill and Samantha were the first to reach the two men as the others lingered behind. Fred laid twisted and disfigured.

Travis was motionless on top of buckets of spilt water while bitterly cold air rushed in from the gaping hole where the kitchen door once existed. Samantha knelt at his side and listened to his labored breathing. His arm was mangled and a hole in the side of his shirt revealed a deep gash at his lower abdomen. She placed her hand under his head and lifted hard enough to straighten his body off the buckets and onto the floor.

"Let's get him into the clinic," yelled Bill, moving to his side while the others came to his aide.

"Oh my God," Julia yelled when she noticed her husband's mangled body. She fell to the floor and placed her hand on his neck.

"Oh Lord," Harold yelled as he went to his knees next to his brother and sister-in-law.

"He's dead Harold," Julia held her bloody hand next to her pale face.

"We can't leave him like this," Harold sniffled, standing and pulling Julia to her feet.

"We'll help," said Adam Jacoby, turning to Breanna and Aaron. "Let's take him into the living room."

Jacqueline and Gina cut off Travis' tattered shirt immediately after he was placed on the hospital bed in the clinic, while he lay unconscious, taking in short, labored breaths. Without the help of the physician assistant, who just lost her husband, they were lost in their effort to save the young pilot.

"We are going to need some lights in here," yelled Gina.

Bill joined his aunts in the clinic and initiated the

emergency battery-operated lights and heating system, bringing bright lights to the room.

Julia watched the Jacobys move her husband to the hard tile on the foyer and cover his body with a sheet.

"I'm going to get Becky," Harold gazed at Julia as she stood rigid as a statue with her eyes fixed on the covered body of Fred. He turned and hurried down the stairs to the basement to find his wife.

Jacqueline crept away from the hospital bed and lingered back into the living room. Lights from the clinic illuminated into the kitchen, revealing blood splattered across the kitchen cabinet. She moved to Julia's side and placed a hand on her shoulder. She knew that the only chance Travis had for survival was for the devastated physician assistant to render immediate medical aid.

"Julia, I'm so sorry," Jacqueline said softly as the newly widowed wife turned her head and stared blankly. She could see the Jacobys standing near the hall with their heads hanging low.

"I need to help the others." Julia took a small step backwards and looked in the direction of the clinic.

Jacqueline nodded; she was relieved Julia made the decision to help Travis.

Gina came to Jacqueline's side while Julia walked to the clinic.

"I would never have imagined the devastation." Jacqueline was breathing hard, trying to catch her breath. "Bobby and Hank are in the middle of all this."

"Believe me Jacqueline, it is something you can't dwell on. In real war reality is bad enough without imagining bad situations," stated Gina.

Becky and Sue dashed up the basement steps with Harold following slowly behind. Sue rushed to Travis' side while Becky lingered toward Julia.

Bill instinctively began to pick pieces of splintered wood and glass off the carpet in the living room. Samantha retrieved two buckets from the kitchen to use as containers for the rubble while Breanna squirted water around the edges of the blast sight, calming some of the dust. Soon, everyone upstairs was working to clear the debris.

***

Deb realized immediately after the explosions that the house was hit. She rested her rifle and glanced at Tommy. His rifle was placed on the blade of the front-end loader leveled in the direction of the southern fields. His undivided focus was on making sure no rebel soldier would get close enough to threaten him or the colonel.

"I'm going to check on damage." Deb moved toward the back door, "I'll be right back."

A metallic smell mixed with dust greeted her as she entered the kitchen. She walked past Breanna, who was wetting the opening where the kitchen door once existed, and into the living room. She hesitated to look at the body covered with the sheet.

"Who is it?"

"It's Fred, Julia's husband and Harold the bricklayer's brother," Bill uttered, moving closer to his aunt.

"Who else?" Deb was looking into the clinic where she could see the back of Julia as she worked on her patient.

"Travis," stated Bill.

Jacqueline moved next to Bill and Deb.

"Have you heard from the others?" Jacqueline asked, holding a shaking finger to her lip.

"Yes, we are all in contact."

"Are Bobby and Hank…?" she swallowed hard as she tried to find the words. "They aren't hurt, are they?"

"Bobby is in the tower and Hank is with Jon on the north side. I haven't heard anything to suggest they are injured in any way."

Jacqueline took in a deep breath and let it out. "Deb are you and Ted going to be able to stop these people?"

"We will stop them," Deb looked into her sister-in-law's eyes. "The foreign insurgent forces are not nearly as structured as I thought they would be."

Jacqueline swallowed hard. She could not believe how anyone could be so calm under the duress of war. The sound echoing from the living room of Becky crying as she clutched Harold's arm while they looked down at Fred's body, fortified her perspective.

"Colonel," Jason Jensen towered over her as he interrupted. "The blast on the front of the house didn't cause as much damage as the one in the kitchen. We were lucky it didn't break the water line."

"We will deal with all the structural damage later. Right now, we need to make sure people stay away from the windows," she acknowledged the carpenter's assessment before turning to Bill. "It might be best if everyone, not helping with the wounded, goes to the basement. There shouldn't be any more mortar attacks, but there are active enemy troops still located close enough to take a shot at someone in the window."

"I will put some of the rifles back into the gun closet," stated Bill.

"That will be a wise choice," Deb looked at Jacqueline. "Be diligent a little while longer. This will be over shortly."

"Aunt Deb are we getting support from the base?"

Bill asked. "They won't leave us here to die without helping, will they?"

"Your dad is in touch with Fort Carson, and they have already given him air support," Deb affirmed. "This enemy is sneaky and much different from an organized army. They are a resistance army, that makes them hard to find."

"I am going to stay upstairs and help." Jacqueline stared inside the clinic at Julia working on Travis, while Sue stayed to the side of the room. She knew that Julia was in shock from just learning of the death of her husband and was working on autopilot.

Eastern Colorado Farm Tower

Bobby and Emilee remained on the third floor of the tower with Terrance and Irving while Dave, Sherry and Caroline went to the second floor to keep watch out the windows.

Sherry held her rifle out the small window to the east as she looked thru the night goggles. Adjusting her eyes to the yellow light emitted by the goggles was giving her a headache. She would remove them every two minutes to allow her eyes to rest.

"I wonder if I should go back to the top and keep an eye to the north," said Caroline. "I could see over the greenhouse from above."

"No, Irving will let us know if he wants us up there," Dave removed his goggles. "Even though we can't see them, I'm sure Bobby is keeping an eye on Coach and Jon on the other side of the garage."

"They are about three hundred meters out with Christian, Shira and Jerry." Sherry flinched as a shot rang out from the room up above.

"Terrance must see someone," said Caroline. "That shot came from the east window."

"They keep shooting but I haven't seen one person yet." Sherry squinted and pulled the back of her hair into a ponytail and slipped on the goggles. She was beginning to wonder if she was looking to quickly over the dark field and missing the enemy. She knew they were out there. Just as she was about to speak, a bullet exploded into the side of the window, creating fragments of jagged concrete block that slammed into the right side her face. She flew back hard onto the floor and screamed loudly.

Dave and Caroline fell to their knees beside her while she clutched the side of her face. Blood was covering the plywood flooring as she rolled over onto her stomach and continued to scream.

"Sherry, let us see," Dave placed his hand on her back.

She remained hunched over as Irving came running down the stairs. He stepped on the rubble from the concrete block as he reached down and lifted, spinning her in his arms. She was limp with blood flowing from the right side of her face. After removing her night goggles, he pulled her hair away from a large gash on her cheek. There were several smaller knicks toward the top of her head that were producing much of the bleeding.

"This was caused by chips from the concrete, not a bullet," Irving hoisted her to her feet. "One of you needs to take her inside the house and have Julia dress the wounds."

"I'll do it," Dave moved next to Sherry and placed his arm around her waist. She clutched his upper back as he all but carried her down the stairs, across the courtyard, to the back door of the house.

Eastern Colorado Farm North of garage

The smell of gunpowder and the wailing from the farm animals was nearly too much for Hank to handle. Never in his life had he felt so vulnerable. If not for Jon's persistence in explaining how important it was for them to protect the northeast flank of the farm, he would have abandoned the area and dashed back to check on the safety of Jacqueline and Bobby.

"Should I go and check on the farmhouse?" Hank seemed like a fish out of water as he held a M-16 rifle pointed straight up in the air.

"Hank, you keep your damn head down and watch for anyone coming across the pasture." Jon took time to shake a finger at his brother before focusing on the murky landscape.

"They are bound to come this way eventually. If it gets much darker, we won't see them until they are right up on us." Jerry glanced at Jon as he aimed his rifle into the abyss of pastureland.

"It sounds to me like they are blowing the shit out of the farm." Christian laid on his belly in the cold snow aiming his rifle. Shira kneeled on one knee with her rifle pointed at the ground.

"Keep the chatter down and concentrate on any movement," said Jon, watching thru tactical night vision infrared goggles past the remains of the old house where Maddy fell into the well. He adjusted his radio head gear with his left hand.

"Have you heard anything from Deb or Ted?" Hank

spoke in a hushed voice. He leaned onto the large wheel of the tractor, looking back in the direction of the farmhouse. The garage, greenhouse and apartment blocked his view of the house, but he could see the top of the tower. "It looks like the electricity has been knocked out."

"Nothing," Jon decided on leaving it there, without telling his younger brother to turn around and help guard for approaching soldiers. The popping of the mortar squad shooting shells toward the enemy in the south and west fields was becoming less and less frequent. The few blasts from enemy mortar shells hitting within the confines of the farm caused him to grit his teeth with each loud explosion. It would take only one well-placed projectile to kill members of his family. He leveled his .50 Caliber rifle on the back hitch of the John Deer Tractor while scanning the flat pasture.

"You need to either get behind the tractor or get on your stomach," scoffed Christian to Shira, who continued to knell on her knee.

"I'd just as soon not lay in the snow," she replied.

"Then go behind the tractor." He shook his head in the direction of Hank who remained staring toward the farmhouse.

She glared at him for a moment before leaning at the waist and scrambling to the tractor. She knelt next to Hank.

"I see movement," said Jon, "five-hundred and thirty meters out."

"How many?" Jerry asked, laying on his belly, aiming his AK-47 into the blackness. He had cleared the snow and was positioned on top of frozen prairie grass.

Jon pulled the night goggles off and tossed them to

Jerry. He then searched the sector using the night scope on his rifle. He waited for Jerry to survey the pasture, before replying, "I'm seeing close to thirty."

"I'm only locating about ten." Jerry remained flat on his belly as he examined the enemy's position. "The pasture is flat as a pancake, so if they want to come this way, they will have to expose themselves."

Christian lifted onto his forearms to look over the prairie grass with his naked eyes. A bullet hit him squarely in the right temple of his head, causing his body to fly a meter to the side. The sound of the single shot lingered before reaching everybody's ears. Shira screamed out as Jon tried to locate where the shot originated.

"Jesus," Jerry yelled. He rolled twice before scrambling to the back of the tractor. He gazed at Christian's still body.

"Keep your heads down," Jon screamed, diligently probing the area thru his scope.

"Can you see the shooter?" Jerry scrambled to the front of the tractor, hearing Shira's gasping as he moved around her.

"No," Jon continued to explore thru his scope as he spoke into the radio. "Irving or Terrance?"

"Yeah, Jon." Irving was looking out the small window on the south side of the tower. His view was directly over Tommy and Deb who were situated outside the egress window on the east side of the farmhouse.

"We have a sniper. From the angle of his shot, he has to be almost directly north of our location."

"I'll check," Irving moved across the tower to the window at the north. "I'm seeing a force assembled north of your location and another group of six, forty meters east of them. I'm not finding a sniper."

"I have visual on the larger force but can only locate two targets east of them." The heads of two insurgents would pop up into the sight of his tactical night vision scope and then quickly disappear. As he brought his scope back to the west in the direction of the larger cluster, he caught the image of a rifle with an oversized scope, one larger than any he had seen in his military career, aimed directly at him. He rolled quickly to the right.

"I found the sniper." He took in two quick breaths. "He's about ten meters to the east of the larger force."

"I see him," stated Irving, "and I have a shot."

"Take him out," Jon yelled into the radio.

The sound from the .50 Caliber rang out from the tower.

Jon glanced at Shira, Hank and Jerry. He knew the rebels were too far away for the M-16 and AK to be effectual. He wanted them to be ready should the enemy advance, but also wanted them to remain hidden. He rolled over, leveled his rifle in the direction of the large group and zeroed in on one target. He pulled the trigger.

Hank jerked from the blast. He was wearing ear protection, but the intensity of the large rifle made him shudder. He remained frozen in place with fog from his breath shooting out from his mouth. The detonation from Jon discharging another round, with the shell casing ricocheting off the side of the tractor, prompted him to let go of his M-16, letting it fall in the snow. The dull sound of Irving shooting from the tower behind them coincided almost precisely with Jon's firing. Jerry was also returning fire with the pinging sound of bullets from the enemy force hitting the metal on the front of the tractor.

"Hank," Jon nodded in the direction of Shira, "get

behind the tire."

"Jon," slobber was on the side of Hanks mouth. "There are too many, we can't win here."

"This isn't a damn football game we are trying to win. We just need for them to know that coming this way is not an option," Jon spoke into the side of his rifle as he continued to look thru his scope. "Now move, get behind the tractor wheel."

Shira rested her head on the tire. Her rifle laid in the snow at her feet. Hank leaned his head into the hard, cold rubber of the tractor tire, next to her, and listened as shots rang out from Jerry and Jon. They remained shoulder to shoulder until the barrage of gunshots stopped. Never again would he diminish the bravery of his brothers and sister, or the ferocity of war.

Jerry stared through his goggles but saw only a darkened mist. He crawled to the back side of the tractor, still wearing the night goggles and moved past Shira and Hank. He remained shielded by the tractor.

"I don't see them anymore," he yelled to Jon. "Did they move out?"

"Irving, are they retreating?" Jon spoke into the radio while continuing to skim the horizon.

"They are running to the west," replied Irving. "Did you suffer casualties?"

"Christian is KIA," Jon glanced over the top of his rifle at Hank and Shira. "We are going to keep our heads down for a bit. I'll let you know when we come your way."

"Roger that, I'll have Bobby and Emilee keep eyes on the area should they try to circle back."

Eastern Colorado Farm Basement

Maddy leaned into Nicole's lap holding a flashlight, with Scotty sitting cross-legged on the floor in front of her. All the other children were sleeping in the gun closet as a slight hum resonated from battery charged heaters.

Irene tucked a blanket around Ed's neck while he slept in the single recliner located in the basement. She plopped down on a metal chair and stared at her husband, wondering how he could have slept through the entire episode of blasts that shook the entire house. Although it had been hours since Sue and Becky were summoned upstairs, her heart continued to beat rapidly. She wished she could fall asleep like her husband.

"Irene," Maddy whispered, looking at her with wide open eyes. "Do you think the kitchen was blown up?"

"If it was, we will build it back." She felt her blood pressure lower from the welcoming sound of Maddy's voice.

"We can make some cupcakes with your special fudge frosting." Maddy moved from Nicole's lap to stand next to Irene. She took hold of her cold, rough hand.

"Aren't you tired?" Irene spoke softly.

"No."

"Me neither," said Scotty, rising to stand next to Maddy.

"I'm going to have to lay down pretty soon and try and get some sleep," Irene sighed. She squeezed Maddy's hand.

"You can lay down in my bed," Maddy tugged on her

arm. "It's really comfortable."

"I might take you up on that," Irene answered.

Nicole rose from her chair as someone approached down the hall. Ted and Corporal Pint dressed in full combat attire entered the room.

Nicole rushed to Ted and threw her arms around his neck.

"Grandpa," Maddy ran into his leg and latched hold.

"Everything is ok now." Ted stared into Nicole's eyes while placing his hand on Maddy's head.

"Sir, 3rd Platoon is fifteen mikes out." Corporal Pint pulled the handless radio down to her chin and smiled at Maddy. "1st and 2nd Platoons are proceeding to Limon."

"When 3rd Platoon arrives have them come all the way down the driveway to the farm," stated Ted.

"Yes sir," Corporal Pint moved back to the hall.

"Why aren't you sleeping young lady?" Ted bent down to one knee as Maddy put her arms around his neck.

"We were too scared to sleep. A bomb hit the house." She leaned back and looked at him, "Weren't you scared Grandpa?"

"Not even a little bit." Ted tightened his eyes and took a breath thru his nose, "Maybe a little scared something would happen to you and Grandma."

Maddy placed her arm around Scotty and pulled him to her side, "Scotty and I still want you to take us to California."

"We have to get things under control before we can get to California. In the meantime, you two need to get to bed." He glanced up at Nicole, "I wanted to check in and let you know the worst is over."

"General Lopez will be available for a briefing in about two hours at 0600," stated Corporal Pint.

"A lot has happened over night on the southern border and in the metro area." Ted rose and looked at Irene, "The FEMA camp in Limon was attacked."

"Were the camps in the city affected too?" Irene was so tired she could hardly stand.

"Yes."

"What does this mean for you?" Nicole licked her lips as she stared at her husband's rugged face.

"I'm going to request a full Battalion to go after the local rebels."

Nicole swallowed hard. She pulled Maddy in close.

"Try to get some sleep, you are safe." He placed a hand on the side of Maddy's face and leaned in and kissed Nicole. "I'll know a whole lot more about what is happening after I talk with General Lopez."

Irene moved next to Nicole as Ted hurried up the stairs. "That man is cool as a cucumber," she said, "he's acting like he's taking a stroll in a park."

Nicole exhaled as she turned to look in the direction of the gun closet. The reality of the day in observing firsthand the devastating magnitude of war changed life at the farm. Hearing the force of the explosions and witnessing the savagery of weapons being fired allowed her to recognize, more than she ever realized in all the years of being married to a Soldier, that her husband was a warrior. A fighter who the enemy feared, and it would never be the other way around.

Eastern Colorado Farm Clinic

Travis lay, covered with a white sheet, on the hospital bed, while Julia used all the medical supplies at her disposal, to tend to his life-threatening wounds. His wife Sue, standing next to Jacqueline, stood to the side. Under different circumstances, in a modern hospital, he would have already been in surgery.

When Dave rushed Sherry into the clinic, Jacqueline hurried to the basement to summon Al and Linda to assist Julia with tending to Sherry's wounds. Al scoffed and bantered about being a dentist and not a medical doctor, but nevertheless followed her up and immediately went to work on the young girl's mangled face. He meticulously removed bits of concrete from the side of her head as she lay on a hospital cot at the back of the small room.

"I think all the pieces have been removed." Al handed Linda the tweezers before leaning in to take a final look at the pellet wounds. He pulled back, "I'm going to let Julia stitch your cheek."

Linda lifted the gauze bandage hanging loosely on her cheek. "It's a pretty nasty cut. You are lucky none of the concrete hit directly on your eye."

"Mrs. Jones," Sherry sat up with her legs dangling and stated, "I'm pregnant."

"Your pregnant," Linda glanced at Al.

"This won't hurt the baby, will it?"

"No, it shouldn't affect the baby." Linda took a quick look at Julia to see if she was listening in on the conversation.

"Have you taken a pregnancy test?" Al asked.

"Yes, I came in here two nights ago and used one of the tests."

"Do you know who the father is?" Linda asked.

"Does it really matter?" she swallowed.

"It does," Al answered categorically, "he has responsibility for the child too."

Sherry squeezed her cracked lips and momentarily glared at Al. She pulled on the back of her hair and turned her head to look away.

Sherry was unaware of the death of Julia's husband but sensed there was something troubling the doctor as she came to her side, placed a thumb on her chin and pushed her face sideways.

"First, I'm going to spray some antiseptic numbing solution on the cut," Julia was breathing hard as she spoke.

Sherry closed her eyes as the spray hit the side of her face. She kept her eyes closed as Julia placed the sutures.

"There we go," said Julia. Bags under her eyes were drooping as she placed a large bandage over the cut. "I'll give you a packet with antibiotic ointment to place over the wound. Unfortunately, I am not a plastic surgeon, so there will be a scar."

"That's no problem. Thank you for fixing my face." Sherry hopped off the cot. Having a scar on her face was something she could care less about.

Julia stared into the living room while she watched Sherry move past the body of her husband on her way back outside. She remained frozen in place with tears dripping from her eyes.

Eastern Colorado Farm

Hank entered the front door of the farmhouse to the humming of a vacuum working to remove fragments of debris from the carpet. He briefly stopped to watch Jason framing the damaged area to the kitchen before continuing into the living room. He moved quickly to his wife's side.

The first thing that hit Jacqueline was that the cheeks on his pale face were sagging. Never had she seen his face so strained. She tossed her arms around his neck. He tensed, so she quickly relinquished the hug.

"Have you seen Bobby?" she tried to look him in the eyes.

"Yeah, he is outside speaking with Jon. He and Emilee will be in shortly," he sniffled and looked away.

"Are you alright?"

"No, I'm really not," he sighed. He ran his thumb and index finger over his eyes.

Jacqueline placed a hand on each of his shoulders and turned him towards her. She leaned back to better look him in the eyes. He shook his head.

"Was it that bad?"

"Yes, I saw Christian lose his life." He swallowed hard, "I learned that I can never be a soldier like my brothers and sister."

"Nobody ever expected you to be."

Hank twisted his head to look in the direction of the kitchen. Bobby and Emilee could be heard speaking with Jason and Dave.

"I know, but..." Hank turned back toward Jacqueline. "I never would have thought that I would completely freeze during a time when my friends and family were facing such a dangerous threat. Jacqueline, I was numb with fear."

"Hank, you are a football coach, not a trained soldier," stated Jacqueline.

Bobby and Emilee walked into the room.

"We just found out about Christian," Bobby held Emilee's left hand in his. He pulled her closer.

"I'm so sorry Emilee," said Hank. He recalled the loud crack of the bullet as it hit his former football player squarely in the head. Then, the vision of him lying in the blood covered snow. He shuffled his feet as he struggled to speak, "He was trying to make some amends and protect all of us."

"I will never know who he really was," Emilee cleared her throat. There was a noticeable wetness around her eyes. "If he had to die so young, I'm glad he came here to do it."

"We saw that Fred lost his life too," stated Bobby.

"Did you see where they took the bodies?" Jacqueline clenched her teeth, wondering if her question was insensitive to Emilee.

"They are in the warehouse," Emilee took hold of Bobby's right bicep.

"I'm sure the plan is to bury them on the hill in the northeast pasture." Bobby noticed Hank looking off in a daze. "Are you okay Dad?"

"I never dreamt we would witness anything like this," Hank wrenched his hands. "I was literally shaking out there today."

"Everyone was scared," Bobby's eyes narrowed as he

replied adamantly to his father. "Dad, you told us we have the power to be in control of our own destiny."

Hank turned toward his son but looked at the floor rather than directly in his eyes. It didn't go unnoticed by Bobby.

"Dad, your positive speeches were always accurate." He pulled away from Emilee and placed a hand on his father's shoulder. "You always preached that it takes hard work and practice to become great at anything. We will all handle the threats better next time."

Bill entered through the front door into the living room and yelled from the foyer, "Aunt Deb and Dad want everyone to meet on the south side of the garage. Make sure to dress warm." He turned and exited out the door.

Rural Colorado

After being stymied in their attempt to defeat the Liscos at their farm, the foreign insurgents retreated to a ranch forty kilometers to the south. They were joined at the location by a small group of thirty dissenters from the FEMA compound in Limon, which was destroyed less than twenty hours earlier.

The thirty malcontents waited in the cold on the farm grounds, separated from the foreign insurgents, while the foreign leader spoke to his assemblage. The superior spoke directly to his troops before addressing the homegrown fighters. His message was that the taking of America was almost certain, and that those who helped at this time would be rewarded greatly after the victory.

Two men standing with the domestic group were especially interested when the foreign leader spoke about a new strategy in seizing the farms on the eastern plains of Colorado. Surprise and ambush tactics were going to be utilized, rather than all out force. When the foreign insurgent finished speaking a man with a baseball cap turned to his blond-haired friend.

"It's payback time," said the blond man, looking at his friend.

"I don't know who I am going to enjoy killing more, the old man Jon, or that gorgeous blond Sherry," stated the man with a baseball cap. As the cold wind gusted, the skinny nose on his oblong face turned bright red. "She would have put a bullet in my head if the old man hadn't stepped in. Now we will see just how brave she is when my hands aren't tied behind my back."

"And Caroline Sanchez, I'm taking her with us when we finish."

A group of ten foreign insurgents, dressed in black with scarfs covering their faces approached the group of renegades. A small woman walked slightly ahead of the others as they all marched in unison.

"Ten of you are to come with us. Those without weapons will be supplied arms," the woman spoke loudly with perfect English.

"Are you going to the farm with the tower?" the man with the baseball cap stepped forward.

The woman stared at him with her big, brown eyes the only part visible from her covered face. She remained silent, surprised someone would ask a question.

"If you are, we want to go with you," said the blond man."

"If you go with us, you must follow orders and fight where you are commanded. The massive region we are directed with securing takes us just east of the Denver metro area all the way east to Hays Kansas. It goes from Clayton, New Mexico on the south to Fort Morgan, Colorado on the north." The tone in her voice was empathetic, with a willingness to clarify, unlike the leader who spoke to the group before her. "We have more pressing issues to take care of first, but the answer to your question is yes, eventually we will strike the farm with the tower."

The woman was glad to have the eager young pawns in her fold. They could easily be manipulated to be used as decoys. She too had personal reasons to go back to the farm. Three of her close friends were killed during the assault on the stronghold.

Eastern Colorado Farm

The morning sky was bright blue with the sun sparkling off the snow. All the occupants of the farm, except for Julia, Sue and Travis gathered in front of the garage. Ted, flanked by four soldiers, stood silently next to Deb while they waited for everyone to assemble. The tents used for housing the platoon were all disassembled, and the combat vehicles lined the driveway.

"Are you leaving Ted?" Al yelled from the front of the group.

"Yes," he looked to the side at Nicole, Bill and Maddy. There was a seriousness about his face which only his wife had seen before. "I am meeting this evening with an FBI counter terrorism task force to work on plans to stop the insurgents."

"Are you gong to be close by if we are attacked again?" Sheriff Bob asked.

"I will communicate with you daily, but my task in fighting the insurgents will take me to different locations which will make it difficult to respond to immediate danger. You have to set security and prepare to protect this farm."

"We want to be as transparent about what is happening as we can," stated Deb. She was dressed in combat fatigues. Tommy remained behind her next to the soldiers. "The war at the border has escalated. Enemy troops have moved northward all the way to northern New Mexico and eastward into central Texas. Yesterday and last night there was a large offensive push coordinated by the embedded rebels."

"Major efforts to create chaos were made by the insurgents in all major cities across the country. None more apparent than that in the Denver metro area where the Cherry Creek reservoir was breached. We don't know the severity of the damage yet," said Ted, glancing at Samantha who was standing next to Jessica with her hand at her mouth, obviously concerned about the safety of her parents. He knew there was major flooding on the south side of the city, but no more than that.

"Colonel, is there a chance the enemy forces could advance here?" Ben Stewart yelled, looking directly at Deb.

"Yeah, Colonel, could we lose this war?" Al asked while turning to face the others.

Deb contemplated the question for a moment. Tommy stood at full attention ready to support any answer she gave to the civilians.

"I won't lie, the challenges are great. The enemy has advanced faster than I believed possible only a week ago, but I believe with all my heart that the United States Military will not be defeated," Deb answered before taking two steps forward. She looked at Jon and Hank. "Tommy and I have been ordered back to Fort Carson and are leaving at 1400 this afternoon. But before we leave, I want to make sure everyone understands that nothing has changed at this farm. Autonomy and freedom come through hard work and responsibility. It's up to each of you to make this a better place for everyone and fight to protect what you have."

Hank felt a sense of pride in listening to both Ted and Deb as they addressed the people with uncompromising confidence. They were true warriors, willing to put their lives on the line to protect America and their loved ones. He made a vow to himself to never make the mistake of quitting or giving up because of fear.

A low humming sound caused all to stop and listen. The sound soon turned into a roar of aircraft flying in the southern sky. Everyone turned to look at the massive force of planes filling the skyline with the sound of explosions causing flashes as enemy missiles intercepted the squadrons of aircraft flying in formation. The planes disappeared into the horizon, leaving the once magnificent blue sky now littered with contrails and smoke.

"War is happening on our soil; it is real, and it is right over the horizon." Ted's loud voice brought the focus of attention back to him. "Deb, Tommy and I will do everything in our power to stop the enemy from advancing. It is up to each of you to secure and make this farm a place to survive until we finish the task. This is not a war for land or freedom. It is a war for our very souls.

CPSIA information can be obtained
at www.ICGtesting.com
Printed in the USA
FSHW021730150921
84783FS